"Now, perhaps you'll tell me what the hell is going on?"

Ghislaine had known that it would come. Of course he would have to know sooner of later, but his menacing manner infuriated her into standing up to him. "If you hadn't walked away from it all, you'd know exactly what is going on, Seth! What gives you the idea that you're entitled to any explanations?"

And as she said it, something fell into place, everything becoming beautifully clear. Ghislaine didn't have to tell Seth anything. He could guess as much as he wanted, and he might even come up with the truth, or something very near it. But as long as she kept her mouth shut, there wasn't a thing he could do.

And even if she did explain, did defend herself, did tell him everything, what would he do with the knowledge? Seth had changed. He was hard, callous and bitter.

"Perhaps I should ask your daughter for some answers, Ghislaine...."

Dear Reader,

The New Year is starting off splendidly here at Silhouette Intimate Moments. Take our American Hero, for instance. Riley Cooper, in Marilyn Pappano's *No Retreat,* is a soldier with a soft side. When his first love walks back into his life, troublemaking son in tow, it's surrender time for this tough guy.

Laurey Bright, long a favorite with readers of the Silhouette Special Edition line, makes her first Intimate Moments novel a winner. In *Summers Past* you'll find passion, betrayal and one all-important question: Who *is* little Carley's father? Allyson Ryan's *Secrets of Magnolia House* takes a few spooky detours along the road to romance; I think you'll enjoy the ride. *Two for the Road* is the first of Mary Anne Wilson's new "Sister, Sister" duo; look for *Two Against the World,* coming soon. Joanna Marks lights up the night with *Heat of the Moment,* and Justine Davis checks in with *Race Against Time,* a tale full of secrets, crackerjack suspense and irresistible desire. In short—I don't think you'll want to miss a single one of this month's books.

As the year goes on, look for books by more of your favorite authors. Kathleen Eagle, Doreen Roberts, Paula Detmer Riggs and Marilyn Pappano are only a few of the great writers who'll be coming your way in Silhouette Intimate Moments. And then there's our Tenth Anniversary celebration in May! Be sure to join us for all the fun.

Leslie Wainger
Senior Editor and Editorial Coordinator

SUMMERS

PAST

Laurey Bright

Silhouette® ™

INTIMATE MOMENTS®

Published by Silhouette Books New York

America's Publisher of Contemporary Romance

SILHOUETTE BOOKS
300 East 42nd St., New York, N.Y. 10017

SUMMERS PAST

Copyright © 1993 by Daphne Clair de Jong

ISBN: 0-373-07470-0

First Silhouette Books printing January 1993

Printed in the U.S.A.

LAUREY BRIGHT

has held a number of different jobs, but has never wanted to be anything but a writer. She lives in New Zealand, where she creates the stories of contemporary people in love that have won her a following all over the world.

Chapter 1

Ghislaine saw him get out of the car. She happened to be standing at the window of her bedroom, having come upstairs to put away some clean clothes. After stowing jeans, shirts and undies in the white-painted drawers in Carley's room, she had automatically straightened the pink quilted cover of the bed that her daughter had made with more speed than skill, and picked up a book, a pyjama top and a lanky decorative rag doll from the floor, restoring them to their proper places before crossing the wide passageway to her own room.

The white lace curtains were blowing inward, and after hanging her newly ironed dress in the satin-polished antique rimu wardrobe in one corner, she'd paused to pull down the window, leaving only a small slit for the spring breeze to penetrate. For a few minutes she stood gazing idly across the top of the scarlet-flowering rhododendron dominating the sloping lawn, and over the tree-bordered farm paddocks at the other side of the road, to the rumpled purple-hazed hills backdropped by white clouds against a lazy blue sky.

The car stopped opposite the formal iron gates that Mrs. Keegan insisted be closed every night.

It wasn't unusual for people to pause and stare at the house. Built in the early part of the century, it was an impressive piece of colonial architecture, carrying strong echoes of British stately homes. Solid, two-storied, with deep verandahs and balconies, boasting a disused tennis court and formal gardens, it spoke of the kind of assured wealth that had been a rare commodity in New Zealand of that era.

Furthermore, it wasn't in the heart of the city, where it might have been less conspicuous, but stood alone four miles from the nearest town. When the original owner had built it—or rather, had it built by the finest craftsmen available—the road it faced had been the main route to Auckland, then fifty-eight miles from Tangihuna. In the sixties the new highway to the encroaching city had shortened the distance, bypassing the small town, and now very little traffic passed the house because the road had become a dead end.

Over the years the English oaks and poplars and other trees the first owner had planted among totara and kowhai, and the scramble of climbing roses, honeysuckle and clematis, of rioting purple bougainvillaea and passion vines that tended to get out hand around the verandahs and trellises, had helped to blend the house into the landscape, but it was still a surprise to tourists or Sunday drivers doing a little exploring. Often a car slowed or stopped, and sometimes people took photographs.

When a rear door of the car opened, Ghislaine expected to see a camera pointed in the direction of the house, but instead a dark-haired, jeans-clad man emerged, hauling a khaki rucksack that he hoisted onto one shoulder. He stooped briefly with a hand on the driver's door, then stepped back, giving a careless wave as the car drew away.

Until then he'd had his head down and his back to Ghislaine and the house, but even before he turned around and straightened to his full height she felt a shiver of premonition, a cold, crawling sensation up her spine, and her fingers crushed the curtain that she'd been adjusting.

As the man stood surveying the house, his long legs slightly apart, a hand tucked into his belt and the rucksack easily held against his shoulder, her mind was still registering surprise that a hitchhiker would ask to be let out here. But at the same time some deep, primitive part of her recognised the tilt of his head as he lifted it and seemed to stare straight at her.

She moved back, her heart beginning a slow, heavy pounding, echoed by a tiny pounding in her head. A wash of heat invaded her body, receding to leave her chilled and slightly shivery.

She could still see the man on the road, but he was too far away at the end of the long drive for his features to be clear.

It isn't him! she told herself fiercely. It can't be Seth.

He had started up the drive, and she watched his rangy, confident stride with a sense of inevitability and increasing panic. Why now? Why, after the years that she had lived in fear of this moment, and more years when with a mixture of relief and aching, angry grief she had finally accepted that he wasn't going to come home, had he turned up now? When he hadn't even been at his father's funeral?

Then, she had been half afraid that he would arrive out of nowhere, and he hadn't, and she'd been glad. His mother, and Ghislaine and Carley, had been allowed to mourn in peace without having to cope with Seth's disruptive presence. It had been a blessing, and afterwards she'd thought: If he didn't come back for this, then that's the end. He'll never come.

She took a long, uneven breath. She could still be wrong. The man had passed out of sight between the poplars and copper beeches shading the drive, and maybe it wasn't Seth at all. Maybe her imagination had been at work again, as it had so often before, when a dark head held in a certain way, a square masculine shoulder glimpsed in the street, a deep-timbred voice heard across a room could make her heart jump, until she realised it wasn't Seth. It was never Seth.

But whoever he was, he was walking up the drive to the door, passing out of sight of the window, and if it was Seth—

She swung round, and almost ran out of the bedroom and along the carpeted passageway to the broad, curving sweep of the stairs. If it was Seth, she must see him before his mother did.

She took the stairs so fast she arrived at the bottom breathless. Crossing the oriental rug set on varnished kauri boards to the panelled door with the coloured glass rose-shaped inset, she forced a couple of deep, calming breaths into her lungs, repeating to herself like a mantra, *It isn't him, it isn't him.*

Then a shadow showed itself on the ruby-and-emerald glass, and the old-fashioned bell burred decisively under a forceful male finger.

Ghislaine had to take another gulp of air before she fumbled with the big porcelain knob and opened the door, the heavy wood swinging silently inward while she resisted a cowardly desire to close her eyes.

Instead she kept them wide open and, while one hand gripped the edge of the door, summoned a blankly polite expression to her face and said coolly, "Yes?"

"Ghislaine!"

Her name was hardly more than a breath on his lips, but it evoked such a flood of old feelings, old memories, that she had to clamp her teeth together to stop herself from crying out his name in return, with all the pain of the past eight years in her voice.

Her eyes were glazed with the effort of keeping unexpected tears at bay, and dazzled by the afternoon sun outside the gloom of the spacious entrance hall, and with his back to the light his face was deeply shadowed. But she knew him with every bone of her body, with her very blood.

"Seth," she said, her voice as steady and expressionless as she could make it. "Welcome home."

Chapter 2

"What are you doing here?" Seth's voice was harsh now, a grittiness underlying the velvety texture that she remembered.

Ghislaine blinked, a slow movement of her lids, giving herself time to think, to adjust. "I live here," she told him calmly.

"*You* live here?" His head lifted, he stared beyond her as though checking for other signs of habitation. He put out a hand and with his palm pushed the door back against the wall. And walked in, brushing past her. Then he turned to face her where she stood in the wide doorway, and she could see his face clearly now, see the narrowness of his eyes, green like the green glass insets of the door. And as hard. "You live here?" he repeated, softly but still with the gravelly, accusing undertone.

She was staring at his face, mesmerised by the changes in him, and the essential sameness. His hair was as thick and black as ever, with the same recalcitrant wave in it, and it hadn't been cut in a while. His lean cheeks and thrusting chin wore a shadowy stubble. Maybe that was what made him look rather older than thirty-two. He seemed taller and broader than she remembered, but none of the broadness was fat. Carelessly rolled khaki shirtsleeves showed sun-browned, muscular arms, and the faded jeans that hugged his hips and legs were tight over a flat stomach.

"Seen enough?" His decisively etched mouth quirked at one corner.

Ghislaine swallowed. "You've put on weight."

He made a scornful, breathy little sound that was almost a laugh. "You haven't." He was giving her a slow, deliberate inspection of his own, his eyes flicking from her rigidly controlled face to the slim body lightly skimmed by a simply cut cream linen shift with short sleeves and a modestly scooped neckline.

She could hardly object, as she had just unwittingly subjected him to a similar scrutiny, but as his eyes returned to her face, her lids lowered and she turned her head a little to the side.

He said sharply, "What have you done to your hair?"

Ghislaine's head jerked up. "My hair?" She just stopped herself from touching it defensively.

"You've cut it!" he said. His dark brows knitted. "Why?"

Her hair had always been very fine and soft, and it was Seth who'd called her an "almost-blonde" in the old days, when she'd worn it long and loose. Too fine to hold a perm or to pin into a sophisticated, mature style, her hair was now cut into a short, sleek bob just level with her jawline that made it much easier to cope with. "That really isn't any of your business."

Seth blinked as though he'd been stung. "Okay," he conceded. Then, returning to the attack, he demanded, "So tell me how you come to be living in my home."

"Your mother's home," she corrected him, playing for time. Panic was setting in again. "It's a long story," she said. "Wouldn't you like to—to freshen up first?"

He looked down at the dusty canvas shoes on his feet, and touched a finger to the incipient beard on his chin. "Too scruffy for you?" he enquired on an ironic note. "I suppose I ought to clean up before I meet my mother. Where is she, by the way?"

"Resting on the back patio. She does that every afternoon now. She's been more tired lately. Especially since your father—" She caught her breath, her eyes suddenly wide on his face. "Your father," she said huskily. "Did you—"

"I know."

"Oh. We—we didn't know how to contact you."

"No, I suppose not," he said indifferently. "I found out—eventually."

"Too late to attend the funeral?" So he'd had some excuse.

He was regarding her thoughtfully. "A bit late, yes. Would I have been welcome?"

She opened her mouth to say, "Of course," but the lie died on her lips in the face of his questioning stare. She gave a tiny shrug and let her lids fall over her eyes again as she looked away from him.

Seth's caustic laugh startled her with its bitterness. "You haven't changed," he said.

As she opened her eyes again and looked at him he stretched out a hand and stroked the back of a finger across her cheek, sensitising the fine, invisible hairs on her skin. "Cat," he murmured. "You still remind me of a Siamese cat, all those graceful angles, the way you blink those slanty sapphire eyes and move your head to the side when you don't want to answer a direct question. And your skin's as creamy and smooth as it ever was," he added, his voice deepening as he watched her. "Strokeable."

Quelling an inward shiver of awareness, Ghislaine jerked her head back. Woodenly she said, "Your old room is in use, I'm afraid, but you could use the guest suite. There are towels in there, and soap."

His brows lifted. "Is that a hint?" When she didn't answer he adjusted the strap of the pack and turned toward the stairs. "Come and talk to me while I clean up," he suggested casually.

She didn't want to, but she followed him up the stairs because of a half-formed notion that there were things she must hide from his too-penetrating eyes.

It wouldn't do any good of course—now that he'd come home everything was going to fall apart. The best she could do would be to salvage something for Carley and herself from the resultant havoc.

Realising she had left the door of Carley's room—which had once been his—wide open, she tried to slip ahead of him before they passed it so that she could unobtrusively close it, but the bulky rucksack he carried made that impossible. He stopped in the doorway, and she held her breath.

He surveyed the pink-covered bed, the chest with the old teddy bear and the rag doll on top, the bookcase filled with horse books and adventure stories and old picture books from Carley's baby days. And the poster on the wall of fluffy kittens peeking from a flower pot, alongside a Degas ballet print that Mrs. Keegan had thought suitable for a little girl's room.

He turned to look at her, with something in his eyes she found impossible to interpret, and she waited for the inevitable questions. She could see them in his eyes, but to her relief he continued down the passageway to the guest room where he dumped the pack on the floor and started undoing the straps. He hauled out a clean shirt and another pair of jeans and some underpants, then a small leather case. "So," he said, straightening with them in his hand, "what are you—some kind of companion to my mother?" He started unbuttoning his shirt with his free hand.

His chest was as brown as his arms, and there was a slight fuzz of dark hair on it, not a thick mat like some men had but more than there had been eight years ago—

Ghislaine wrenched her gaze away. "Yes," she said hastily, seizing at the suggestion, staving off the time when he would learn the truth. "Sort of. Look, I'll come back later—"

He pulled the shirt from his pants, glancing at her with irritated surprise. "I told you, I want to talk to you." He walked into the bathroom that was part of the guest suite, tossing the clean clothes onto a stool. Turning just inside the doorway, he stripped off his shirt and said, "How is she?"

"Not well."

He cast her a sharp look, and tossed the shirt onto the bedroom carpet.

Automatically Ghislaine went across to pick it up.

"Leave it!" he ordered. "I'll deal with it later."

She straightened with the shirt in her hand. "If you throw out the rest as you undress, I'll put them in the washing machine." She turned away from him, going to gaze out of the window. She didn't want to watch him.

The shirt was plucked from her hand, startling her. She hadn't heard his footsteps on the carpet. "I said, leave it," he told her evenly. "Is washing clothes part of your duties?"

Ghislaine shrugged. "I wash your mother's. It's no trouble to add yours."

"Thanks," he said, turning away, "but no thanks. I hope she pays you well."

Ghislaine opened her mouth, then bit her lip.

Already he was back in the bathroom. She heard him shuck the jeans, the rasp of the zipper and the soft putter of the harsh fabric falling on the tiled floor. Then he was running some water into the basin. "Is her health worse than it was?" he asked through the open door. "What does the doctor say?" The rush of water from the tap stopped abruptly.

She didn't want to be yelling to him about his mother's health. Ghislaine crossed the room to lean on the door frame of the bathroom with her back to it, arms folded. She heard the faint scrape of a razor. "He says her heart is getting weaker."

She added, almost to herself, "If you really cared, you could have written."

"In your own words," Seth told her, after a few moments of silence, "that's really none of your business."

Ghislaine bit her lip. Bastard! she thought dispassionately. The shock of his coming was wearing off, displaced by a slowly building but deeply seated anger. "Your mother's health is my business," she said tightly. "It's the business of everyone who lives in this house."

His breathy grunt seemed to have a sceptical quality. "Yes, it always has been."

Angry at his callousness, she half turned, her lips parting on a stinging retort, but the sudden gurgle of released water down the plug hole, followed by the hiss of the shower, stopped her.

"Don't go away," he said. "I won't take long."

Ghislaine stood seething while he thumped shut the glass shower door and presumably began soaping himself under the hot water. She thought of marching into the bathroom and turning on the hot tap over the basin full pelt. Or better still, the cold one.

No. That would be going too far. And he'd see her through the glass if he was looking that way. She wouldn't put it past him to barge out of there naked as he was and stop her.

Picturing Seth naked, she was suddenly having trouble breathing, and disturbing thoughts began to drift through her brain.

Fiercely, she shook her head. She couldn't help the erotic dreams that sometimes made incursions on her sleep, but in waking life there was no need to give in to such shaming images.

She debated going downstairs, leaving him alone and letting him find his own way, but she needed to talk to him, too. Only she'd not had a chance to frame how she was going to do it. Looking at her watch, she saw that it was well past two o'clock. A dampness cooled her temples. Soon after three, Carley would be home from school.

She closed her eyes, dropping her head onto her hands. What could she say? What was she going to do?

Dimly she was aware of the shower stopping, and the thud of the door. She lifted her head and found Seth beside her, his hair and body dripping as he knotted a towel at his waist.

"What's the matter?" he asked her.

"What's the matter?" she repeated, on the edge of hysteria. "What do you think? You come waltzing in here out of the blue, after three years without a word, without—anything," she tacked on lamely. "You might have been dead, for all we knew! And you ask me what's the matter? What the hell do you think?"

His green eyes were piercing, watchful. "Would you have cared," he asked her, "if I'd died?"

Ghislaine swallowed, her throat raw. "You haven't," she said flatly. "Unfortunately."

Again that flick of something showed in his face, behind the wet droplets that chased each other down his now clean-shaven cheeks. Close up like this she saw tiny lines at the corners of his eyes, and a permanent crease etched by his mouth. Then he smiled. "Well," he said lightly, "now we know how *you* feel about me."

Conscience gnawed. It had been a filthy thing to say, to anyone. But her anger was stronger. "How would you expect me to feel?" she demanded, coming away from the door frame to confront him.

"I've learned not to expect anything," he said, "from people—from life. It helps."

He turned away from her and she followed him into the bathroom, watching him pull another towel from the rail and start rubbing his hair and face. "Helps what?" she asked. The past eight years hadn't been easy for her, but some of them at least must have been hell for him.

He was drying his chest now, and his cool eyes met hers. "Me," he answered. "It helps me. I don't expect—so I don't get disappointed."

"You mean—you have no hope?" A stirring of something other than anger was trying to make itself felt.

But Seth laughed. "Let's not get melodramatic," he said. "Are you going to stay while I dress?" He was tugging at the knotted towel at his waist.

Ghislaine walked out into the bedroom, and he laughed again. "Still shy?" he called after her. "How old are you now? Twenty-six?"

She didn't answer, going back to the window, to blindly watch the trembling leaves of the oak tree by the gate. A long time ago Seth had helped her climb that tree; she still remembered sitting in its solid branches and surveying the ground below, terrified but triumphant. "You see?" he had told her, in the light, deepening voice of a boy turning into a man. "You can do anything if you try hard enough."

And if Seth was there to encourage her.

He came out of the bathroom, his jeans on but not fully zipped, swinging a creased stone grey shirt in his hands. As he shrugged into it she transferred her gaze again to the view, the green lush paddocks spreading across the valley floor beyond the road, and the shadowy pockets of dark bush huddled in the folds of the faraway hills. But with her peripheral vision she was aware of him buttoning the shirt, tucking it into his pants and pulling up the zip.

She said, "Your mother will be waking from her nap soon. She'll wonder where I am. We can talk downstairs." Even a guest bedroom had an unwanted intimacy about it. There was only one chair.

He raked a hand over his hair. "Hold on a minute." He rummaged in the pack again and brought out a comb.

He used it without looking in the mirror, ruthlessly sleeking his hair down, but even damp the stubborn wave fought to assert itself. "Do I look presentable now?" he asked her, catching her fascinated stare.

"Probably as much as you ever do," she told him crisply.

Seth grinned, his eyes kindling with some kind of challenge. "Not impressed any more?" he queried softly.

There had been a time when she'd thought he was God's gift. "I'm twenty-six," she reminded him. "Not fifteen any more."

"Nor even seventeen," he agreed. "All grown up, huh?" An edge of regret coloured his voice.

"That's right. It takes more than a handsome face and a few kisses now to bring me to a man's feet."

"Were you ever at my feet?" He looked at her intently, the smile gone.

"Metaphorically speaking," she said. He must have known it, she wasn't giving anything away. She'd been an ardent teenager, with no more ideas of hiding her feelings than of giving up breathing.

"Well," he drawled as she crossed the room ahead of him and he followed her to the passageway, "whose feet are you falling at now?"

She hoped her laugh was convincing. "No one's. I had an extended adolescence, but it's over now. I lost my illusions a long time ago. I don't need anyone, now."

"What does that mean?" He caught her arm as she started down the stairs. "There's no man in your life?"

Ghislaine hesitated, but what could she lose? "No."

She freed her arm so that she could turn away from him and proceed down the stairs.

"But there was once."

"You know there was," she said. "You."

"Apart from me." He was at her side, but she wouldn't look at him. "After me," he insisted.

"What do you want?" She stopped to look at him briefly, then continued on her way. "An ego boost? You're the only man I've ever loved, Seth," she simpered mockingly. "Is that what you want to hear? Except it wasn't love, really. Just a stage in my growing up."

A stage that had gone on too long. She'd not been able to see any other man because Seth filled her life, her dreams. She'd scarcely known that other men existed.

"You didn't get married?" he asked, an odd trace of urgency in his voice.

She saw that his eyes were on her unadorned left hand, trailing down the broad, polished balustrade. "No," she said. "Did you?"

"Never."

They reached the bottom of the stairs, and he swung down to the floor, his hand on the newel post, trapping her in the circle of his arm but not touching her. "So," he said, and her skin prickled at the deep, glittering light in his eyes, her breath coming shallowly. "No man in your life, huh?"

Unable to speak, she shook her head, defiantly holding his eyes with hers, making her mouth firm, willing it not to tremble.

"Well, I've got news for you, lady," he said very softly. "There is now. Me."

Her mouth parted, she couldn't help it. Her quick intake of breath almost choked her. He was watching her, taking in her reaction.

Which was one of pure, blessed fury, a white flame that burned somewhere in her chest and shot up to her head, making it feel hot and tight. It was years since he'd walked out of her life and now he thought, did he, that he could walk back in?

She scarcely recognised her own voice, low and husky and filled with rage. *"Don't you dare touch me!"* she threatened. "Ever again!"

For a moment he remained staring into her eyes. Then he stepped back, ostentatiously lifting his hands away, palms outwards.

"That's a different tune," he said. "I remember when you purred like a kitten if I so much as stroked your hand."

She remembered, too. The memory was gall and wormwood. "A long time ago," she said. "And didn't you know how to play me?" she admitted bitterly.

His head inclined sideways, his eyes narrowing. "Explain."

But a distant voice called, "Ghislaine? Are you there, dear?"

And Ghislaine said hurriedly, "Let me talk to her first—please! The doctor—her heart—"

She realised she'd said none of the things she'd meant to, made none of the revelations she'd planned. But right now the major problem was to spare Mrs. Keegan the shock of meeting her son unprepared. "Please!" she repeated.

"If you think it's necessary."

"It is," she assured him tersely, and as Mrs. Keegan called again, she hurried to answer the summons.

"Oh, there you are, dear. I thought I heard voices." Mrs. Keegan raised her head from the cushions that Ghislaine had earlier arranged for her on the lounger, and fumbled for her glasses on the table beside it.

They hadn't been speaking loudly, but the door to the vine-shaded patio had been open, as Ghislaine always left it in the afternoon. And she'd noticed before that in spite of her age, Mrs. Keegan's hearing was remarkably acute.

"I'm sorry if we woke you." Ghislaine crossed the tiles under starry passion flowers and clematis and thick sheaves of purple bougainvillaea scrambling over open beams. Picking up the glasses she handed them over.

"Thank you, dear. I was only dozing. Do we have a visitor?" Adjusting the glasses, the older woman directed a curious gaze at her.

"Not exactly." Ghislaine went down on her haunches and put her hand over the thin, veined one that rested on a grey mohair afghan. "This may be a bit of a shock."

"A shock?" The eyes behind the glasses sharpened, blinked. A quiver of apprehension passed over the lined but still aristocratically beautiful features. "What kind of shock?"

"Well, a surprise," Ghislaine said. "Nothing dreadful. It's—I suppose it's good news." She moistened her lips, and forced the words out. "Seth's home."

For a moment his mother didn't react at all. Then Ghislaine felt a tremor in the hand under hers. "Seth," Mrs. Keegan whispered. "You're right. It is . . . a shock. After all this time." Her eyes were on Ghislaine, obviously not seeing her.

"Are you all right?" Ghislaine queried anxiously. "Can I get you anything?" She ought to have made the usual afternoon coffee and brought it out, but she hadn't expected Mrs. Keegan to wake yet, and she'd been afraid of her coming inside and finding Seth there.

"Yes, yes I'm all right."

"I've put him in the guest suite," Ghislaine said, giving her time to recover. "Is that all right? If you'd rather he had his own old room, I'll move Carley's—"

"No!" Mrs. Keegan removed her hand from Ghislaine's, smoothing the afghan over her legs. "Don't be silly," she added more gently. "We redecorated that room for Carley." Pausing, she clasped her restless hands together on her lap. "Have you talked?"

"No." Ghislaine swallowed. "No, I . . . haven't told him anything. He knows about his father," she tacked on.

Mrs. Keegan was gazing over the clear blue water of the swimming pool, its locked iron-railed enclosure softened by ferns and bright-faced impatiens and climbing geraniums, staring beyond it to the white post-and-rail fence that separated the house from smooth-cropped green paddocks. "I see," she said. Her head went up. "I see."

"Shall I . . . bring him out to you?"

The older woman's nostrils dilated on a deeply drawn breath. "I suppose I must see him. Bring him to me. And then would you make coffee please, dear. For three of us?"

"Yes, of course."

In the dimness of the house after the bright light outside, Ghislaine almost cannoned into him. He had moved down the passageway toward the back door. She stopped inches short of his dark bulky form, and stepped back immediately. "She'll see you now."

"It isn't a royal audience," Seth said, following her.

Ghislaine waited at the door, letting him go alone to meet his mother. Mrs. Keegan watched him cross the weathered tiles, her perfectly groomed white head held high, her eyes cool and critical.

Seth stopped by the lounger, and she said, "Well. So you've come home at last."

"Yes." For a moment he stood stiffly, then he bent and touched his lips to her cheek.

She accepted the kiss without moving. When he straightened she said, "You'd better sit down."

He took a chair from a set arranged about a wrought iron table, and placed it a few feet away. "How are you, Mother?"

Ghislaine left them, going inside to prepare the coffee.

When she brought the tray out Seth got up to take it from her and put it on the table. She wondered if he welcomed the excuse. His mother was looking austere. There was no way of telling what his feelings were. It was as though he wore a mask.

"I made yours black," she told him. "But there's cream and sugar on the tray in case your taste has altered."

"My taste is the same as ever." He was looking at her, but she wouldn't meet his eyes. He picked up his mother's cup that Ghislaine had already mixed sugar and a generous dollop of fresh whipped cream into, and handed it to her. "With your heart," he said dryly, "should you be having so much cream?"

"Doctor Turner is quite happy about my diet, thank you."

"Turner? Is that old . . . man still in practice?"

"He's semi-retired, but he attends a few of his long-standing patients." Mrs. Keegan's voice was tart. "And I mean attends. He's one of the few doctors about these days who really does the job. Try to get the younger ones to make house visits—" she added scornfully.

Ghislaine unobtrusively seated herself at the table.

"Do you need house visits?" Seth queried his mother.

"I told you, my health has deteriorated. I'm not a young woman any more."

"I realise that." He sat down again and took a sip of coffee.

"That doesn't mean that I don't have all my wits about me," Mrs. Keegan warned sharply.

"I've never known a time when you didn't," Seth agreed. "And I don't perceive any change."

"Of course, physically I'm not as strong as I would like." Her voice wavered. "Ghislaine has been a big help to me."

Seth flickered a glance at Ghislaine. She tried to keep an indifferent expression, one arm resting on the table, the other hand lifting her cup to her lips. "I gathered," he said.

"She's a wonderful girl."

"I always thought so."

Ghislaine directed a look at him that raised his black brows slightly. "Has she been living here since my father died?"

Ghislaine put the cup down on its saucer. He was still looking at her, and she answered. "Long before that."

"I see."

But he didn't, of course. He didn't see anything, know anything. And didn't care, Ghislaine reminded herself, or at least he certainly hadn't until now. And if he did now—why?

"Tell me," he was saying quietly to his mother, "about his death?"

"I don't wish to discuss it," Mrs. Keegan said, "with you."

Seth was staring into his cup. He stayed like that for several seconds, then he put both hands about the cup and leaned forward, his elbows resting on his parted thighs. ''I think,'' he said levelly, ''that I have a right to know.''

Ghislaine saw with concern the coins of burning colour that appeared on Mrs. Keegan's pale cheeks, heard the quiver in her voice. ''You forfeited your rights in this house years ago,'' she told him thinly. ''It's too late now to start claiming them.''

''He was my father,'' Seth reminded her. After a short pause he said, ''Tell me one thing. Did he leave you well provided for?''

''If it's any of your business, yes!'' Mrs. Keegan said peevishly. She put a hand to her chest, her breathing becoming uneven and loud.

Ghislaine stood up to go to her side, brushing past Seth as he straightened in his chair, frowning.

''It's all right,'' Ghislaine soothed, removing the coffee cup from Mrs. Keegan's hand and taking a firm grip on her wrist. ''It's all right. Deep breaths, now. One—two—three, that's right, four—five. Relax. Better?''

The older woman's face was drawn, her lips a tight line. She nodded weakly. ''A little...I think. Oh, I do feel dreadful.''

Seth had got up and placed his cup on the table. Quietly he said to Ghislaine, ''Can I do anything?''

''You've done enough!'' she snapped, her eyes glancing off him. Returning her attention to his mother, she coaxed, ''Three more deep breaths, now. One, two, three...good. Could you take a little more coffee?''

''I'll try,'' Mrs. Keegan gasped.

When she had drunk most of it, in tiny sips, Ghislaine took the cup from her hand, only to have it plucked away by Seth.

His mother lay back on the cushions, her eyes closed. ''I'll be all right,'' she said tiredly after a while. ''Just...leave me alone.''

Ghislaine patted her hand. ''All right. I'll come and check on you in ten minutes.''

She turned to the table to put the coffee cups back on the tray. But when she made to lift it, Seth picked it up and went ahead of her into the house.

Ghislaine lingered, looking at the steady rise and fall of Mrs. Keegan's chest, checking the colour of her cheeks, before she followed.

"I didn't know you were a nurse," he said to her as she joined him in the kitchen where, ignoring the big old dishwasher, he already had the cups in the sink.

"I'm not. The doctor says all you need is common sense."

"Turner?" Running the hot water, he said, "The old fool ought to take some of his own advice. He must be well past the age, himself, where he ought to be expected to go running round after his patients."

"He doesn't have many, now. Your mother and some other elderly people who are used to Dr. Turner and don't want to start with someone new." Automatically she picked up a tea-towel and began drying as he washed.

"Maybe we should."

"Should—?"

"Start with someone new," he said impatiently. "Turner must be in his dotage—he always was, as far as my mother was concerned," he added, his mouth twisting.

"What do you mean?"

"Oh, for heaven's sake! The man's been besotted since he first clapped eyes on her thirty years ago, or whatever it was. She's been twisting him round her little finger ever since. Her health might have been much better if she'd had a doctor who wasn't prepared to pander to her every time she developed a twinge or a dizzy spell."

"*Pander* to her? Dizzy spells? She has a weak heart!"

"Does she?" Seth's voice was flat, almost disbelieving.

A sound from the road penetrated Ghislaine's consciousness. The school bus accelerating away from the gate with a roar and a heavy gear change. She'd forgotten to listen for it, not realising what time it was. Horrified, she glanced at her watch, then looked at Seth who was obliviously letting the water out of the sink, twitching a towel off the rail on the wall to dry his soapy hands. Too late now to say anything to him. If she could get to Carley before—

"Excuse me," she said, throwing down the tea-towel on the counter. "I have to—there's something I have to do."

When she opened the front door, Carley was halfway up the drive, running, her long fair hair flying in the breeze, a bright red schoolbag bouncing on her back. When she saw her mother a smile appeared, showing the front teeth that were still too big for her face. Ghislaine met her at the bottom of the broad steps and hugged the slight, warm body to her, felt the softness of her daughter's hair against her cheek, breathed the sweet childish scent of her skin with closed eyes.

Nothing must hurt Carley. Whatever went on between the adults in this house, none of it was Carley's fault, and she must be sheltered at all costs from the storm that was about to break over their heads.

Ghislaine pulled away a little, her arms still protectively curled about the child. "Carley," she said urgently, "something's happened. There's someone here that...that you haven't met before. He...he may be going to stay."

"Who?" Carley asked. Blue eyes, very like her mother's, stared into Ghislaine's under fine, straight brows. "Who is it?"

"Well...it's...Granna's son. He...he went away a long time ago, before you were born. But now he's back."

"Can I play with him?"

Ghislaine shook her head. "He's not a little boy, darling. He's a man. And Carley, if he...if people say anything that sounds funny—odd—don't worry. Some grown-up talk is hard for little girls to understand, but I promise everything's going to be all right. If anything bothers you, just ask me about it when the two of us are alone, okay?"

"Okay." Carley looked puzzled at her mother's obvious tension, but she nodded, and Ghislaine relaxed slightly.

She took Carley's hand in a firm grasp and stood up, ready to mount the steps.

And found Seth standing on the top one, looking down at them both, his jaw tight and an enigmatic look on his face.

"Well, well," he drawled, leaning back against the verandah post and tucking his thumbs into the belt loops of his jeans. "No need to ask whose kid this is!"

Chapter 3

Ghislaine's hand tightened on Carley's, her eyes pleading with Seth.

He returned her stare coldly, and his look at Carley was unsmiling. Ghislaine whispered, "Please, Seth!"

Carley looked up at her mother, then turned back to Seth. "Are you Granna's son?" she asked him.

"Granna?"

"That's what she calls...your mother," Ghislaine explained quickly.

His eyes on Carley, he said, "Yes. My name's Seth."

"Hello, Mr. Seth."

"Mr. Keegan," Ghislaine corrected her, as Seth said, "No, don't call me that."

Ghislaine seized a quick breath, her whole body stiffening.

Carley's head twisted round to her mother again. Seth, straightening away from his pose, dropped to his haunches, bringing him almost level with Carley, so that she looked at him again. "You can call me Seth," he told her, his eyes meeting her solemn gaze. "And what's your name?"

"Carley. Caroline, really, but everyone calls me Carley."

''Hi, Carley.'' He held out a hand, and she freed herself from Ghislaine's and stepped forward to put her small one into it.

He smiled then, a faint quirk of the lips. Carley cocked her head to one side, watching him with curiosity. The breeze blew her long hair across her face, and she screwed up her eyes.

Relinquishing his gentle grip on her hand, Seth brushed the wayward strand aside for her. ''Your mother's hair used to be just like that,'' he said.

Carley looked again at Ghislaine, then back to him. ''Did you know her when she was a little girl?''

''Yes. Yes, I did. A little girl just like you.'' He was staring at her intently, as if he couldn't take his eyes off her. Ghislaine momentarily closed hers. She felt sick.

''Did she ever talk to you about me?'' Seth asked.

Ghislaine's eyes opened. She moved forward as though to shield her daughter, but Seth shot her a look that stopped her in her tracks, inwardly trembling.

Carley shook her head. ''No.''

Seth kept his eyes on the child. ''How old are you, Carley?''

Ghislaine held her breath.

''I'm seven.''

''Seven.'' Seth didn't look at Ghislaine, his entire attention apparently centred on Carley.

''Nearly eight,'' Carley said proudly.

The man's face might have been carved in stone, his eyes suddenly narrowed.

Ghislaine said, ''I have to check on your mother. I told her ten minutes. Come on, Carley, and say hello to Granna.''

She grabbed Carley's hand again, sweeping past Seth as he stood up, avoiding his hard, questioning gaze.

He followed them along the passage to the back of the house, and stood in the doorway.

Mrs. Keegan turned her head as Ghislaine and Carley approached the lounger.

''Are you feeling better?'' Ghislaine enquired.

"Yes, dear, thank you. Hello, Carley." She held out her arms, and Carley gave her a hug and a quick kiss.

"Hello, Granna. Were you sick again?"

"Just a little. I'm feeling better now."

"I've got a new *School Journal*." Carley swung the red bag from her shoulders and began to open it. "I'll read it for you, if you like."

"That would be lovely. We'll be fine, dear," Mrs. Keegan said dismissively to Ghislaine.

Ghislaine reluctantly turned and went back to the house. She wasn't sure if Mrs. Keegan was ignoring Seth or if she hadn't seen him because she wasn't wearing her glasses.

He swung round before she got there, and went inside himself. But almost as soon as she entered, he gripped her arm and marched her along the passageway to the seldom-used formal drawing room at the front of the house, as far from the patio as they could be. He thrust her into the cool, dim room before letting her go, then thumped the door shut with his hand and stood against it, folding his arms.

"Now," he said, "perhaps you'll tell me what the hell has been going on here?"

She'd known that it would come. Of course he'd have to know sooner or later, but his menacing manner and the way he had manhandled her infuriated her into standing up to him. She shivered. This room with its heavy green velvet drapes and dark solid furniture always seemed cold to her. "If you hadn't walked away from it all you'd know exactly what's going on!" she said. "What gives you the idea that you're entitled to any explanations?"

And as she said it, something fell into place, everything becoming beautifully clear. She didn't have to tell him anything. He could guess as much as he wanted, and he might even come up with the truth, or something very near it, but as long as she kept her mouth shut, there wasn't a thing he could do.

And if she did explain, defend herself, tell him all the details, what might he do with his knowledge? Seth had changed. He was hard and callous and bitter, perhaps even with a streak of real cruelty, although she had to be grate-

ful for the way he had treated Carley. She said, "But thank
you for not upsetting Carley."

"Perhaps I should ask her—"

"No! She doesn't know anything!"

"But you do."

"It's not your business, Seth!"

"Not my—" He looked furious. He stepped toward her
and she started back, cannoning into a round oak occa-
sional table behind her.

"I'm not going to beat you," he promised harshly.
"Tempting though the thought is."

"Don't you threaten me!"

"I thought I was doing just the opposite."

"You have no right to question me. No right to come
barging in here, turning everything upside down, making
your mother ill—"

"And what rights do you have?" he enquired softly,
dangerously. "I am a member of this family," he reminded
her. "What's left of it. And you are the hired help. Whatever is between me and my mother is just that—a family
matter."

Ghislaine swallowed the hurt of his brutal summing up.
It wasn't true, anyway, and he'd find that out soon enough.
"I won't allow you to endanger her health!" she said hotly.
"She's old and frail, and I won't stand by and see her bul-
lied!"

"Did I bully her?" he demanded.

Ghislaine hesitated on her retort, and he said flatly, "No.
And I've no intention of doing so. But she's not so very old,
you know. Plenty of women her age are leading active, ful-
filling lives."

"They don't have her health problems," Ghislaine
pointed out.

"No," he agreed. "I sometimes wonder about the chicken
and the egg."

Ghislaine was bewildered. "She's your mother! Why are
you so snide about her?"

"Snide?" He seemed to consider the word. "I don't mean
to be. Has she ever, to your knowledge, seen a specialist?"

"No. Do you think she should?"

"Possibly. Do you think you could persuade her?"

"I suppose I could try." They both knew that if the suggestion came from him it would be vetoed.

"Do," he said. "You're fond of her, aren't you?"

"Yes. I owe her—more than I can say. She's been wonderful about Carley."

A line appeared between his brows. "They're obviously attached to each other. Perhaps she should have had a daughter, herself."

"Perhaps."

"Is that where you come in?" he asked her. "As a surrogate daughter?"

Ghislaine shrugged. "Maybe. In a way."

"I'm sorry for that crack," he said abruptly. "About being hired help. Below the belt."

"It doesn't matter. It isn't true, anyway."

"I know—"

"I'm not paid," she said.

His brows contracted further. "Aren't you doing the housekeeping?"

"Well, I suppose you'd call it that. But this is my home, now. I only do what I'd do wherever I lived."

"You got my mother's coffee. You cook the meals?"

"Well, yes, but Carley and I eat, too."

"And you do her washing. She hasn't done any housework for years other than cooking, and maybe arranging a few flowers. This is a big place. Do you have someone come in to help?"

"A man does the windows, and we have a gardener once or twice a week, depending on how much needs to be done."

"That's all?" As she shrugged, he said, "She's made a slavey of you."

"She has not! You just said yourself, she's made a daughter of me. And I'm grateful."

"Grateful!" He sounded as though the word were loathsome.

"Yes!" Ghislaine lifted her head. "And I'll thank you to keep out of it! I'm happy, she's happy!"

"I'm sure she's very happy!"

"And my daughter's happy. And as far as I'm concerned, that's the most important thing. And if you do anything to hurt Carley, I'll kill you, Seth. I swear it!"

"I'm not in the habit of attacking children! Do you think a few years in prison turned me into some kind of monster?"

"I just...I just don't want any...differences we may have to spoil things for her," Ghislaine said. "She's a happy child, and I'd hate to see that change." Unconsciously, she was pleading with him again.

"So would I," he said. "Hard though that appears to be for you to believe. I promise you, I won't do anything that might distress her."

"Thank you." He'd always been a man of his word, although he'd proven to have feet of clay in other ways. If she had Seth's promise to keep Carley happy, she'd be able to negotiate the minefield that lay ahead.

"Mummy!" Carley's voice came from the passageway. "Mummy, where are you?"

Ghislaine started for the door, stopping in front of Seth who stood in her way for a couple of seconds, then moved aside.

"Mummy!" Carley ran to her when she opened the door. "Look at my new *Journal*. I read the first story all by myself. Granna only had to help me with three words! Can I have an apple?"

Usually Ghislaine would have insisted that first she put away her bag in her room, but today she took her into the kitchen, found an apple and poured her a glass of milk, and admired not only the colourfully illustrated *School Journal* but the drawing Carley had made of her teacher. Mrs. Keegan came inside and went upstairs to her room, and Ghislaine at last told Carley to put away her school things while she looked in the freezer and the pantry for something to make for dinner.

A bowl of soup and an egg or salmon salad would have done for the three of them, but she supposed that Seth would require something more substantial. She found some frozen home-killed lamb chops and put them in the microwave to thaw, before Carley came down again, asking if she could ride her pony in the paddock behind the house.

Ghislaine supervised her for nearly an hour, then scrubbed half a dozen potatoes and switched on the oven of the big stove, calculating that the time taken to bake six potatoes in the microwave would just about equal what they would take in the conventional stove.

Dinner was ready by six. Carley had set four places at the dining room table where Mrs. Keegan preferred to have dinner, rather than at the kitchen table they used for other meals. But when Ghislaine brought the food into the dining room Seth was absent.

"I'd better go and call him," she said. "I suppose he wouldn't know when dinner is."

His mother said nothing, but Ghislaine was well aware that the family had eaten at the same time every day for more than thirty years.

She knocked at his door and got no reply, even when she knocked a second time, more loudly. A faint hope entered that he had packed up and left, immediately followed by a pang of guilt that he hadn't been made more welcome, and a swift, piercing desolation that she quickly crushed.

Quietly she opened the door. The rucksack wasn't on the floor where she had last seen it, but Seth lay on the bed, sprawled across the cover, fully dressed even to his worn rubber-soled canvas shoes, as though he had just lain down for a minute and fallen asleep.

Ghislaine stepped into the room. "Seth?"

His chest rose and fell rhythmically. She could hear him breathing. His head was turned aside on the pillow, eyes closed, his lips just barely parted. A moist sheen lay on his forehead and in the hollow of his throat. Obviously he was exhausted. For the first time she wondered where he had travelled from today. He had appeared so suddenly, like a genie from a bottle, that she'd just accepted his presence without questioning how he'd got here. She crossed to the window, pushing it up a little to allow a cooling breeze to waft over to the bed, glancing at him when the slide grated, to see if she was disturbing him. But he slept on, looking curiously defenceless in his oblivion.

* * *

"He's asleep," she reported on her return, removing his plate from the table. "I'll put this back in the kitchen."

Carley looked disappointed, and seemed inclined to ask questions about Seth and where he'd come from, and why he'd been away. But Mrs. Keegan made it clear she didn't want to talk about him, and Ghislaine firmly steered the conversation into other channels.

After dinner Ghislaine and Carley cleared the table and stacked the dishwasher, and Mrs. Keegan made her evening tour of the garden. The older woman went to bed early, looking more tired than usual. Carley, of course, had long been tucked up.

Ghislaine was restless, knowing she wouldn't sleep if she went to bed. And that she couldn't concentrate on reading tonight. The November night was warm, almost summery, and as she went to open the window of Carley's room a little further and let some more air in, the faint gleam of the swimming pool caught her eye. Until now the water had been too cold for swimming, although last year she'd had her first dip as early as October.

In her own room she put on her swimsuit, wrapped a big towel about her waist and went quietly down the stairs, crossed the patio and slipped into the pool.

She breaststroked up and down its length for about twenty minutes, and the water had a cooling and soothing effect. The scent of a flowering bead tree nearby floated on the warm air, mingling with the perfume of the yellow climbing roses on the fence. She turned over, floating and watching the stars as the sky darkened, then backstroked to the poolside where she had left her towel.

As she turned and fumbled for the ladder, a pair of denim-clad legs met her vision, and a hand came down to grasp hers.

Seth pulled her easily up to stand before him. He had her towel, but when she reached for it he put it around her shoulders instead, and retained a hold on it, imprisoning her.

Ghislaine shivered, staring at him. His eyes in the moon-light were deeply shadowed and colourless.

He tightened his grip on the towel, bringing her closer, and Ghislaine strained backwards, breaking his hold. She lifted the slipping towel and rubbed at her hair. "Thank you," she said breathlessly. "Did you have a good sleep?"

He ignored the question. "If I hadn't seen the evi-dence," he said, "I'd never believe that you'd had a child."

He was staring at her body, the wet black lycra doing nothing to hide her lithe slimness, the flat stomach and neat, rounded breasts.

Ghislaine held the towel in front of her, wiping her face on its softness. "I kept some dinner for you," she said. "You must be hungry."

"Oh, I'm hungry," he said. His eyes, which had been lingering on the length of her bare legs, flicked to hers, but she wouldn't meet the challenge in them.

"I'll get changed and come down to the kitchen," she offered, backing away from him. "You won't mind eating in there?"

Seth shook his head. "I don't mind."

When she came down he was lounging against the kitchen counter. She had put on blue cotton trousers and a navy sweatshirt, and rubbed her hair almost dry and combed it so that it lay sleek and slightly water-darkened against her head.

"You don't need to wait on me," he said as she took three chops from the fridge to place them in the microwave oven.

"It's no trouble. I cooked these before, but I didn't like to wake you." She turned on the stove and found a small pan.

"Very considerate of you."

He watched her as she heated a little oil and dropped two eggs into the pan, covering them with a lid before turning down the heat. The salad had wilted, and she set about making him a fresh one.

"Have you had a long journey?" she asked, shaking wa-ter from some lettuce.

"From Perth."

"Perth? Western Australia!"

"That's right. You always were good at geography," he said with faint sarcasm. "I seem to have been travelling forever."

No wonder he'd been tired. He'd have had to fly over the Tasman Sea from Sydney to Auckland, of course, but she wondered if he'd hitched his way across Australia—about four thousand kilometres.

"How long had you been in Perth?" she asked, putting the lettuce on a plate and picking up a tomato, hunting in a drawer for a slicing knife.

Seth shrugged. "Couple of years."

"Have you been in Australia since—" She began slicing the tomato.

"Since getting out of prison?" he completed for her. "Pretty well. Once my parole ran out there didn't seem much to hang about here for."

The knife slipped in Ghislaine's hand, and she surveyed the ragged piece of tomato and pushed it into the sink to go down the waste disposal. Carefully she sliced the rest onto the plate.

"Was it...all right over there?" she asked him. "Did you find a job?"

"I lost count of the jobs I found," he said. "There's still a place for unskilled labour if you're willing to work in atrocious conditions—in the outback, or the mountains, or down a mineshaft. But the pay's usually good."

"You're not unskilled labour," Ghislaine protested. "You have degrees in science and commerce!"

"Yes, well, people who are looking for science and commerce graduates usually require some background information and references. A criminal record doesn't impress them much. Manual workers can get by on willingness and a strong back, and no one asks too many questions. I took what I could get, and believe me I was bloody grateful."

The microwave beeped, and she removed the chops and added them to the plate, then slid the perfectly cooked eggs from the pan. "Do you want dressing?"

"No, thanks. This looks good."

She gave him a knife and fork and he sat down at the table. "Are you having something?"

"I ate hours ago."

"You look as though you could do with fattening up. As usual." He gave a faint, reminiscent grin before turning his attention to the steak.

"You know I've never been able to put on weight." Ghislaine moved restlessly, unwilling to be drawn into a session of "Do you remember." There was nothing she wanted to remember of those old days when life had been a golden dream. The dream had been too rudely, irrevocably shattered, and memories held too much pain. "Coffee?" she queried, veering to something safe.

"If you'll join me."

It would give her something to do instead of hovering over him. She took her time over measuring the spoonfuls into the percolator, and pretended that making the coffee needed her undivided attention until it was ready. By the time she poured it, Seth had almost finished the meal.

"Thank you," he said as she put a cup in front of him. "Sit down." Because she was still hesitating, debating if she could drink hers leaning on the sink counter.

He pushed away the empty plate and curved his hands about the cup before him, looking down at the gently steaming liquid. Then he raised his eyes, coolly enigmatic, and said, "Are you going to tell me about it, Ghilly?"

The old pet name was nearly her undoing. A soft, treacherous yearning unfolded inside her, mingled with grief that hurt her throat and made her eyes sting.

She blinked, and took a quick gulp of the hot coffee to hide the unwanted emotion. Putting the cup carefully down on the table, staring into it, she said in a voice that sounded hoarse with the effort of keeping it steady, "I have nothing to tell you, Seth."

He leaned toward her, and now his eyes leaped with angry flame. *"Yes, you damn well do!"*

She couldn't look away from him, her own eyes frightened but defiant. "No."

"Why?" he asked harshly. "Just tell me why!"

Ghislaine shook her head, unable to speak.

"You should have told me!"

"You were in prison! What could you have done?" she cried before she could stop herself. And then she cringed inwardly, because that was a remnant of earlier times, when she'd have expected Seth to fix anything, solve any problem.

"Is that why... was it because I was in prison?"

"It wasn't that simple."

"How *simple* was it, then? How complicated? I want to know." There was a simmering anger behind the questions.

"Stop hectoring me, Seth!" She stood up. "I'm going to bed, it's been a long day."

As she turned, leaving her almost untouched drink on the table, she heard the scrape of his chair on the floor, and before she reached the door his hand was on her arm, swinging her round to face him.

She pushed against him, and his hands tightened, holding her shoulders so that she was brought close to him. His green eyes blazed with temper.

For what seemed an age they stood there, breast to breast, thigh to thigh. And then he bent his head and took her mouth in a kiss of ferocious passion, his lips forcing hers apart, his fingers digging into her flesh.

It only lasted a couple of seconds, but the effect was devastating. The blood pounded in her head, and a burning thrust of desire seared her body. When he released her she almost lost her balance.

His face had flushed, but the colour suddenly receded, leaving a sallow pallor under his tan.

Breathing fast, Ghislaine stared at him with hatred, all the more hot and acrid because a moment before she'd been consumed with wanting him. "I told you," she said, her voice shaking, "don't touch me! If you do that again I'll slap you clear across the room!"

Seth gave a bark of laughter. "Just try it," he said. "Don't tempt me, Ghislaine!" His eyes were still a brilliant, glinting green.

Ghislaine swallowed, clenching her teeth. Then she swung on her heel and left him.

Chapter 4

He must have cleaned up and washed the dishes after she left, because in the morning when she went down to supervise Carley's breakfast and make Mrs. Keegan's tray the kitchen was tidy and spotless.

She hoped that he'd slept in, but on leaving Carley to her cornflakes and milk to take up the tray, she saw that the door of his room was open and the bed neatly made up.

"Where's Seth?" Mrs. Keegan asked as Ghislaine deposited the tray and went to draw up the blinds.

"I don't know. He's up." Ghislaine hesitated. "Shall I find him for you?"

"No, but I'll have to talk to him later. I haven't slept well. I think . . . I need my pills."

Ghislaine glanced worriedly at Mrs. Keegan's drawn face and took the bottle from the bedside drawer, shaking a couple onto the woman's outstretched hand. As Mrs. Keegan swallowed them, Ghislaine said, "Perhaps you ought to see a specialist."

"Specialist? What kind of specialist?"

"Well, a heart specialist, I suppose—"

"Nothing can be done for my heart, my dear. If Roger—Dr. Turner—had thought there was any chance, he'd have sent me to a heart surgeon years ago."

"I'm sure he would. But it's a long time since Dr. Turner did his training. Perhaps another opinion—"

"I don't want another opinion. I have the greatest faith in Dr. Turner's ability. Has Seth been talking to you?" Mrs. Keegan demanded angrily.

Ghislaine flushed. "He's concerned—"

"The only person he's concerned about is himself."

"Surely that's not true," Ghislaine protested. "Just the fact that he's here—"

"He wants something. I don't know what, but he's after something. Possibly he thinks that his father might have left this place to him. Well, he has another think coming." She picked up the small jug from the tray and poured fresh cream liberally over her plate of home-preserved peaches.

Ghislaine tamped down a sense of shock. Mrs. Keegan must have been very much hurt by her son, and hurt, as she herself well knew, bred anger.

"I think he just heard recently about his father's death," she said. "He told me that he got the news too late for him to come to the funeral."

"Well, he's five months too late now. Why come at all?"

"I don't know," Ghislaine admitted. "But he's travelled a long way."

"Oh?" Mrs. Keegan looked up, a silver spoon poised in her hand. "How did he get here, anyway? Does he have a car? I haven't seen it."

"He hitchhiked. I saw him arrive."

"Hitchhiked!" Disgust coloured Mrs. Keegan's voice. "From where?"

"Well, Auckland, I suppose. At least, I assumed. But maybe only from Tangihuna. He could have got a bus that far. He's been living in Australia. He didn't tell you?"

"He's told me nothing. What's he been doing in Australia?"

Ghislaine hesitated. "A variety of jobs, I gather. Labouring, mostly."

"Labouring!" Mrs. Keegan's lips pursed. "A son of mine!"

Ghislaine refrained from pointing out that labouring was a perfectly honourable occupation. Mrs. Keegan had been Lucille Delbridge before her marriage to Roald Keegan, who had brought her to this house after their wedding, about the same time that he took over a farm machinery retailing business in Tangihuna, later expanding to service other farming communities throughout the North Island. Keegan was a well-known name, going back to pioneer days, and Roald's grandfather had once served in parliament. The Delbridges, too, were one of Auckland's oldest families, with connections in the British aristocracy, and Mrs. Keegan never forgot her ancestry. It was a foible that Ghislaine found easy to forgive.

"I'd better get Carley off to school," Ghislaine said. "Then I'll bring your coffee." Mrs. Keegan liked her coffee hot, and Ghislaine always gave her time to finish her fruit and toast with marmalade before taking her drink upstairs.

Carley, her cornflakes apparently forgotten, was chatting to Seth who lounged in a chair opposite her.

"Carley, you'll be late!" Ghislaine said. "Come on, finish your breakfast."

Seth stood up. "My fault. Anything I can do to help?"

"Just keep out of the way," Ghislaine suggested shortly.

He accepted that apparently equably. "See you later, Carley," he said, and ambled out.

"What was he saying to you?" Ghislaine asked her daughter.

"Funny things."

Ghislaine's heart stopped.

"He said there used to be a fish pond in the front lawn and you fell into it once, and you had to wear his brother's clothes because yours were all wet. And did you and his brother really have a midnight picnic in the garden?"

She'd cycled out to the big house alone, and after Seth had discovered them gorging themselves on chocolate bars and fizzy drinks in the summer-house, he'd taken her home in the dark, sending Darrell back to bed, and helped her to climb undetected back in through her bedroom window.

"We did, and it was very silly and naughty of us," Ghislaine said firmly. "I was scared stiff the whole time, and it rained before I got home. It wasn't nearly as much fun as it sounds."

When she had given Mrs. Keegan her coffee Ghislaine took Carley down to the road and waited with her until the bus came along. Then she collected the tray and took it back to the kitchen, and was stacking the dishwasher when Seth reappeared.

"Do you want a cooked breakfast?" she asked him.

"If I do, I'll make it. Carley gone to school?"

"Yes, and your mother's having a shower. She'll be down soon."

"You don't need a chaperon." He sounded nettled.

"I thought you might want to talk to her."

"There's plenty of time."

Did that mean he intended to stay?

"Have you had breakfast?" he asked her.

"Not yet." Usually she got herself toast and coffee while Mrs. Keegan had her shower. But if Seth was going to remain in the kitchen, she'd prefer to skip it this morning.

There was a tap on the outside door and she went to open it, for a second staring blankly at the middle-aged man in overalls and boots.

"Oh, Mr. Wallace! I'd forgotten you were coming today."

"'Morning, Ghislaine. Mrs. Keegan said something about shifting a few plants."

"She isn't down yet."

"Well, I'll start with the lawns and see her later."

Seth's voice said, "Jerry?" And he came to stand beside her. "Jerry Wallace! Is this what you're doing with yourself these days?"

Surprise and quickly hidden dismay crossed the other man's face. "Seth! How long have you been home?" He hesitated before taking the hand Seth held out to him. "I didn't expect to see you here."

"I just arrived yesterday. How are you? And the family?"

Ghislaine turned back into the kitchen. She heard the note of false heartiness in Jerry Wallace's voice as he answered Seth's social enquiries. He didn't ask what Seth had been doing. It was obvious he felt awkward, and when he'd gone off and they heard the harsh drone of the mower, Seth leaned back against the door, a wry twist to his mouth.

"Well, what did you expect?" Ghislaine asked, against a sharp sense of pity. "People are going to find it difficult, they're bound to."

"I told you," he answered, "I don't expect anything. It's going to be…interesting, watching the reactions I get, though. You must have experienced something like it, yourself. Being an unmarried mother."

"Everyone was very kind, actually. It's not like it used to be."

"No, but in a community like Tangihuna…" Even though it was no longer the self-contained country village it had been before the roading system made Auckland more accessible, Tangihuna retained some qualities of its earlier isolation. Against the fact that the community would rally round in a crisis, and neighbours still stepped in to help when someone needed it, gossip spread like wildfire and the conservatism that bred solid, responsible citizens also bred those who were quick to judge and condemn their less admirable fellows.

"Your mother didn't throw you out, did she?" Seth asked.

"Throw me…? No, of course not! She was…disappointed, but very supportive."

"Is she still living in Tangihuna?"

Ghislaine stared at him. She hadn't realised how cut off he must have been. Hadn't his father—? But there were several reasons why Mr. Keegan might have withheld that news. "She died."

Shock pinched his face. "Died?" His hand came up as though he would have touched her, and he took a step toward her. Then he stopped and his hand dropped to his side. "I'm sorry," he said. "I didn't know. When?"

"A long time ago," Ghislaine said evasively. Then, thinking it could do no harm, she tacked on, "Before Carley was born."

Ignoring the small sound he made, she said, "It's all right. I've done my mourning." She would never forget her mother, of course, but it was possible to speak of her now without the tearing grief of the early days.

"She must have been quite young. Was it an accident?"

"Apparently she had an unsuspected heart condition. One night she said she felt tired and wanted to go to bed early. She had a bath, went to bed, and…died. I found her when I went in to say goodnight. I asked the doctor, if I'd gone in earlier…but he said it wouldn't have made any difference. She couldn't have known what was happening."

"You've had rotten luck, haven't you?"

"No worse than lots of people. I've been very fortunate. Your parents were good to me and…and Carley. I don't know where I'd have been without them."

"Your mother had worked for them for a long time."

But his look was puzzled, and Ghislaine was relieved when Mrs. Keegan appeared in the doorway, saying, "I see Mr. Wallace is here. I'll just go and talk to him about the roses and those shrubs—oh. Good morning, Seth."

Seth returned the stiff greeting, not offering to repeat the kiss of yesterday. But when his mother reached the outer door and clutched at the frame to steady herself going down the steps, he swiftly went to her side and offered his arm. She dropped it as soon as she had reached the path, but he strolled beside her as she went in search of Jerry Wallace, and Ghislaine breathed a sigh of relief, hastily slotting two slices of bread into the toaster for her breakfast.

She didn't see him for the rest of the morning. At lunchtime she set three places at the kitchen table. Jerry Wallace always brought sandwiches and a thermos of tea and had them either sitting in the garden or in his battered truck. Sometimes he would accept one of Ghislaine's cakes or a biscuit and chat to her about his family who had been her schoolmates, but despite her invitations he never set foot inside the house.

On the dot of twelve Mrs. Keegan sat down at the table and Ghislaine placed a chicken mousse in front of her.

"That looks lovely, dear. Are we expecting someone?" She looked at the third setting.

"I assumed Seth would be coming in for lunch."

"Oh, yes," Mrs. Keegan said vaguely. "I suppose—do you know where he is?"

Ghislaine shook her head, about to offer to go and find him when the back door opened and he stood there, cutting off the light.

"I've made lunch for you," she told him as he kicked off his shoes on the steps.

"Thank you." He came inside, his hands soiled and a film of sweat on his forehead. "Don't wait for me. I'll shower and change first."

"What have you been doing?" his mother asked.

"Helping Jerry shift those plants for you."

"I pay Mr. Wallace to do that," she informed him. "He doesn't need your help."

He stopped halfway across the room and looked down at her disapproving expression. "It's quite a job for one man."

"If he needs help—"

"It's quicker with two, that's all. Excuse me."

When he had gone Ghislaine put a salad and a dish of new potatoes on the table and seated herself. "He might as well make himself useful," she suggested, "while he's here."

"I don't want him interfering." Mrs. Keegan picked up her knife and fork.

I'll second that, Ghislaine thought fervently. "How long is he going to stay?" she asked.

"I don't know what his plans are. Seth never did tell me anything," the other woman fretted.

He had never been close to his mother, Ghislaine knew. Seth had always seemed something of a loner, even as a boy. She remembered when he'd been a lanky, sullen-browed eleven-year-old, a ferocious football player and always first in most of his races on sports days, but not one to join in ordinary playground games. Sometimes he'd spend the whole of the lunch hour perched in a fork of one of the old macrocarpas that ringed the school grounds, only coming down when the bell rang.

The year that Ghislaine started school, her mother began working for Mrs. Keegan three times a week, cleaning the big old house. In the holidays she packed Ghislaine into her ancient Morris and took her along.

Mrs. Keegan's younger son was nearly Ghislaine's age, a sunny-faced child with guileless blue eyes, true golden curls and a sweet, mischievous smile. Ghislaine initiated games for them both, and although her mother was anxious that she didn't encroach, Ghislaine was a well-trained child and Mrs. Keegan seemed happy for Darrell to have a playmate. A lively four-year-old, even one as easy to manage as Darrell, was taxing for someone who had never enjoyed the best of health.

Seth was usually off riding his bike somewhere, with a bunch of schoolmates or more often on his own, but sometimes he'd be perched on a the branch of a tree. Once when Darrell was confined to bed with a tummy upset and Ghislaine was told to play outside and be good, she had come across Seth lying on his stomach on the daisy-dusted lawn of the orchard, reading a book.

"Go away, kid," he said abruptly when he saw her regarding him.

Ghislaine blinked and started to back off, but curiosity got the better of her. The book was large, and she caught an interesting glimpse of glossy coloured pictures. "What are you reading?" she asked him.

He scowled, but she stood her ground and after a second or two he sat up and said, *"Animals of Africa."* He held it up so that she could see the photograph of a group of elephants on a wide yellow plain.

Ghislaine dared to come closer. She looked at the print on the facing page. It seemed dense, the words long and close together. "Can you read all that?" she asked, awed. At five, she thought she was pretty smart being able to read the eight-page large-print primers, with half a dozen words to a page, that the teacher gave her to take home.

"Yes, of course I can," the boy answered. He smiled suddenly. "You're a funny little thing."

"Show me!" Ghislaine demanded.

She thought he was going to refuse, but although he scowled again at first, he shrugged and said, "Sit down, then."

Ghislaine sat among the daisies and listened. "What does that mean?" she interrupted when he read out a word she didn't understand.

"Habitat?" he said. "It means, where they live."

"Africa?"

"Well, yes. But it's more the kind of place they live in. This big park is their habitat."

"Like you live in the big house." She always called it the big house in her mind. The rented two-bedroom bungalow she shared with her mother didn't compare.

"I suppose so."

"Show me." Ghislaine wriggled closer to him, peering at the book.

"What?"

"Show me the word," she said impatiently. "Habby-at."

"Habitat," he corrected her. "See?" He put his finger under the letters. "Hab-i-tat."

She sounded it out, then pointed to another word. "What's that?"

It was the first of many things that Seth taught her. He wasn't always patient, and sometimes he couldn't be bothered with a little girl hanging about, especially as he entered the teenage years. But if she was really in trouble, she knew that she could rely on Seth to help.

When Darrell started school she took her turn at being the elder, easing him into his first days. More outgoing than his brother, though less brilliant at both schoolwork and sport, Darrell made friends easily. Everyone liked him, he was the golden boy, and as he grew older the girls vied with one another to attract his attention, but none of them kept it for long.

"Are you all right, dear?"

Ghislaine blinked, realising that Mrs. Keegan had finished her mousse and was speaking to her. "Sorry," she said. "I was daydreaming."

She'd eaten her own meal without even tasting it. Hastily she pushed back her chair and picked up the empty plates.

"There's no hurry," Mrs. Keegan assured her.

Seth appeared in the doorway and wordlessly took the place that was obviously his. His mother said, "It would make it easier for Ghislaine, Seth, if you could come to meals on time."

"I didn't know she was making anything for me," he said. "I told her there's no need."

"Well, perhaps she'd rather do that than have you trailing in and out of the kitchen at all hours, making a mess."

Ghislaine said quickly, "I told you I'm cooking anyway, one more is neither here nor there."

Seth shrugged, tasting the mousse. "Okay. Thanks. And I'll try to arrive on time. This is very good."

"Thank you."

"And I hope you have something more presentable than jeans to wear at the dinner table tonight," Mrs. Keegan added as Ghislaine spooned coffee into the percolator.

By the time she'd poured for herself and his mother, and put one of Mrs. Keegan's special chocolate biscuits on the side, Seth was just finishing his meal. She put the cups on the table and made to take his plate.

"Sit down," he said curtly. "I'll do it." He got up, slid the plate into the dishwasher and filled the cup she had left on the bench.

Returning to the table with it, he said to his mother, "Ghislaine tells me she's not paid for what she does here."

"Paid?" Mrs. Keegan repeated blankly. She turned a startled gaze on Ghislaine. "My dear, do you expect—"

Horrified, Ghislaine flushed. "No, of course not! I told you, Seth, it isn't *like* that! And it's my business!"

"If you're going to be waiting on me as well, it's my business."

"I don't think you understand the situation."

"All right, so you get bed and board for yourself and your child—"

"It's a lot more than that."

Mrs. Keegan interrupted. "I don't think that either Ghislaine or I wish to reduce our—relationship to the level of dollars and cents."

"Certainly not!" Ghislaine supported her. "Just leave it alone, *please.*"

Mrs. Keegan said, "Seth, I don't know what you imagine your position is in this house, but I have asked Teddy Trounson to come around this afternoon and explain to you the provisions of your father's will. I hope you will make yourself available."

Seth shot her a glance, inclining his head. "Isn't that unnecessarily formal? You could just tell me yourself."

"I prefer to do it this way. Then there will be no room for recriminations and misunderstandings."

"If that's what you want. I would like to know how my father left things."

"I suggest you postpone any plans you may have until you've seen Mr. Trounson."

"Yes, of course. I don't have any plans anyway—until I've checked out what's happening here. That's why I came. To find out."

"Yes, I imagined that it was."

Seth's gaze rested thoughtfully on his mother. "You will be present as well?"

"I don't see the necessity—"

"There may be things we both need to discuss with the lawyer."

"I think you will find there is nothing to discuss."

"Perhaps. But I imagine Mr. Trounson will expect you to be there. What time is he arriving?"

"About two. If I'm to be there, then Ghislaine will accompany me."

Ghislaine tensed. "I don't think—"

"It concerns you too, dear," Mrs. Keegan said firmly, causing Seth to shoot a sharply surprised glance at her. "And besides, I may need you. Especially if I'm to forgo my little rest."

"Perhaps we should ask him to make another time," Seth suggested.

"No, no. I don't want to put him out any more than necessary."

After helping Ghislaine clear the table, Seth said drily, "My mother's become used to your being her little helper."

"She needs someone." Ghislaine sensed a criticism in the remark, which was very unfair. He hadn't been here and, particularly after his father died, there had been no one else.

Almost as if he'd read her thoughts, he said, "She doesn't want to talk about my father's death. Can you tell me?"

Drying her hands on a towel, Ghislaine hesitated. He had a right to know. "He wasn't ill for long. Probably he'd been ignoring the symptoms for some weeks. Once the doctors diagnosed cancer, it was only six weeks. He refused treatment to prolong his life because they said it couldn't save him and it would have made him feel rather dreadful a lot of the time. So they just gave him painkillers when he needed them. I can't tell you much more."

"Thank you. I'm glad it wasn't prolonged. He'd have hated that."

"Yes." She remembered a tall, loud-voiced but taciturn and easily irritated man whose usual way of coping with children, unless they actively annoyed him, was to ignore them. Seth in turn had regarded his father with wary respect rather than affection. Mr. Keegan had learned to unbend a bit with Darrell, but then Darrell won over most people. Certainly the younger son had been treated with more indulgence than Ghislaine had ever seen their parents bestow on Seth.

"How did my mother take it?" Seth asked.

"She was very brave. Of course she grieved, I'm sure she still does. But she's had to bear grief before." Ghislaine's voice shook in sympathy. "You said I've had rotten luck, but your mother..."

"Yes. You think I'm hard on her, don't you?"

"I think...it's a pity that you couldn't be closer to her. You are her only son now."

"I was for six years, before. We weren't close even then." He shrugged. "I guess I wasn't an easy child. Not like Darrell."

"Were you jealous of Darrell?"

"Jealous?" He laughed, then seemed to give the question some thought. "Envious sometimes, perhaps. I don't remember harbouring any dark thoughts. Darrell was too good-natured to engender any. A golden child. Beautiful, even as a baby. I recall the first time I saw him, I thought he was a miracle all of his own. My parents were very old-fashioned about the facts of life, I had only the haziest idea of how he'd actually been produced. It was a total surprise to me. Jealous? One might as well be jealous of the sunshine."

"You loved him," she remembered. Seth had been fiercely protective of his little brother, and endlessly patient with him. More so, sometimes, than with herself.

"Yes." His lips twisted, his eyes sombre, the vivid green darkened to the colour of a stormy sea. "Yes, I loved Darrell."

Ghislaine let the lawyer in. He was an old friend of Mrs. Keegan's, having been retained by her husband for both business and private legal matters over many years.

"Mrs. Keegan and Seth are in the front room," Ghislaine told him. "She . . . she wants me to stay."

"Yes, of course," he said, and waited at the door of the room to allow her to go first.

Seth stood with his back to one of the long windows between the floor-length green velvet drapes, his tall figure dimly reflected on the polished mahogany top of the baby grand piano nearby. Mrs. Keegan sat upright on the flowered sofa, her hands clasped in her lap.

Mr. Trounson bent over her hand almost as though he meant to kiss it. As the lawyer straightened, Ghislaine went to sit beside Mrs. Keegan. Seth strolled forward, holding out a hand to Mr. Trounson.

Clasping it briefly, Mr. Trounson asked, "How are you, Seth?"

"Not bad. And you?" Seth responded politely. "I'm sorry we've brought you out here. It seems a bit unnecessary."

"Well, Lucille thought it best." Glancing at Mrs. Keegan, he said, "You want me to explain."

"If you would," Mrs. Keegan nodded.

"As briefly as possible, please," Seth added.

"Please sit down, Teddy."

Mr. Trounson cleared his throat, sitting on the edge of a huge armchair and fishing in his briefcase. "I have here a copy of your father's will, but in short," he said, sitting back a little as he pulled out a folder and opened it, "the fact is, your father left you nothing at all." He glanced up at Seth, then down again as though afraid to meet his eyes.

Seth didn't blink or move. His unswerving gaze remained on the uncomfortably fidgeting lawyer.

Mr. Trounson cleared his throat unhappily. "You will understand the reasons, of course, most of which are spelt out in the will. He was very determined that you should not be a beneficiary, I'm afraid."

Seth gave a short laugh. "I knew my father too well to suppose he left his money to a cat's home," he said. "So my mother gets the lot?"

"Well...not exactly." The lawyer hitched himself forward again, took two pages from the folder and held them out. As Seth moved to take them, Mr. Trounson added hurriedly, "She gets the use of the house and all income from the farm, the business, and various stocks, bonds and shares during her lifetime. Then...the whole of the estate passes to your—well, to her and Roald's—grandchild."

Ghislaine's hands clenched whitely in her lap. She should have told Seth, should have—

Seth stood with the thick white pages in his hand. "You mean, if I should marry and have children..."

Mr. Trounson cast an agonised glance at Mrs. Keegan, who was sitting with her back upright and her hands tightly folded together in her lap. "Not exactly," he said. "That isn't what's meant. No, not at all."

Seth's brows contracted. "Well, then, what the hell does it mean?"

"Perhaps," Mr. Trounson suggested, "you should read it for yourself."

Seth stared at him, then frowned down at the will that he held, skimming it for an answer. Ghislaine held her breath, a pulse hammering painfully at her temple.

Seth whipped the top page away, and shook his head in apparent disbelief, then as the seconds ticked agonisingly by, he went to the window as though he needed more light, and read the whole again, more slowly. Mr. Trounson hunted for a handkerchief and dabbed at his upper lip before returning the white square to his pocket.

Then Seth, his fist crushing the pages, turned back to the lawyer. Holding them up, he said, ''What the *hell* is this all about?''

Without waiting for an answer he took two swift strides into the room and fixed a cold, savage stare on Ghislaine, who was trying to sit calmly and not tremble. ''You know about this?'' he demanded incredulously.

''Yes,'' she whispered through stiff lips. She couldn't meet his eyes. Why, oh why, hadn't she at least warned him? ''I'm sorry,'' she said miserably.

''*Sorry!*''

Mrs. Keegan's hand covered hers, light and comforting. ''Ghislaine has nothing to be sorry for,'' she said, ''but a youthful moment of weakness and compassion for a man who failed her in every way. A man who should have had the decency to refrain from seducing a girl much younger than himself. She has more than made up for that lapse. Your father has merely arranged that our granddaughter will be provided for.''

''Roald wanted to ensure that the future of his family was secured,'' Mr. Trounson said. ''You were not—around, and his descendants had to be cared for.''

Seth hadn't even looked at either of them. ''I'd never have believed it of you,'' he said to Ghislaine, his voice low and vibrant with anger. ''Never.''

With an effort, Ghislaine looked up, to find him staring at her as though trying to fathom some strange being. Speaking to his mother, though still looking at Ghislaine, he said with brutal clarity, ''Carley—'' his eyes went again to the will ''—Caroline Lucille Pargiter '*Keegan*'—is not your granddaughter. I don't know what story Ghislaine cooked up to persuade you that she is, but I'm damned if she's going to saddle me with the responsibility for another man's bastard child.''

Chapter 5

Ghislaine winced. "Don't call her that!"

Seth swung away as though he couldn't bear to look at her any longer, and thrust the copy of the will at the lawyer. "This is nonsense."

Mr. Trounson reinserted the crumpled pages into his folder. "It is legal. Roald recognised the child as his grand-daughter."

Seth's face tightened with disbelief. "How could he do that, when I decline to admit paternity?" He threw a glance of cold fury at Ghislaine.

"You're denying that you're Carley's father?" Mr. Trounson's voice held scornful distaste.

Seth looked at the man, his mouth in a tight, angry line. "Yes," he finally bit out. "I'm not the child's father." He turned to stare at Ghislaine, and she dipped her head, her eyelids coming down against the force of accusation in his gaze.

He said grittily, "I don't know who she was sleeping with at the time, but it certainly wasn't me!"

Mrs. Keegan got to her feet. "How can you?" she demanded of her son. "How can you stand there and deny the obvious? Carley is my granddaughter. I recognise her, Roald recognised her. And he would have made you sign your name to the birth certificate if Ghislaine hadn't begged him not to.''

"I'll bet she did." His mouth curved contemptuously.

Mrs. Keegan made a disbelieving sound. "It's fortunate that your father had a keener sense of honour than he managed to instil into you! At least Ghislaine has no need to worry that her child will be denied her rightful inheritance.''

"Ghislaine's child," Seth insisted, "has *no* rights to my father's estate." His gaze went to Ghislaine again, and he suddenly strode toward her.

Hastily she got to her feet.

He stopped before her, breathing hard, his eyes blazing. Perhaps he saw apprehension in hers. Softly, almost gently but with an underlying implacability, he said, "You can't keep this up, Ghilly. I suppose you did it for Carley, but you'll never get away with it. You're going to have to tell them.''

Her mouth firming with determination, she stood dumbly before them.

"Damn it!" he said between his teeth, his hands shooting out to grip her arms. "You *know* she's not entitled to use my name—to any of this!''

Ghislaine threw her head back, her eyes defiant now. "Yes, she is," she said clearly.

His hands dropped. For long seconds he stared at her as if trying to see into her soul. "You lying, mercenary, greedy, little cheat!" he said flatly.

His mother said, *"Seth!"* But he ignored her.

Ghislaine, white and shaking, bit her lip. She said huskily, "I'm telling the truth.''

Seth had paled, too. He stepped back, breathing heavily. "I think I need some air," he muttered. "Thanks for coming, Mr. Trounson. You'll be hearing from me.''

"I don't think—" Mr. Trounson sounded alarmed, bleating after him, but Seth was already out of the room, and shortly afterward the front door banged behind him.

* * *

After Mr. Trounson had left, Mrs. Keegan declared she had a headache, and Ghislaine, whose own head was pounding insistently, got her a Disprin and a glass of water, then made her some coffee and accompanied her up the stairs to her room. "I would just like a little time alone," Mrs. Keegan said fretfully, sinking down on the bed, a hand to her chest. Ghislaine gathered that she was reluctant to rest on the patio in case Seth came back.

She wasn't the only one who preferred to keep out of his way. Ghislaine lay on her own bed for half an hour, thoughts reeling in her head. Then she got up, rinsed her face in cold water and combed her hair in time to meet Carley from the schoolbus.

Seth had not seemed inclined to embroil Carley in their differences, but he had until this afternoon been unaware of the implications of Carley's presence in his family home. Now he knew, and he was furious. Ghislaine meant to stick by her daughter like glue, at least until he had calmed down and she could see what might be his next likely move.

"Granna's not feeling well," she warned the little girl. "Put away your things quietly, and don't disturb her."

Matiu Hemi, the farm manager who lived with his young family in a modern bungalow further down the road out of sight of the main house, brought in a side of mutton for the freezer and seemed inclined to linger while Ghislaine put the meat into labelled plastic bags.

"Hear Seth's home," he commented.

"Yes, he is." The news must be all around Tangihuna. "Staying?"

"I don't know. He hasn't said."

"Funny, that business." Matiu's dark eyes were on Carley who was carefully peeling the next label off the roll for her mother, her small pink tongue showing at the corner of her mouth.

Ghislaine wanted to put her arms about her daughter, to shield her from the speculation in the man's eyes.

"Everyone thought," Matiu mused, "that the minute he got out he'd have been over here to—" He caught her eye and cleared his throat, looking down at the floor. "After the way you stood by him," he said, "you'd have thought . . ." He glanced again at Carley, and shook his head. "I don't understand it."

"No one does," Ghislaine suggested crisply. "People shouldn't jump to conclusions."

He grunted, obviously not convinced.

That was something else that Seth would have to cope with if he stayed, Ghislaine realised. The silent disapproval of a small community, not only of what he had done, but what he had not done. The elder Keegans had accepted Carley into their home and given her their name, tacitly acknowledging that in their eyes Ghislaine's daughter was one of them. No one doubted that if Seth had been free at the time, his father would have made sure he married the mother of their grandchild before its birth.

If he had returned home four years ago the people of Tangihuna would have welcomed him back, if not effusively, at least with the recognition that he had taken his punishment like a man and paid his debt to society. And they'd have given him a fair chance to redeem himself and become a useful member of it again. But instead he had chosen to stay away, to run off to Australia, ducking the responsibilities that awaited his release from prison. And that was going to take some living down.

Carefully, Ghislaine said, "Things aren't always as they appear, Matiu. Maybe I don't—didn't fancy the idea, myself."

"Yeah, I s'pose you might not have been keen to be tied to him anyway, after—all that." He looked at her and then away. "Well, I'll be off, then. 'Bye, Carley." He touched the child's fair head with a broad brown hand. "Ask your mum if you can come and play with the kids again sometime."

Seth arrived in the dining room promptly at six. He wore a white shirt and dark olive slacks. Both looked brand new. Catching Ghislaine's eyes on them, he said, "Keegan credit is still good in Tangihuna. I gathered Mother doesn't approve of my jeans."

His mother glanced at him sharply but said nothing. Ghislaine, too, refrained from comment. If he was buying new clothes on credit, how did he propose to pay for them? Or did he think that Mrs. Keegan would take care of the bills? She probably would, Ghislaine surmised, simply to keep the family's good name in the town. Seth had certainly changed. But then, he had never been the man she'd thought he was. Surely he'd proved it that dark night when her world and his had been split apart?

She couldn't help a condemnatory glance at him, and he lifted his brows and smiled.

Ghislaine went to bed when Mrs. Keegan did, conscious of the frustrated green glare that followed them up the stairs. When she slipped on a nightgown after a long, relaxing soak in the bathroom she shared with Carley, she heard him come up, and his soft footsteps stop outside her door. She paused by the bed, her skin prickling with panic, but after several seconds he moved on and she heard the click of the guest room door.

Of course it wasn't possible to avoid him forever. Ghislaine kept Carley by her side for most of Saturday. But she was aware of Seth prowling about the house like a tiger scenting prey. When Carley reminded her of Matiu's invitation, she took up the suggestion with relief, and walked down the road with her to spend a couple of hours in the Hemis' kitchen, helping Matiu's wife to pickle some onions while Carley played outside with the children. She was grateful that Donna refrained from mentioning Seth's name.

On Sunday, as was Mrs. Keegan's unbreakable habit, they went to the little white wooden church in the centre of Tangihuna. To Ghislaine's surprise Seth joined them as they climbed into the big car that Roald Keegan had bought a year before his death. It had been his custom to trade in his used car for a new one every two years. Seth got in the back with Carley, and Ghislaine, made nervous by his presence, forgot about the automatic transmission and neglected to place her foot on the brake when selecting the gear, so that the car unnervingly leapt out of the garage.

After the service Mrs. Keegan usually chatted with the minister and exchanged greetings with other worshippers.

This morning Ghislaine sensed she would have liked to get away quickly, but with Seth at her side there was no chance of that. The minister had been in the parish for only eighteen months, and when Mrs. Keegan stiffly introduced her son, a courtesy he obviously expected, he shook Seth's hand with alacrity and welcomed him.

Other people hung back staring or came forward to greet him. One man clapped him on the shoulder while his wife, a pretty young woman with dark hair, stood by disapprovingly. Turning to her, Seth said, "How are you, Jinny?" And put out his hand, forcing her to acknowledge him.

Driving home, Ghislaine wondered if he had enjoyed the attention—or notoriety. He had certainly seemed reluctant to leave, and very ready to say hello to anyone who showed the slightest inclination to speak to him. She suspected that some had done so much in the same spirit that people might have wanted to boast they had shaken hands with Jack the Ripper.

When he got out and opened the front passenger door for his mother, Mrs. Keegan stopped before him and, looking up into his face, said, "I hope you're pleased with yourself."

Returning the look quizzically, he said, "I thought *you* might be pleased with me. I recall in my teenage days you were very anxious for me to attend church."

"I hoped it might do you some good, then."

"Am I beyond hope now?" he asked her. "What about Christian forgiveness?"

"What about atonement?" Mrs. Keegan snapped. "If you had shown any sign of wanting to put things right, instead of denying the obvious truth..."

"Obvious?" Seth's eyes went to Ghislaine, who was out of the car now and holding Carley's hand, tensely afraid of what Carley might overhear. "It was Pilate, wasn't it, who said, 'What is truth?'"

Mrs. Keegan made a disgusted sound and stalked toward the house.

After lunch Ghislaine helped Carley groom her pony and watched while she rode it round the paddock. Then she prepared the usual Sunday chicken for the oven, wondering if it would be enough for Seth as well, and turned to peeling potatoes and kumara.

Carley popped broad beans out of their pods into a pot, chatting about school, friends and life in general while Ghislaine listened with half an ear, until Carley said, "Midge Hemi says Seth killed a lot of people and he had to go to jail."

Ghislaine dropped the kumara in her hand and had to fish it out of the waste disposal. "Midge shouldn't be saying things like that!"

Carley said timidly, "Are you angry?"

"No, darling." Ghislaine rinsed her hands and dried them on a towel, sitting down next to her daughter. "I'm glad you told me what Midge said, but I don't want you repeat it to anyone else, okay? Seth was in prison for a while, but that's all over now. Midge must have overheard her parents discussing it, but I'm sure they won't talk about it to other people."

"Was he bad?"

"He did a bad thing," Ghislaine explained. "When people do bad things they sometimes have to be locked up for a time, to teach them that they mustn't do it again. And when they come out, everyone should help them not to do anything more that's bad. Talking about them behind their backs doesn't help them."

"If he killed people," Carley said, "that was very, very bad, wasn't it?"

"Yes, but he didn't mean to. It was an accident."

"Then why did they lock him up?" Carley's smooth brow furrowed. "When I break something or spill something and it's an accident you say I didn't do it on purpose and it's all right."

"This was a bit different. Seth was driving a car, and when people drive they're supposed to be very careful, so as not to hurt other people on the road. He wasn't careful, and that made it his fault, even though he didn't kill anyone on purpose."

"Did they lock him up for a long time?"

"Five years," Ghislaine said huskily. "Almost." Parole had shortened the sentence by a few months. "But it was a long time ago, and I'm sure he won't ever drive dangerously again."

"I like Seth," Carley announced. "Is it all right to be nice to him, then?"

"It's always all right to be nice to anyone. Just remember what I told you about sick people who might want to hurt you, though, won't you?"

Carley nodded. "Seth isn't sick, is he?"

"No! I'm sure he isn't." She wasn't worried about him on that score.

She managed to avoid being alone with him until Monday morning when she got out the car to drive into Tangihuna for groceries.

"Give me a lift?" he enquired, opening the passenger door as she paused after backing out of the garage. "I take it you're going into town."

Ghislaine swallowed, unable to think of a valid excuse to say no, and trying to control her panic. In the end, she nodded, and he got into the seat beside her.

"Thanks," he said, fastening his safety belt. "I have some things to do. How long will you be?" he enquired as they left the drive and headed toward the town, past the scattered farmsteads, some of them solid old timber houses with painted corrugated iron roofs, others modern brick and tile set in fenced, landscaped gardens.

"About an hour and half," she guessed.

"If I'm going to stay I'll have to see about getting myself some transport."

"What with?" she asked sarcastically, and then flushed under his thoughtful stare. It wasn't any of her business that he seemed to have arrived practically destitute.

He grinned suddenly. "Do you think my loving mother might help me out with a loan?"

"No, I don't! She'd be crazy to—" Ghislaine stopped herself. No use getting into a slanging match with him. "*Are* you staying?" she asked him.

"Oh, I think so," he said. "For a while, anyway. There are things I intend to find out."

She didn't rise to the bait, keeping her eyes fixed on the road ahead. They passed a large paddock where a herd of Friesian-cross cows grazed, some near the wire fence lifting their heads curiously as the car passed. On the hills farther away from the road a flock of sheep were distant white blobs on the green slopes.

"Not interested?" Seth questioned softly.

"In what you want to do? Why should I be?"

His voice hardened. "You ought to be. Because a lot of it concerns you. And that child of yours."

The car swerved toward the side of the road. Hastily Ghislaine righted it.

He was looking at her narrowly. "Do you want to tell me, now that we're alone?"

The road wound downhill and over a narrow bridge crossing a small, sluggish stream fringed with pussy willows and ponga ferns. "Tell you what?"

"Cut out the games, Ghislaine! You can lie to everyone else but you can't lie to me!"

"I haven't lied to anyone."

He turned, thumping a fist on the back of her seat so that she flinched, and the wheel jerked under her hands. An oncoming car veered nervously to the left.

"Don't!" Ghislaine said sharply. "You of all people ought to know better than to startle a driver! I need to concentrate, please."

He sat back in his seat. "All right. This isn't the place to talk about it. But we are going to talk, Ghislaine," he warned. "You can't keep ducking it forever."

"There isn't anything to talk about," she muttered, concentrating fiercely on her driving, the speedometer needle hovering just on the speed limit. She was tempted to put her foot down and get them there more quickly. The tension and frustration emanating from him was palpable. The car was a large one, but it seemed a very small space to be trapped in with this big, angry man.

He didn't speak again until they'd passed the dairy factory on the outskirts of the town and reached the parking area outside the supermarket in the main street.

"I'll leave the car here," she told him. "You can meet me if you want a lift back."

He said, "Don't wait if I'm not here. I can walk."

"Four miles?"

"I got used to walking when they took away my licence."

He'd lost it for two years commencing when he was released from prison—the judge had been ready to throw the book at him after the accident. And he must have already walked or hitched into Tangihuna yesterday after storming out of the house.

She hurried through her shopping, filling her supermarket trolley as quickly as she could and stowing the bags in the car. Lifting out a bundle of library books, she walked under the wide verandahs shading the footpaths outside the shops to the public library just around the corner and returned them, replacing them with several chosen almost at random for Mrs. Keegan and Carley, grabbing one from the "returned today" trolley for herself without even looking at the cover copy, although the author's name was familiar.

When she emerged from the library she saw Seth descending the steps from a two-storied building on the other side of the road, the office of Trounson, Dunkling and Cottle, Solicitors. Looking grimly preoccupied, he swung on down the street without seeing her.

Don't worry, she told herself. Mr. Trounson wouldn't have been able to tell him anything. There was no need for this sick fright that made her clutch at the iron railing alongside the library steps, taking a deep, shuddering breath.

"Hi, Ghislaine! Are you all right?"

Ghislaine blinked, trying to smile at Jinny Price who stood nearby, a toddler hanging on one hand, and a look of concern on her pretty face.

"Yes, I'm fine," she lied. "How are you, Jinny? Hi, Melinda," she added to the toddler, who hid her face behind her mother's denim-clad legs, peeking at Ghislaine with one eye.

"She's having a shy stage," Jinny explained. "You're looking peaky. A bit of a shock having Seth home, is it?" she asked bluntly. "Could have knocked me down with a feather when I saw him at church. Were you expecting him?"

Ghislaine shook her head. Jinny had always been outspoken. For a few years in their childhood they'd been best friends, but at high school they'd gone into different classes and the friendship had become intermittent. Jinny had married a local boy who now owned a car maintenance business, and the last time Ghislaine had bumped into her in town they'd had coffee together.

"Time for a coffee?" Jinny asked now.

"No, sorry, I'm in a rush today. Another time?"

"Sure." Jinny looked down at her daughter who was now pulling impatiently at her hand. "Stop it, Mellie! Look, Ghislaine—Ralph says I should have been nicer to Seth on Sunday. Only after what he did to you...and Carley and all...I know you were crazy about him before, everyone knew. Are you going to get mixed up with him again?"

"I've no such intention," Ghislaine assured her. She couldn't be offended, Jinny's anxious eyes made her genuine concern all too clear. "I have to go. Next time, coffee," she promised.

She had to go to the chemist to fill a prescription for Mrs. Keegan. If she'd thought of it she could have dropped it off first and picked it up when she'd finished shopping, but now she had to wait fifteen minutes while the pills were counted and the bottle labelled. When she got back to the car, Seth was lounging against the side, waiting for her. Surprisingly, he had a large suitcase with him, obviously not new although the leather had once been expensive. He'd probably picked it up secondhand.

"D'you mind?" he asked her.

"It'll have to go in the back," she said. "I bought a lot of groceries."

He swung it in easily, and she forbore asking where it had come from, but he volunteered the information. "It arrived on the ten o'clock bus," he told her. "I'm going to need it now that I know I'm staying on."

"Have you asked your mother about that?"

He cast her an amused glance. "I spoke to her yesterday. She said, and I quote, 'Of course you may stay. You are, after all, a member of the family.' Generous of her, wasn't it?"

"Yes, it was!" Ghislaine said passionately as they left the carpark. "I hope you appreciate how generous!"

He inclined his head with mock humility, jerking forward as she applied the brake to avoid running into a car passing along the road.

"I can see we can't talk while you're driving," he said.

Seething, Ghislaine changed gear. She was a good driver, but with him sitting beside her all her skills suddenly left her.

He heaved the suitcase out of the car and left it on the drive while he helped—despite her assertion that she could manage alone—to carry in the groceries. As she began putting them away he said, "I'll take my case upstairs. Will you be free when you've finished here?"

As she hesitated, he added in a hard voice, "You can't run away forever, Ghislaine. It might as well be today."

"You won't get anywhere," she muttered despairingly, looking down at the jar of peanut butter in her hand.

His face was bleak and determined. "We'll see about that," he answered. "We're going to have a showdown whether you like it or not. So when? And where?"

Ghislaine's teeth touched her lower lip. "Fifteen minutes," she said. "In the front room. But—"

"Thank you," he cut in. "Fifteen minutes it is."

His mother was dozing on the patio. If Ghislaine needed anyone—

Of course she wouldn't. Seth had never laid a finger on her in anger, even when they were children. He was simply not the violent type.

But was that still true? She shivered. The Seth she had known—thought she had known—wasn't the same as the man who had spent nearly five years locked up with all kinds of criminals, and three more bumming about doing rough jobs that must have brought him into contact with equally rough people. He'd lived among men to whom violence was a way of life. It had to have changed him. She could see that he was hardened, embittered, all the softness in him rubbed away.

She made coffee for them and carried it into the front room normally used only on formal occasions. That was why she'd chosen it, she supposed, hoping that its faintly oppressive atmosphere might dampen down any raw emotions.

When Seth entered she was sitting on one of the deep armchairs flanking the unused fireplace that was screened by a polished brass fan, the coffee on a small table before her.

"Very cozy," he said, closing the door behind him, "but I don't want coffee, thanks. Are there still drinks in this cupboard?" He crossed to a kauri cabinet, the rich mottled wood gleaming with the mellow gold patina of well-polished age, and turned the key in the door. "Ah, that's more like it. Brandy, I think. Some for you?"

"No—yes." The glitter in his eyes as he turned to enquire changed her mind. If he was in this mood, she needed to fortify herself. "A small one," she said.

He handed it to her, holding it so that their fingers needn't touch, and sat facing her.

Ghislaine looked down at the dark amber liquid and took a sip to brace herself. He had engineered this tête-à-tête; he could start the conversation.

But he was silent for so long that she was forced eventually to look up, finding him surveying her with a speculative stare. "How long did you think you'd get away with it?" he asked curiously. "You took a risk, didn't you?"

Ghislaine touched her tongue to her lower lip, tasting the brandy on it. Her spine tingled with tension. "What do you mean?"

His brows snapped together. "You know damn well what I mean! Don't play the innocent with me, Ghislaine! When did you cook up this story of yours? When you realised I wasn't coming home after I got out of prison? Decided I was never going to show my face again, did you? It never occurred to you that I might change my mind, and come back to blow your little scheme to kingdom come?''

''There was no scheme!'' she said, stung into defending herself. ''I never cooked up any story.''

''Oh, come on!'' he said impatiently. ''You're sitting pretty here in this house, waiting on my mother hand and foot, worming your way into her good graces—she never could see through anyone who was willing to treat her like a queen. And you've got what you were out for—my mother really believes that when she dies Carley is entitled to inherit all this!''

''She *is!*'' Ghislaine insisted, banging down her glass on the table and jumping to her feet. ''Mr. Trounson told you, your father was adamant that you weren't to inherit. I'm sorry about that, but—''

''Sorry?'' he shot at her, standing up to face her. ''When you persuaded him to leave it all to your daughter?''

''I had nothing to do with that! As a matter of fact I tried to tell him it was unfair to cut you out of his will. But—your father wasn't an easy man to talk to, once he'd made up his mind. And you *know* I couldn't have persuaded him into anything, even if I'd wanted to!''

He was gazing at her, lynx-eyed. ''No, you wouldn't have needed to, would you?'' he said slowly. ''You're too clever for that. Just feed him the right lies, and he'd make up his mind all by himself.''

''I told no lies!''

He stared at her white face, her unswerving eyes. ''You sound very convincing, but I'm calling your bluff, Ghislaine,'' he said. ''You might have told everyone that Carley's mine, but I'm denying it. And I'll keep on denying it—''

''No one will believe you,'' she said.

It stopped him for a second. She saw that he remembered his mother's disbelief, and the lawyer's. People he'd known all his life weren't going to accept his denials.

''You think you've got it all sewn up, don't you?'' he said. ''But there are tests—''

''Carley isn't having any tests.''

He smiled thinly. "Because you know they'd prove you're a liar and a fraud."

"I said, I'm not a liar. Carley's entitled to her name—Keegan—to her home—this house—and to anything your father wanted to leave her. I won't have her put through any tests. She's terrified of doctors and needles."

"You're making that up."

"I'm not. It's true!" When she was three Carley had been hospitalised with a stubborn, dangerous infection, and the treatment, despite the best intentions of the doctors and nurses, had been painful and traumatic. "I won't have her frightened. And it wouldn't make any difference, anyway."

There was bafflement in his dark stare. "Have you been living this fantasy of yours for so long that you believe in it yourself?" he demanded.

A bitter smile touched her mouth. "It's no fantasy." This nightmare was all too real.

He was watching her broodingly. "Sit down," he suggested abruptly. "You've hardly touched your drink."

"I don't need it. If you'll excuse me—"

"I haven't finished with you yet. Sit down."

Ghislaine's head lifted. She debated ignoring him and walking out, but that would only lead to a continuation of the uncomfortable tension of the last few days. So she shrugged and sat down, picking up her brandy.

Retrieving his, Seth remained standing, putting her at a disadvantage. He prowled restlessly across to one of the long windows and then back to pause before the fireplace, looking down at her. Under his hard stare, Ghislaine drank some more brandy and tried to appear relaxed and unconcerned.

"Did you have a chip on your shoulder all along about us, and this place?" he asked her. "About the fact that we had money? And that your mother worked for us?"

"No." She looked at him warily, wondering what he was getting at. She'd always known the Keegans were wealthy, but she hadn't particularly envied them. Her own mother had worked hard but she'd taken a pride in that, in being independent. And she hadn't seen housekeeping as demeaning, but as a skill that deserved her time and talents and was worth the price she put on it when she placed those talents at the disposal of others.

There was some truth in Seth's allegation that Mrs. Keegan liked being treated like a queen, but Ghislaine's mother, while cheerfully performing any task demanded of her, had never allowed herself to be treated like a servant.

"I know she wore a wedding ring, but your mother wasn't married, was she?" Seth asked.

"No." Ghislaine had begun to suspect that, even before she found her birth certificate tucked into a drawer full of papers after her mother died. "I suppose everyone knew she wasn't really a widow."

"Guessed, maybe. I don't think anyone knew for sure. Did it bother you? Is that why you're so determined that Carley's going to have what you never had—why you keep saying she's entitled?"

"It never bothered me," Ghislaine answered truthfully. "I didn't know until I was grown up. And then—well, I was in the same boat myself, expecting Carley." And she'd had more immediate worries to deal with.

"Exactly."

She looked up at him and laughed. "You're on the wrong tack, Seth. This isn't some grand plot to revenge myself on the Keegans, or society, or anybody."

"Then what *is* it?" he asked her, leaning forward, a hand on the arm of her chair, his eyes piercingly intent. "Why are you doing this?"

Perhaps, if she told him everything . . .

Once she'd have trusted him with her life, but now . . .

While she hesitated, his eyes hardened. "All right," he said. "But I'll find out. I'll find out if I have to tear you limb from limb."

Chapter 6

Ghislaine blinked, recoiling from him.

He straightened, with a short, harsh laugh. "Oh, not literally. But you learn a lot in prison about getting information from people who don't want to give it."

"'Ve haf vays?'" Ghislaine suggested sarcastically, trying to allay her unease.

He laughed again, a more genuine sound this time. "You never did scare easy." He ran an appreciative glance over her, but with a kind of insulting impersonality that made her hackles rise.

Ghislaine gulped down the rest of her drink and put the glass carefully on the tray with the now cold coffee. Before she could pick up the tray, he had placed his empty glass beside hers and, with his fingers about her wrist, almost casually hauled her to her feet, crowding her against the chair.

"On the other hand..." he said softly.

She pushed at his shoulder, flinging back her head with a stinging rebuke on her lips.

But she never got a chance to utter it, because his mouth covered hers, hard and warm and ruthless, a hand on the small of her back forcing her close to him.

She kept her lips clamped together, her body rigid, and when his mouth momentarily left hers she muttered, "Let me go, Seth!"

"Not until you respond," he muttered back, and kissed her again, this time more gently, but still she refused to give in.

She deliberately opened her eyes, but his dark brows and closed lids, the lashes thick and black on his cheek, filled her vision as he concentrated on the kiss, and it didn't help. When he lifted his head and saw what she was doing, he laughed quietly, and a calculating expression crossed his face before he transferred his attention to the shallow groove just under her ear. She felt the tip of his tongue on her skin, and in spite of her determination she shivered. It wasn't fair, he knew too much about her—

His arm tightened about her waist and he released her wrist at last, to place a hand on her breast, caressing her as his lips returned to hers and they reluctantly parted for him.

She tried to fight the sweet, wild sensations, tried to stop her body from pressing itself closer to his, from melting into a fluid, delicious heat that turned her bones soft and liquid. But the scent of his skin was an aphrodisiac that filled her nostrils, the movements of his mouth on hers, the hidden, muscled strength of his body waking old familiar yearnings that finally overwhelmed her, and brought him the response that he'd wanted.

When she made a despairing sound of surrender low in her throat, and slid her arm about his neck, he shivered, too, giving her a small stab of satisfaction. The kiss became deeper and fiercer, until her head was pushed into the cradle of his shoulder and arm, and they swayed, locked together in a fury of desire.

Seth's mouth lifted fractionally. "Come here!" he murmured, and turned to drop into the chair, pulling her down and scooping her legs across his knees and over the padded arm.

But the shift had allowed just enough sanity to penetrate the fog of passion that had engulfed Ghislaine. "No," she said, struggling to get up. "No, Seth! Leave me alone!"

He watched her stand up and straighten her clothes, her cheeks on fire. His eyes glittered, the lids narrowed as he laid his head against the high back of the chair. "As I was saying," he drawled, "you were easy in other ways."

She felt as though he'd punched her in the stomach. The hectic colour receded in a rush from her cheeks, leaving them white. "That's not true and you know it," she said, her voice shaking.

"I'm beginning to wonder if I knew anything about you at all," he told her, still lounging in the chair. "I played the little gentleman with you for so long—a waste of time, wasn't it?"

"What—" She swallowed. "What are you suggesting?"

He smiled then but without warmth. "I think you know. When exactly was Carley born? And don't bother to lie on this one. I can find out easily enough, even if you faked a date for my parents' benefit. There'll be records."

She gave him the date, woodenly. "I didn't fake anything. If you don't believe me you can check." Her voice shook, but she spoke with confidence. If that was the tack he was on, he'd come up against a blank wall of irrefutable evidence. "I had Carley at the local maternity hospital. Your father filled in the registration papers himself. All I did was sign them. The records will only confirm the date."

He said, frowning, "You must have been pregnant that last time I saw you, when you came to visit me."

Ghislaine swallowed. It had been among the worst days of her life. "You told me . . . not to come any more. To find someone else."

Something flickered in his eyes. "So I did. But you'd already done that, hadn't you?"

Ghislaine shook her head. She hadn't found someone else.

"You hadn't been hoping to talk me into putting my name on the child's birth certificate, had you?" Seth demanded.

"I wasn't hoping for anything," she said. She'd been beyond hope at that time, her whole world in pieces about her. She recalled the scalding tears that had run down her cheeks all the while Seth's father, his face set like granite, was driving her home from the prison.

She'd told herself that Seth was saying he didn't want her to visit only to spare her from the prison environment. But he'd been very convincing when he'd said ruefully, almost shamefacedly, that the truth was, she was beginning to bore him before the accident, she was too young for him and he should have told her so before, only he hadn't liked to hurt her. Now it was only fair to tell her that there was no point in her waiting for his release. And, cruellest of all, when she reminded him, "Crystal Summerfield was only a year or so older than me!" he'd looked at her with his green eyes suddenly opaque, and said, "Yes. But much older in the ways that count. She knew how to give a man what he wants."

Perhaps she'd been unthinkingly cruel, herself, to remind him of Crystal in the first place. Perhaps subconsciously she had wanted to hurt him, as he had already hurt her. But if so his revenge had been swift and brutal. "Go away, little girl," he'd added roughly, "and grow up."

She'd done that all right, Ghislaine thought grimly. The events of that year of blood and tears, each one painfully engraved on her memory, had dispelled the last remnants of childhood.

"Why did my father do the registration?" Seth asked her abruptly, yanking her into the present again. "How far back does this fairytale go?"

She winced at the sarcasm but let it pass. "After my mother died he...asked me to come and live here. Carley was born from this house."

He absorbed that, his face blank and watchful, thoughtful. "And he believed *then* that Carley was his granddaughter?"

"Yes." She met his eyes defiantly.

"Why?"

She said starkly, "He took my word."

Mr. and Mrs. Keegan had attended her mother's funeral, and she'd noticed their covert, startled glances at her burgeoning figure. She was four months pregnant by then and unable to hide it any more. After the burial in the old, windswept cemetery, the Keegans hadn't come back to the house where the neighbours had arranged food and drinks for the few mourners. But later that evening when she answered the door, Mr. Keegan was standing there, tall and forbidding, asking if he could come in.

She stood in the living room with him, her face wan and her eyes dull and disbelieving, but dry. And he'd looked at the swelling mound under her cheap black dress and said, "Is it my son's child you're carrying?" He had never been a man to waste time in small talk.

"Yes," Ghislaine said. Numbed by the multiple griefs of the past months, culminating in the death of her mother, she didn't even feel relief or surprise that he knew, didn't elaborate on the bald answer.

And he'd shifted his bleak green eyes to hers and said, "I'm very sorry. You should have told us."

"You've had enough troubles," Ghislaine said.

Something else entered his eyes then. Grief, she thought, and then unmistakably, compassion. "So have you," he told her, his deep voice almost gentle. "Haven't you?"

She hadn't cried through all the comforting hugs and expressions of sympathy that friends and neighbours had heaped upon her. But the rare flash of kindness from a man she'd always found distant and a little frightening crumbled her composure.

When the tears spilled unexpectedly, he'd taken her clumsily in his arms and let her cry against him for a long time. Then he'd given her his handkerchief and sat her down on a chair and said, "Now, this is what we're going to do."

He'd arranged it all for her. The sale of her mother's things, except for those Ghislaine couldn't bear to part with, the payment of the month's rent and the bill for the funeral and the other outstanding accounts, even informing her supervisor at the bank that she wouldn't be coming back to work. Almost before she could turn around she was ensconced in the Keegans' home and Mrs. Keegan, putting aside her own recent sorrow, was taking her shopping in Auckland for baby clothes and a bassinet. Once she said to the older woman, "You're being so kind to me…I'm sorry you had to find out that way—"

But Mrs. Keegan merely said, "We won't talk about that, dear. Of course I wish things had not been quite as they are, but nobody is blaming you." Then she'd turned to a book of wallpapers that they'd been discussing for the baby's room, and Ghislaine knew the subject was closed.

She'd accepted gratefully everything they did for her. She was just eighteen and alone, and the prospect of having a baby without the support of her mother or anyone close had been little short of terrifying. The only time she'd jibbed was when Mr. Keegan was preparing for his monthly duty visit to Seth, and he'd asked her quietly, "Have you told Seth about your pregnancy?"

"No!" She looked at him apprehensively. "You won't tell him, will you?"

"He ought to be told, Ghislaine. I thought perhaps you'd prefer that I—"

"No! Please don't say anything to him! Please?"

"He'll have to know eventually, my dear."

"Not yet!" She was so agitated she took hold of his sleeve. "I don't want him brooding over it while he's locked up. Think how awful that would be—he'd go mad."

His father said grimly, "You credit him with a good deal of sensibility that I doubt he has."

"You never understood him!" Ghislaine exclaimed. "I'm sorry," she added breathlessly, dropping her hand from his arm. "I shouldn't have said that."

"As a matter of fact, you're right," Mr. Keegan admitted. "I was never close to my elder son. And I'm afraid it's too late now. You're still fond of him, aren't you?"

"Yes." But so much more than fond. He'd been the centre around which her world revolved, until that world had tipped on its axis. But with the accident and its aftermath, she had to wonder if anybody, herself included, had ever understood Seth. Perhaps she'd made an idol of something that had never really existed.

"I'm not sure that he deserves your devotion," Mr. Keegan told her drily. Then he asked, "Do you want to marry him?"

"I...did." Ghislaine hesitated. Once she would have been utterly certain of her answer, certain of Seth's too. Now nothing was certain any more.

"It may be possible to arrange it," Mr. Keegan murmured, almost to himself. He was frowning as though working something out. "A wedding in the prison chapel..."

"Oh, no!" How could he suggest it?

"I could enquire—they might even let him out for a day, perhaps a registry office..."

"No!" Ghislaine recoiled.

"It would legitimise your child."

Ghislaine shook her head. "No. I couldn't! I don't *want* to marry him now!" Her voice rose. "How could I?"

"All right, my dear. I'm sorry, I didn't mean to upset you. It would...comfort my wife, you see, to know that her grandchild has our name."

"I...I'm sorry too. But I couldn't! Please, don't ask me, and don't mention it to Seth!" She felt ill just thinking of it, her face cold and sweaty.

"No," he agreed heavily. "I don't blame you for feeling like that, after all that's happened. No doubt it was a very bad idea. I won't press it."

When Carley was born, she sensed that the Keegans were disappointed the baby wasn't a boy, but they hid it well and were as kind to her as ever. And to Carley, who was named Caroline for Ghislaine's mother and Lucille for Mrs. Keegan. Her surname on the birth certificate was registered as Pargiter, Ghislaine's name, but with Ghislaine's consent, Mr. Keegan ensured that "Keegan" was added to Carley's name by deed poll.

"We could change your name, too, if you want," he had told her.

But Ghislaine steadfastly refused. "I'm happy that Carley has your name," she said, "you've both been very kind. But I don't feel that I'm entitled to it."

"My father left his entire estate in trust for your child on the strength of *your word?*" Seth demanded.

"Yes."

"I can't believe it," he told her flatly. "He was such an astute businessman. How could he have allowed a pretty face and an innocent smile to take him in?"

"I didn't take him in." Not deliberately, at any rate. And if he'd known the full truth he wouldn't have acted any differently. Seth's father had lacked the ability to express affection, but he'd possessed a strong sense of right and wrong, a sense of justice.

Seth snorted with disbelief. "Of course you did. He was no altruist, my father."

"He was a fine man." Ghislaine flared with temper in defence of the man to whom she had so much reason to be grateful.

"I'm not disputing that. But soft he wasn't—in head or heart. I'm wondering why he didn't insist on some kind of evidence."

It hadn't been necessary. Because he'd taken it for granted that the baby was Seth's.

Everyone knew that Seth was the only male who interested Ghislaine at sixteen, seventeen, almost eighteen. Even his father couldn't have failed to miss that. She'd wondered sometimes if his mother disapproved. She knew she didn't have the background that Mrs. Keegan would have wanted for her son's wife. Occasionally she'd sensed a slight coolness in the other woman's manner when she was at the big house with Seth that last summer, although she still smiled at Ghislaine and called her "dear" as she had always done.

Ghislaine and Darrell had both left school and were enjoying their last long Christmas holiday before Darrell was scheduled to go to university and study law. Ghislaine intended to follow him a year or two later, having got herself a job, starting in February, in the local bank where she hoped to earn enough to help pay her tuition fees for a degree in music.

Starting in November, when final exams were completed, there were end-of-school parties, river picnics, beach barbecues and excursions to Auckland nightspots as, with an almost feverish awareness that life would never be the same again, a lively crowd of young people crammed as much fun as they could into the weeks leading up to Christmas.

Even Mrs. Keegan, who had previously discouraged her sons from bringing home more than one or two friends at a time, with notice properly given and an invitation extended from herself, seemed to catch the prevailing mood, perhaps poignantly aware of how soon she was to take a less central part in Darrell's life. She made only the mildest protest when without any prior arrangement Darrell brought a dozen of his friends home to swim and laze about the pool all afternoon with cans of beer and soft drinks; when he laid on a party at two days' notice, carelessly assuring her, "They'll bring their own booze and food, don't worry!"; and even when he stayed out all night and in the morning arrived in a battered car driven by an erstwhile classmate and accompanied by three girls who were several years older, requesting breakfast for all of them.

"Dad had a piece of me for that, though," he'd told Ghislaine a few days later as they lay on towels beside the pool in the afternoon sun, while a cicada chirruped in desultory fashion nearby. "Gave me a blistering lecture on the evils of wine, women and song, and implied that not remembering to tell my mother I wasn't coming home that night could have killed her."

"You should have phoned," Ghislaine said. "She must have been worried. You know how she gets."

Darrell grimaced. "I was having a good time," he said. "I forgot. Anyway, at my age I shouldn't have to account for every minute I spend away from my mother."

"She is a bit over-protective with you," Ghislaine admitted. "You being the baby of the family, I guess."

"Yeah. Seth never copped it like I do—how come she never got worked up about him hurting himself or getting into an accident?"

Ghislaine said thoughtfully, "Seth's always given the impression that he could look after himself."

"So can I!"

She grinned at him affectionately. "He doesn't have your angel face and baby curls."

"Ugh!" He reached for her, scattering a cloud of tiny grey-blue butterflies hovering among the flowers, and she dodged away from him, laughing. His hair was no longer golden but it curled more than Seth's and wasn't as dark as his brother's. And his handsome, boyish features were as sunny and open as when he was four years old.

"Anyway, I don't think you've had it tougher than Seth," Ghislaine chided. "You know you can wind your mother round your little finger, and even your father is softer on you than he ever was on Seth."

"That's because Seth will insist on having head-on confrontations with them," Darrell said shrewdly. "Not so much now, but before he left home to go to university."

"Whereas you smile sweetly and obediently and then do what you like, as long as they don't find out," Ghislaine told him.

He grinned. "Makes for a quieter life. Why make waves?"

"Did Seth make waves?" Ghislaine asked curiously. She had only a hazy knowledge of Seth's teenage years. That was the time when they'd drifted apart, while Seth was growing up and she'd still been a little girl.

"Not a lot, compared with some. He had friends that the parents didn't care for much, and a couple of what Mother called 'unsuitable girls.' But don't we all?" Darrell gave a wicked, leering grin, and Ghislaine made a face at him. "They wanted him to take medicine or law at university, and he opted for science and commerce, so there were a few rows over that. I don't think Dad minded so much, but Mum thought it was a waste. And Dad was pretty livid about Seth's speeding tickets. Remember that rust-heap he bought in his first year away, that he used to drive home in for the holidays?"

"It was all he could afford at the time. I'm surprised it could go fast enough to warrant a speeding ticket."

Darrell laughed. "Seth got clocked at a hundred and twenty. I reckon he took it for a burn now and then just to get rid of his frustrations. When he'd been arguing with the parents he slammed out of the house and took off in the car. Bit unlucky, really, getting caught. It wasn't as though he was on the main road. Hardly anyone comes down here, and on River Road you can see for miles until you get near the water and those trees at the end. And you know why the traffic cop was lurking down *there*—perving, I reckon.''

''Mr. Stanhope?'' Ghislaine had laughed. ''Rot, he's not the type.'' The traffic officer's daughter was a friend of hers, and she couldn't imagine him as a Peeping Tom in the local lover's lane. ''More likely he knows about the carloads of teenagers that go down there, drinking.''

''I don't think Seth had been drinking. Not much, anyway. They only did him for speeding, so he can't have been over the limit. And he's a fantastic driver—a natural. He taught *me*,'' Darrell added modestly.

Ghislaine contented herself with a sceptical raising of her brows.

He grinned. ''I hope I can talk the old man into giving me a set of wheels next year. Tell him I can't come home and see me mum if he doesn't.'' He dropped his chin on linked hands in front of him. ''Auckland,'' he said longingly. ''Freedom at last!''

''Won't you miss this place?''

''Nah.'' Darrell rolled over on his back, looking up at the big house. ''Can't wait to get away from it. I don't know why old Seth keeps coming back for weekends.'' He turned, grinning at her. ''I *do*, though. He's cut you out of the herd lately, hasn't he? I reckon he's been waiting for you to grow up.''

Ghislaine blushed, looking away from him. When she was fifteen, and Seth had come home from university for the holidays, she'd already begun to look at him with a new, sweet stirring of excitement. She made every possible opportunity to be in his company, hoping he would see that she was no longer the little girl he was used to, but he treated her with the same mixture of offhand friendliness and the superiority of greater age that he always had.

When she'd turned sixteen she'd been invited to a twenty-first birthday party that Seth, now in his final year, had come from Auckland to attend. Dressed in a pale blue lace party frock that her mother had made, her hair twisted into a loose knot, and with more makeup on than she'd ever worn, she'd seen the surprised admiration in his eyes before he said, "You look very grown-up all of a sudden!" and asked her to dance.

That night she'd dared to try flirting with him, no doubt ineptly because she'd never attempted it with anyone before. He seemed at first embarrassed, and then distant. A few weeks later Darrell was saying, "Have you seen Seth's latest girlfriend? Wow! Talk about legs! And boobs like you wouldn't believe!"

"Don't be such a male chauvinist swine!" Ghislaine had snapped at him. "You're disgusting, you know that?"

After his first surprise, Darrell had hooted with laughter. "You're jealous!" he diagnosed accurately. "Poor old Ghilly, never mind. She won't last—they never do."

Ghislaine, her cheeks aflame, said, "I'm not *jealous*. I just think you should take your mind out of the sewer!" And walked off.

But they'd been friends too long for a tiff to last, and maybe Darrell had realised that he'd been less than tactful. He never teased her about Seth again until that day by the swimming pool, the year they left school.

It was true that around that time Seth had been home more than usual. He had confounded his parents by getting a well-paid job in the development section of a large pharmaceuticals company after completing his double degree. And the weekend after Ghislaine's last exam he'd arrived in an almost new silver car, sleek and sporty, the envy of his brother and all Darrell's friends. He'd let Darrell, who had a new licence but was seldom allowed to drive his father's car, take it for a spin along some of the country roads while Seth sat in the passenger seat.

"Wouldn't let me try it out for speed, though," Darrell reported indignantly. "Talk about 'Do as I say, not as I do!' Anyone'd think he didn't trust me!"

Later Seth had called at Ghislaine's house and asked her if she'd like to go for a ride.

It was the first of several invitations, all apparently casual and spur-of-the-moment, nothing that could be called a real date. He returned to Auckland but the next weekend, and the next, he was back home.

Whenever the crowd gathered at the big house Seth seemed to be there, talking quietly and pleasantly with everyone, but in the end unobtrusively singling out Ghislaine. He even attended the Keegans' annual pre-Christmas gathering, when they traditionally invited their friends and business contacts and Tangihuna's tradespeople with whom they dealt to come for drinks and socialising. Ghislaine and her mother were always invited, but it was the first time since he'd left home for university and flatting in Auckland that Seth had bothered to turn up.

Ghislaine and Caroline were late, because they'd had some trouble starting Caroline's ancient car. In the end Ghislaine, trying to avoid soiling her best dress, had pushed the Morris down the slight slope of their rough driveway while her mother kept turning the starter. Caroline had suggested doubtfully that perhaps they'd better stay home, but a look at her daughter's crestfallen face changed her mind.

The party had overflowed from the house to the patio at the back. The minute Ghislaine stepped out of the door onto the faded red tiles, she saw Seth talking to Mr. Trounson— the solicitor—and his wife. As she watched him he lifted his head and his eyes went straight to her, and a second later he was moving through the crowd under the intermittent shadows cast by the climbing plants overhead, smiling at her as though they were the only two there.

She knew she was smiling the same way, and was vaguely aware of her mother beside her staring as Seth reached them and took both her hands in his.

"Ghislaine," he said, and the intimacy in his quiet voice sent a shiver of pure pleasure dancing up her spine.

Then he bent his head and brushed her lips fleetingly with his, his eyes holding hers for another second before he turned and put out his hand to her mother. "How are you, Mrs. Pargiter? Nice to see you again."

He found a seat for Caroline and got them drinks, and stayed at Ghislaine's side until everyone was leaving. And then, because Caroline's car refused to start, even with enthusiastic assistance from Darrell and several of his friends, he took them home in his own car.

When he got out to open the doors for them, Caroline thanked him and said casually, "I'm going to bed, but I'm sure Ghislaine wouldn't mind making you a cup of coffee, if you'd like, Seth."

Ghislaine refrained from giving her mother a grateful hug.

She made the coffee and they sat and talked, and she saw the banked green fire in his eyes, and waited for him to kiss her again, properly.

He didn't until he was leaving, and then he stood on the doorstep and framed her face in his hands and lowered his lips gently to hers, in a kiss that was long and tender and like nothing she had ever experienced.

She lifted her hands to put her arms about him and bring him closer, but he caught them in his and held her away from him. "Did you like that?" he asked gruffly.

"Yes, of *course* I liked it!" she assured him. "Let's do it again!"

He laughed then, and put his arms about her and hugged her to him, his cheek rubbing against her hair. "We will," he promised, "very soon."

She wanted to say, "I love you," but sensed that he preferred not to rush things. And she remembered how he had cooled last year when she'd been too forward. She just smiled in what she hoped was an enigmatic, Mona Lisa fashion, and let him walk to his car alone. When he'd gone, and she'd come inside and shut the door behind him, she leaned back against it, clasping her hands before her with lifted eyes, and then danced all the way to the kitchen and the dirty coffee cups. It was after that night that they began seeing each other exclusively, became tacitly recognised as a couple.

"What are you smiling at?"

The harsh voice recalled her again to the present, the dim, dankly cool room, and the angry, baffled man standing before her.

She blinked at Seth—the new, different Seth who didn't trust her word and thought his father a fool for having done so.

"Smiling?" she said blankly, unaware that she had been doing so.

"That little cat-that-got-the-cream look," he said. "What's it all about?" As she didn't answer, he looked at her with narrow, calculating eyes and she saw him stiffen, his face going pale. "No," he said to himself. "It's not possible."

"What's not possible?" Her heart was thumping with fright, she didn't like the suddenly ugly look on his taut face.

He said hoarsely, "You didn't—you couldn't—was it my father? Did you actually get round *him* that way?"

It took several seconds for his meaning to even start to seep through her stunned brain. When it did, her first thought was to hit him, but shock paralysed her, although her hands curled into fists as she stared up at him. Almost choking on the words, she whispered, "I—I—have to go—"

And he stood like a stone looking after her as she turned with her hand over her mouth and fled for the downstairs bathroom.

Chapter 7

When Ghislaine emerged from the bathroom, white and shivery, there was no sign of Seth. She peeked at Mrs. Keegan dozing on the patio, and then went upstairs and lay down until she felt less sick, although the leaden burden of misery and fear that had been constantly with her since Seth's arrival was still there.

She tried to relate the man whose every word and glance seemed inimical and threatening, to the boy she'd once known, patiently teaching her to read well ahead of her age; and to the considerate young lover who had briefly, tenderly, begun to initiate her into the mysteries of sexual passion.

But she had changed, too. Then she'd been an eager but frightened young virgin. Now she was a mother and a woman, and if Seth had become hardened, events had toughened her as well. With his parents' help she had built a life for herself and Carley, and his mother needed her now. Perhaps more than ever since he'd come home. She wasn't going to walk away from that.

By the time she went downstairs to make Mrs. Keegan's afternoon tea, she'd pulled herself together, forced a mask of serenity to her face, and determined that whatever Seth's next move was, she'd meet it without flinching.

It seemed he was biding his time. For the next couple of days she hardly saw him, and when she did he treated her with a remote, mocking courtesy that set her teeth on edge but left her powerless to retaliate. She didn't ask how he was spending his time, and so far as she knew neither did his mother. Mrs. Keegan scarcely acknowledged her son's presence in the house at all, but her brief attacks of breathlessness and nervous tension increased, and her voice had taken on a fretful tone.

Ghislaine was tense, too. The only person not adversely affected by Seth's presence was Carley. Carley liked him, and Ghislaine gradually ran out of excuses to keep them apart. She was afraid that Seth would rebuff the child, but he never did. Whenever Carley ran to meet him he would smile at her in much the same tolerant way that he used to smile at Ghislaine when she was Carley's age and he was entering his teens. He never sought her out but he talked to her and listened to her with grave attention, and when Ghislaine warned her daughter not to be a nuisance, he flashed her a look over the little girl's head and said curtly, "She's not a nuisance. Leave it."

Ghislaine left them together and went into the kitchen to prepare the dinner, her emotions so churned up that it was a while before she identified with a sickening jolt the source of her rage and pain.

She slammed down the bowl she'd taken from a cupboard and slumped into a chair, her elbows on the table, burying her head in her hands. She was jealous—jealous of her own daughter. Because Seth was still capable of a gentleness with children—with Carley, anyway—that he couldn't or wouldn't give to her.

Appalled, she took a couple of deep, calming breaths. This was ridiculous. You're not a child any more, she reminded herself grimly, so stop acting like one. Be thankful that he hasn't directed any of his antagonism toward Carley.

At dinner his mother said to him, "Matiu Hemi tells me that you've been . . . advising him about farming matters."

Seth looked up from his plate. As far as she could read his masklike expression, Ghislaine thought he looked wary. "Did he say that?"

"He said that you'd been talking to him about trying a new breed of beef-cross cattle."

"When I was helping Matt ear-tag some of the stock we discussed a couple of herds I'd seen in Australia. He thought they sounded interesting."

"We are not in Australia."

Ghislaine felt herself stiffen with tension. Seth put down his fork and leaned back a little, surveying his mother with a faint curl at the corner of his mouth. Ghislaine looked away, watching Carley separating her carrots from her peas.

Mrs. Keegan added, "I wasn't aware that you'd been 'helping' Matiu. You were never interested in the farm before. I don't know what you hope to gain from it."

"Gain?" Seth cocked his head. "Perhaps I thought I might learn something."

Ghislaine looked up quickly at him.

"And actually," he said, "I spent quite a lot of time on the farm when I was a boy. Perhaps you didn't notice—or you've forgotten."

"When you were too young to be of any use," his mother said.

"I suppose. Maybe I can make up for it now. Earn my keep?"

"That's quite unnecessary. And if you think I'm going to pay you wages—"

"That isn't what I meant," he said shortly.

"If you need money," Mrs. Keegan said, "I'll see Teddy Trounson and make some suitable arrangement."

Seth looked momentarily startled. "Thank you," he said.

"But don't expect a fortune," Mrs. Keegan warned him. "And I won't keep you forever."

"Of course not." Ghislaine couldn't read his expression now, but she thought it held a touch more warmth than she'd seen him yet direct toward his mother. "That's very generous of you," he told her.

Mrs. Keegan was a generous woman, Ghislaine wanted to tell him. She'd been a recipient herself. He shouldn't have been surprised that his mother was willing to help him financially, or any other way. She found herself hoping that this was the beginning of a new phase for the two of them. They'd never communicated well, but they were mother and son, and there must be some bond that would help them bridge the gap that so obviously existed between them.

Having been close to her own mother, she had always been puzzled and occasionally disturbed by the distant nature of Seth's relationship with his. They seemed constantly to be at odds with each other, not overtly but on some deeper level, as though they were trying to communicate across some invisible barrier.

The days had grown longer. Carley jibbed a bit at going to bed while it was still light, but with school the following day, Ghislaine insisted.

"Can't I have a swim first, then?" Carley begged. "Please?"

Ghislaine gave in, and went up with her to change. Carley was a good swimmer, but Ghislaine always stayed in the pool with her or at least watched her from the side.

They played about for half an hour before Carley scampered inside, wrapped in a big towel, to get ready for bed. Ghislaine locked the gate to the swimming pool and followed more slowly, tying the belt of her terry-cloth wrap and pausing to dry her feet before stepping into the house.

She locked the back door, too, and rubbed her wet hair with a towel on her way down the passage, dropping the towel about her shoulders as she came into the big front hall.

Seth was at the bottom of the staircase, and for a instant in the fading daylight that penetrated the gloom of the hall, she thought he was naked.

Then she saw that he was wearing hip-hugging swimming briefs, and swinging a towel from his hand.

"I thought I'd join you in the pool," he said, "but I see I'm too late."

"You can still swim," she said, proffering the key as he walked across to her. "Just remember to lock up afterwards." She concentrated on his face, trying not to study the tapering masculine lines of his body, the broad shoulders and narrow hips, the deep, lightly furred chest and long, muscular legs. He had tanned all over in the Australian sun. He'd been nice to look at before, but now he was magnificent, brown and unscarred.

"Thank you." He took the key from her, their fingers brushing.

"You were very lucky," she said involuntarily, desperately trying to distract herself from the tingling shock of that light, unintentional touch.

"Lucky?"

"That you weren't injured." She bit her lip. She hadn't been going to bring up the subject of the accident. It had just slipped out.

"Lucky," he repeated, a feral smile momentarily showing his strong teeth. "I suppose you could say that."

Ghislaine made to pass him, and he shifted slightly, but not enough for her to walk by easily. He tossed the key in his hand. "Can I persuade you to come back in with me?"

She shook her head. "I have to put Carley to bed."

In fact Carley was quite capable of putting herself to bed, but she liked Ghislaine to read to her and kiss her goodnight.

He knew by now that it took less than fifteen minutes, but he didn't suggest again that she join him, just nodded, his eyes letting her know that he recognised the excuse for what it was, and then went on down the passageway.

He had been incredibly lucky, she thought, climbing the stairs. Physically, at least. Although no doubt the fact that he'd walked away unscathed while four people had died and another was critically injured had been one consideration that led the judge to impose a heavy sentence on him.

Not the most damning one, though. Ghislaine still couldn't believe that, when he'd found Crystal Summerfield was bleeding to death beside him while two other cars lay wrecked on the lonely stretch of road, he had just deliberately walked away.

"No, I didn't know Officer Stanhope was injured," he'd said in the witness box. "I didn't know the Witehera family were dead. I didn't know they were in the other car. I never saw the other car.

"I don't remember," he'd said over and over. "I don't remember anything about it. I don't remember the accident."

He must have been in shock, Ghislaine had thought. Because the police doctor had found no injuries on Seth beyond a couple of scratches and a slight swelling of one ankle. He'd been adamant there was no sign of concussion.

"You *wouldn't* have just left them," she'd said to him in the weeks awaiting his trial when he'd been home on bail. "Unless maybe to go and get help? And anyway, you came back later! Surely they'll take that into account. Try to remember, Seth—maybe if we go over it together—"

But he'd said harshly, "I don't want to talk about it. I can't remember anything about it. Just shut up, will you? There isn't anything you can do, Ghilly."

She'd put out her hands to him and he'd taken them in a crushing grip, saying, "Sorry, I didn't mean to snarl. I know you're doing your best and it's good of you to stick by me—"

"I *love* you," she'd said, tears stinging her eyes. She was bewildered and shocked and sickened by what had happened, and she'd had to readjust her view of him, accepting that he'd reacted less than heroically in a crisis.

"Ghislaine!" He took her in his arms then and kissed her mouth hard, then kissed away the tears. "I don't deserve you," he said. "I'm sorry I've been such a brute lately." And then he covered her mouth again, with the fierce, hungry desperation that lately she had come to expect.

It was just as well, she'd told herself stoically, that she'd learned to see him as a normal, fallible, person instead of the shining hero she'd created in her own mind and worshipped since childhood. That shouldn't stop her loving him. It ought to make her love stronger and more durable, based on reality rather than starry-eyed romance. For better, for worse was what love was about, wasn't it? If she deserted him when he needed her most, what sort of person would that make her?

But sometimes, while they waited with increasing dread for the trial date, she couldn't help weeping in the privacy of her own room for the loss of the person she'd thought he was.

That leaden suspense, the sense of dread that was the chief feeling she recalled of those awful weeks, had returned with Seth's homecoming.

After tucking Carley into bed and reading her a chapter of *The Hobbit,* she went to draw the blinds to dim the room, and stopped with a hand on the tasselled cord. Carley's room overlooked the pool, and looking down she saw Seth powering through the water from end to end and back again. Water sleeked his hair, and she felt a shiver of desire as she watched the taut muscles of arms, legs and back under the slick wet skin.

Lust, she thought. Not love—that had died along the way while they were apart, turning into the two different people that they were now. And perhaps it had never been love on his part anyway, just a young man's natural carnal appetite for a nubile girl.

Because if he'd been the only man she could even see, let alone think of loving, it hadn't been the same for him. For Seth, she'd been just another girl, perhaps a bit special because he'd known her and been fond of her for so long. But basically no different.

She'd been stupid enough to think that once he saw her as a woman instead of a child, he would forsake all others. Knowing there'd been girls before her, why hadn't she realised that what he didn't get from her he could easily get from someone else?

Someone like Crystal Summerfield.

"Mummy? What are you looking at?"

Ghislaine pulled the blind down and turned to smile at her daughter. "Nothing. Go to sleep."

"Is Seth swimming?"

"Yes, how did you know?"

"I can hear him. He splashes more than you. Like Grandad used to. He looks like Grandad sometimes." Carley looked wistful.

"That's because he's Grandad's son. People tend to look like their parents."

"I look like you, everyone says."

"Yes, I know." Ghislaine crossed to the bed and sat on the edge. "Do you miss Grandad?" Knowing his impatience with children, Ghislaine had largely kept Carley out of Roald Keegan's way. But he had been a very positive presence in the house, and occasionally he had smiled at the child and gruffly talked with her, although Ghislaine thought that Carley had rather gone in awe of him.

"Sometimes," Carley said consideringly. "But Seth is here now."

Not sure how her mind was working, Ghislaine said, "He may not stay very long."

"Why not?"

"Well, for one thing, it's Granna's house and she might not want him to."

Her fair hair spread on the pillow, Carley regarded her mother with grave blue eyes. "But Granna's his mother!"

"Yes, but when people are grown up their mothers don't need them around all the time."

"When I'm grown up won't you want me?" Carley's eyes were enormous.

"Yes, darling, of course I will!" Ghislaine slipped down to her knees and put her arms around the child. "I'll always want you. You'll be home just as long and as often as you like. But when you grow up you'll want to go away sometime, and have a home all your own."

"No, I won't. I want to stay with you for always."

Ghislaine smiled and didn't argue. "I'm glad," she said. "If that's what you want, I'd like it, too."

Ghislaine was still wearing her thick towelling wrap over her swimsuit. She showered and changed into a cool cotton nightgown, tying on an embroidered silk dressing gown that had been her mother's.

The material had faded with the years from sky blue to palest duck-egg, and it was very thin, but she loved the feel of it and it had been part of her childhood. She remembered stroking the hand-sewn butterflies and flowers when her mother wore it, and Caroline saying smilingly, "When I die, it's yours."

After Caroline's death she hadn't been able to wear it, because each time she looked at it she'd think, But I don't want it, Mum, I want *you!* Until the grief had passed, and she'd been able to put on the lovely gown and smile because it evoked good memories.

The daylight had faded at last. Mrs. Keegan would soon be going to bed. She had always retired early in the evening, to read one of her favourite biographies or detective novels for a couple of hours before switching off her light.

Barefoot, Ghislaine went down the stairs to lock up the lower floor for the night. When she'd come out of the shower the splashing from the pool had stopped, and she supposed Seth would be in his room changing.

She was halfway down when the back door shut, and she hesitated, suddenly conscious of being in her nightwear, and wondering if she had time to go back to her room until Seth was out of the way.

But while she debated her chances he strode into view, a towel wrapped about his waist, his hair rough-dried and pushed back. He waited at the bottom for her, although there would have been plenty of room to pass on the broad stairway.

He watched her descend, his gaze going from her bare feet up over the soft, clinging blue silk to her throat, and lingering on her mouth, only meeting her eyes when she reached the lowest stair that made them level with his.

She stopped there, because he was standing with a hand on the balustrade, swinging the pool key from one finger of the other hand.

She put out her hand for it, palm up, and after a pause that seemed interminable, he dropped the key onto it.

She closed her fingers on the cold metal. "Thank you."

His eyes were sombre, his face stark with his hair damp and back from his forehead. She made to walk round him, but as she stepped to the floor at his side he caught her arm. "Wait a minute."

His fingers were hard and strong, and through the worn silk she could feel that they were cool from his swim. She pulled against his hold but he didn't let go, still looking at her face. "Tell me something," he said.

She lifted her chin, staring at him with hauteur.

"Did you suggest to my mother that I could do with some money?" he asked her.

"Of course not!" Her surprise was unfeigned. "Why should I?"

His mouth twitched, his brows rising. "I thought perhaps you were sorry for me."

She said, "What your mother does with her money is her business, but I certainly wouldn't encourage her to spend it on you."

He dropped his hand from her arm at last. "At least I'm her own flesh and blood."

"So is Carley!" Ghislaine flashed, backing from him as Mrs. Keegan appeared in the doorway of the little sitting room they used in the evenings.

"Ghislaine? I was wondering where you were. I'm ready for my hot milk and chocolate biscuit now."

"I'll get it."

Ghislaine hurried toward the kitchen as Mrs. Keegan said, "Seth, I wish you wouldn't stand about dripping on the carpet."

He hadn't been dripping, he must have dried himself before he came inside. But she heard him say, "Sorry, Mother," and go on up the stairs.

Almost ready to climb into bed later, Ghislaine realised she'd forgotten, after all, to check the doors and windows.

She thought about leaving it. She was fairly sure that Seth would have locked the back door when he came in from the pool, and that she had shut the kitchen windows after she and Carley had done the dishes. What about the window in the sitting room? Had they opened that tonight?

Sighing, she retied the belt of the embroidered wrap and opened the door to the landing. There was a line of light under Mrs. Keegan's door, but downstairs was in darkness.

She didn't need light on the stairs, but she snapped on the switch in the passageway and checked the front and back doors, made sure the kitchen windows were latched, then went into the sitting room. It was in darkness but there was moonlight filtering through the curtains, and she crossed to the windows and satisfied herself they were secure.

She turned to go back to the door and drew in a startled breath at the tall, bulky figure standing there.

"Ghislaine," Seth said.

"What do you want?"

"I heard noises and thought I should investigate. What are you doing in the dark?"

"Checking. I forgot to lock up before. Your mother gets agitated if she finds we've left something open overnight."

"I made sure everything was locked," he told her. "You can leave it to me in future."

That sounded awfully permanent. She went slowly towards him. Toward the door.

Instead of moving back to let her through, he stepped into the room. "Was that remark of yours for my mother's benefit?" he asked her.

"What remark?" she queried blankly.

"About Carley being her flesh and blood. You saw her standing in the doorway, didn't you?"

She stopped in front of him. They were a foot apart and she discerned that he was wearing a light shirt and dark trousers, but she couldn't see his face. And she was shaking, she realised. She said huskily, "You won't believe me if I say no. Why bother to ask?"

"Maybe because I'm still hoping that one day you'll tell the truth."

"I've never done anything else."

His breath hissed. "What *is* it with you? You think if you stick to your story religiously, everyone will believe it?"

"It's worked so far." Let him think what he liked, she was too tired to argue.

His hands clamped on her shoulders and he shook her. "You deceitful bitch! How many men were you sleeping with, that summer, when I thought I was the only man in your life?"

"None!" She stumbled back as he released her, but he followed, a dark, avenging shape looming over her. "You know there wasn't anyone else!" she cried. "You *know* it!"

"Then where did your damned cuckoo in the nest come from?" he demanded. "Because it was sure as hell no virgin birth!"

Blindly, unthinkingly, she swung her hand at his face, and heard the slap land with a satisfying crack.

But her satisfaction was shortlived. He grabbed at her wrist and yanked her toward him. Her fist thudded on his shoulder and she fought him.

His strength was much greater than hers and she knew she'd made him thoroughly angry, but she was too angry herself to take the safe, sensible way out and give in. Her fists flailed and she got him a glancing blow on the chin before he captured both wrists and twisted them to one side until she was off balance.

She didn't understand at first why he was backing, until he gave a sudden pull and turn and she found herself sprawled on the sofa. And heard the distinct, heartbreaking sound of tearing silk through their laboured breathing as Seth knelt over her.

She gave a despairing cry and stopped fighting, and hot tears scalded her cheeks, falling to the pillows.

Seth said sharply, "Are you hurt?"

"My gown," she whimpered. "My mother's gown—you tore it!"

Sobbing, she hit at him again, but without force, her hand beating uselessly at his chest until he caught it in his.

He made a low, smothered exclamation, sat down and pulled her against his shoulder, his arm round her while he stroked away the tears with a thumb. "Stop it, Ghilly. Stop, now. I'm sorry. I just wanted to stop you attacking me."

"You started it!" she accused him like a child who'd got into a playground spat.

"I suppose I did." He was smoothing her hair now, and she felt his lips on her temple. "How bad is the damage?"

"I don't know!" She sat away from him, wiping her nose and her cheeks with the back of her hand, and he got up and switched on a table lamp.

Ghislaine fumbled in the pocket of the robe and produced a tissue, rubbing at her face with it.

"Let's see," Seth suggested, coming back to her.

Stuffing the tissue back into the pocket, she tried to peer over her shoulder where she thought she'd heard the fabric tear.

Seth said, "Take it off and come into the light."

She slipped out of the robe and carried it to the lamp, finding the long slit that followed the line of the seam.

"Can you fix it?" he asked her.

"I think so," she said with relief. "It's very close to the stitching, and there's room to make the seam a bit bigger."

"It was your mother's?"

"Yes. I loved it when I was kid." She folded the gown carefully, reluctant to put it back on in case the tear got worse.

"I liked your mother." He put out his hand and traced the line of a flower stalk embroidered on the silk. "I always thought you were very lucky." He looked up, his eyes meeting hers. "Ironic, I suppose. You had none of the material and social advantages that I did. But I envied you."

Ghislaine swallowed. "Your mother—would like to be closer to you, I think."

He shook his head, his mouth twisting. "Once, perhaps. It's too late now. Oh, I'm not blaming her. No doubt I was a repulsive child. I vaguely remember some fairly horrific tantrums when I was small. I have no idea what about, but I can still vividly recall the consuming rage and total frustration. My father soon put paid to that sort of behaviour."

"All children have tantrums."

"I suppose so, though I don't recall that Darrell ever had my nasty temper. When he cried because he didn't get what he wanted, he sounded heartbroken rather than angry. Except for my father, who was made of sterner stuff, I think all of us found it almost impossible to withstand."

"He was spoiled," Ghislaine said. "He could always make you do anything he wanted you to when you were children." And later, she had suspected that the reason Seth came home quite often was to provide a buffer between Darrell in his independence-asserting teenage years and their father.

"It didn't matter." Seth's face softened in remembrance. "He was so sweet-natured from the time he was a baby, spoiling didn't harm him, except perhaps—" His eyes had suddenly gone bleak.

"Except what?"

"Perhaps he might have been stronger, if we'd been a bit tougher on him. I don't know. I'm no psychologist."

He meant emotionally stronger, of course. Ghislaine knew what had brought the look of remembered pain to his face.

"He was at a vulnerable age," she said. "Teenage suicide is common. Sometimes it seems the only way out."

He was looking at her intently. "Did you think of it?" he asked. "When you found you were pregnant? You weren't much older than Darrell."

"It crossed my mind," she said. But finding she was pregnant had been only the culmination of the trauma that had gone before. And then there'd been the final, crippling blow. "Especially after my mother died," she added.

"God!" Seth breathed.

"And then your father came to the rescue . . . I'd always been rather afraid of him, but he was kind that night."

Slowly, Seth said, "I think I'm beginning to understand." He raised his hands and cupped her shoulders, bare except for the ribbon straps that curved around to tie in a bow in the front of the pale blue cotton nightgown. "You must have been so frightened and alone."

"Yes," she said, shivering. There had been no one to share her anguish and despair over the past, or her terror of the future.

Seth stared frowningly down at her. His hands moved over her skin, along the line of her neck until they framed her face. He bent and touched his lips to her forehead, and Ghislaine closed her eyes, pierced by the tenderness of it, a tear sliding from the corner of one eye to her cheek.

Seth's tongue caught it, and he whispered, "Don't cry."

She opened her eyes then and looked at him, and tried to smile. He was still frowning, but there was taut desire on his face, a glitter in the green eyes. His fingers slid into her hair, and he said, "I wish you hadn't cut it. It was beautiful, before." Then he lifted her face further, and she closed her eyes again as his mouth came down and claimed hers, passionate, questing, nurturing.

Ghislaine savoured the kiss, not responding but standing quiescent in his hands. Her heart increased its rhythm, and there was fire in all her veins. Unconsciously, her hands tightened on the silk garment she held, crushing the fabric. When Seth at last raised his head, he looked down and carefully took the gown from her hands, placing it on the table by the lamp.

They stood inches apart, Seth's eyes narrow and questioning, Ghislaine's darkened with apprehension and desire.

"You look frightened," he said, touching one of the satin straps, sliding his fingertip to the bow between her breasts, his eyes following its path.

"I am."

"Don't be." He looked up into her face, and repeated, "Don't."

His finger trailed up her skin, along the line of her throat to her chin, resting under it. "Please don't," he whispered, as he lowered his mouth to hers and began a slow, erotic exploration of its outline.

When her lips at last trembled in involuntary response he fitted his mouth firmly over hers and kissed her deeply, his hand on her waist drawing her snugly into the curve of his body as her mouth opened for him, inviting the warm thrust of his tongue.

When he withdrew it and lifted his head she kept her eyes closed, her lips still parted and moist while she felt his mouth on the taut arch of her throat and his hand slipped the strap from her shoulder.

Then his hair brushed her skin and the warmth of his lips flowed over the swell of her breast where her nightgown was pushed down, and she cried out wordlessly, swaying in his arms.

He laughed then, a low, pleased, breathy sound, and returned to her lips, but as he kissed her again with increasing abandon his hand was on her breast, teasing the soft flesh into a feverish response.

Wild sensations cascaded through her body. She felt she was about to go out of control, her breath quick and uneven, her limbs heavy, heated, liquid, even while small shivers passed over her skin.

Seth's mouth left hers again, but only to press hot, openmouthed kisses down the side of her throat, and to nuzzle into the angle of her shoulder. His palm was still stroking her, and then she felt the gentle nip of his thumb and forefinger, and her breath escaped in a sharp sound of pleasure.

"You like that," he murmured, and did it again, and she shuddered against him, her head thrown back, eyes slitted so that she could barely see his smile as he felt her reaction.

"You know I do," she told him, her voice scarcely audible. He'd always known exactly what she liked, as if by instinct.

He held her away from him to watch his own hand on her body, and what it was doing to her. Suddenly shy, she turned her head into his shoulder and moved closer to him, but his hand was still touching her.

"We can't stay here," he said in her ear. His lips grazed along her temple. "Come up to my room, Ghislaine."

Chapter 8

Seth eased her away a little and reluctantly drew the strap of her nightgown up, dropping a kiss on her bare shoulder as he did so. With one arm still hooked about her waist he picked up the folded robe from the table before urging her toward the door and the lighted entrance hall.

The light made her blink and as they passed the switch he reached out a long arm and flicked it off. She was glad that the stairs were now in darkness, and at the foot of them he turned her in his arms and kissed her, then whispered, "Shall I carry you up?"

"No." Her voice sounded shockingly loud, although she had spoken very quietly, and she felt his silent laughter before he loosed her and they climbed the stairs together, their hands entwined.

It was the line of light under Mrs. Keegan's door that stopped Ghislaine in her tracks and made her fingers stiffen in his, automatically trying to free herself from his grasp.

"What is it?" he murmured, and Ghislaine shook her head, less in denial than trying to clear her brain of the dark enchantment that still lingered.

As he urged her along the passageway with an arm about her waist, all the reasons why she couldn't do what she'd been going to do came crashingly to mind, and outside her own bedroom door she pulled away from him, gasping, "No! I'm sorry—"

She backed from him and fumbled for the handle of the door, pushing it open. But as she stepped inside the room he followed her in the darkness, scooping her into his arms. "Ghislaine—"

She shied from his kiss, shoving against him in something like panic. "Don't!"

He let her go and turned, as though he would have left, but instead he shut the door, then snapped on the switch beside it.

Ghislaine flinched from the sudden flood of light and the taut anger in his face.

"You've changed your mind." His voice was flat and wary. Leaning back against the door he invited, "Tell me why?"

She said hopelessly, again, "I'm sorry."

He straightened suddenly, taking a step toward her. "I said, why?"

"I—" Ghislaine spread her hands. Where could she start? The fear of Mrs. Keegan overhearing, of knowing they had gone to his room together, had been the catalyst. But there were myriad reasons. A deeply felt instinct based on her early training was one. Her mother might not have been married but, perhaps because of her own experience of raising a child alone, she'd instilled into Ghislaine a traditional, conservative view of the relationship between love, sex and marriage.

And besides that, more immediately, sharing Seth's bed would be far too dangerous. "You must see," she tried to reason, "that it would never work."

"It seemed to be working pretty well downstairs," he reminded her.

"Please keep your voice down! Your mother's still awake."

"We're both adults." Cynically he suggested, "Are you afraid she'll throw you out if she knows you've been making love with me?"

She hadn't thought of it. "I suppose it's a possibility," she acknowledged.

"If Carley's my daughter, why should she object?" he enquired with deadly logic. "But if not—" he added slowly, "suppose she started wondering about the authenticity of this granddaughter you presented her with. No wonder you're afraid to risk offending her."

Ghislaine put a hand to her forehead. She didn't know how to answer him, where safety lay. For a little while he'd seemed like the Seth she'd always known—patient, kind, passionate. But now she remembered that he didn't trust her, and that she mustn't trust him, she didn't dare. "Oh, can't you just accept that I've changed my mind? We'd been talking about old times and I suppose I wanted to turn the clock back, but we can't pick up where we left off, Seth. Too much has happened for that, too many years have come between us."

"They don't seem to have made a lot of difference."

She looked at him in bleak despair. Almost gently, she said, "It *was* different then, Seth. We can't recapture what we had when we were young. We have to let go of our dreams."

"Is that what you've done?"

"My dreams were shattered a long time ago. They weren't worth holding on to in the end."

"None of them?" he asked harshly.

Ghislaine shook her head.

He said, "Do you know what I dreamed of, in prison? You. Always you. Sometimes I dreamed of us having children—a child. A little girl who looked like you."

Ghislaine swallowed, going white. "You told me—not to wait."

"So I don't have the right to find it—distasteful that you'd already found someone else." He paused, looking at her broodingly. "Was it some kind of revenge? Did you give yourself to the first man who crossed your path? Or did you become totally promiscuous? Is that why you couldn't name Carley's father, and settled on me as the scapegoat, because I was in no position to fight it? Crystal Summerfield's death left quite a gap in the local scene, I imagine.

Were you the girl who filled it? Did you comfort all the young men who were missing her?''

Shaking with sick, cold rage at the sudden, vicious attack, Ghislaine said, ''Get out of my room. Get out!''

For a split second she thought he might be going to apologise. Then he gave a brief, contemptuous laugh, and turned to throw the door open and walk out, leaving it swinging behind him.

Ghislaine closed it and leaned her forehead against the panels, still shaking.

How could Seth—*Seth*—say those things to her? It was as though there were two people living inside his skin. One was Seth, whom she'd known and loved from childhood, and the other was some monstrous stranger, a man capable of using words as deadly weapons, of deliberately hurting the people who'd been closest to him. Surely that about-face from tender lover to savage accuser had been more than the piqued reaction of a man who'd been sexually thwarted by an unexpected rebuff?

Of course it was, she acknowledged tiredly as she finally got into bed. He'd come home, perhaps taking for granted that his years of hardship and poverty were at an end, only to find that Roald Keegan had added his own punishment to the impersonal judicial retribution already inflicted on his son. What Seth must have always regarded as his birthright had been taken from him in favour of a child of whose very existence he had been unaware.

It was understandable that he should strenuously deny the presumption of his paternity, that he would fight it.

Perhaps it had been wrong to refuse to allow him to be told of her pregnancy. At the time it had seemed the only way to handle what had happened to her—and to him. She'd sometimes lain awake wondering fearfully if some unknown visitor would casually mention it, if she should have tried to break the news to him herself, perhaps in a letter rather than in the far too public atmosphere of the prison visiting area.

She need not have worried about that. Everyone in Tangihuna must soon have drawn their own conclusions, but Seth had never made friends very easily and, as with most small towns, school leavers who didn't find jobs locally had to move away to get work or higher education. By the time he was twenty-four, his few childhood friends had lost touch with him or were out of the country. Perhaps he was visited—she hoped he had been—by some of the people he must have met since moving to Auckland. But it seemed no one had brought him news of his home town except his father. Mrs. Keegan had never visited. The strain of seeing her son in such surroundings would have been too much for her.

Ghislaine had braced herself to face the inevitable when he was released, rehearsing over and over what she would say, how she would tell him. Because she'd asked to be allowed to do it herself.

Everyone had assumed he would come home, until Mr. Keegan returned grim-faced and said, "He's not coming. He thanked me for meeting him, shook hands and said he was all right and if I liked I could drop him off in the city. I suppose when he's sorted himself out he'll be in touch."

But he hadn't. Not until he'd come swinging up the drive five months after his father's death, shouldering a shabby backpack and without, apparently, a cent to his name.

And he'd come back changed. Once she would have entrusted her deepest secrets to Seth with perfect confidence. Now that was impossible. If the old Seth might have suffered unbearably from her revelations while he was locked up and unable to act on them, the new one was capable of inflicting suffering himself, not only on her but on his mother, and perhaps even on Carley.

She was still shocked at the speed with which he'd changed from one to the other. Supposing the new Seth was the real person, now. A person who could don the skin of the old one at will when it suited his purposes. If he was capable of turning on her and savaging her with such suddenness, might he do the same with Carley? His patience with the child might be just a façade—could he have some ulterior motive in making friends with her?

Ghislaine lay awake shivering for a long time in spite of the warm November night and the feather and down duvet that covered her.

* * *

"We should be sending out invitations to our end-of-year gathering," Mrs. Keegan said at dinner one evening.

"Are you still planning to have it?" Ghislaine was surprised. She had expected that Mrs. Keegan would drop it now that her husband had died, especially with Seth's unsettling presence in the house.

"It won't be the same, of course, but Roald would have expected the tradition to be maintained. And people were very kind after his death. I would like to repay them in some small way."

"It's a nice thought," Ghislaine said warmly. "If you think you're up to it, I'll make the arrangements."

Seth looked up from his steak. "Have you done that before?" he asked Ghislaine.

"Yes," she answered briefly.

"Ghislaine is a wonderful organiser," Mrs. Keegan said. "I can safely leave it all to her. And I hope that you will endeavour not to disgrace your father's memory."

Seth leaned back a little in his chair, his expression wary and perhaps surprised. "I'll do my best. Am I expected to play host?"

"You are family. And there is no one else."

Seth inclined his head ironically.

The next day Ghislaine found the previous year's guest list and took it to Mrs. Keegan after she'd had her afternoon rest.

Hesitantly, Ghislaine said, "Are you sure you want to do this? Everyone will understand if you'd prefer to leave it this year."

"No, it's best. There is bound to be a great deal of curiosity about Seth being here."

That was already evident. Two ladies from the Women's Division had called yesterday to discuss their annual garden visit, although a phone call from the secretary had sufficed in other years. And there had been other casual visitors, too many for it to be coincidence.

Mrs. Keegan said, "Heaven knows I don't condone what he did, but he has, after all, paid the price. And he is my son. This is his home, at least until I die. Of course, after that it will be up to you what to do.''

It had not occurred to Ghislaine that eventually it might be in her power to refuse Seth the right to live in his family home. ''Or Carley,'' she said.

''My dear, I'm not likely to live that long,'' Mrs. Keegan assured her pragmatically. ''Anyway, he has apparently decided to stay for now, and the best way to kill gossip and speculation is to show people that he's been accepted back into the family. He ought to be able to make something of his life, and perhaps he'll find someone among Roald's friends and business contacts to help him with a new start.''

So it was for Seth's sake that she wanted to have the party, Ghislaine thought. She smiled at Mrs. Keegan with affectionate admiration. ''I see. Well, if you'd like me to go through the list, you can tell me if there are any changes you want to make.''

Seth came across her rummaging in the big desk in the room that had been his father's study. This was the one Mr. Keegan had preferred to use, although in another corner a custom-built rolltop made to complement the older furniture held a hidden computer.

''What are you doing here?'' Seth asked, closing the door behind him.

''Looking for some addresses,'' she told him, pulling a leather-bound address book from a drawer. She wondered if she'd imagined the accusatory note in his question. ''What are *you* . . . ?''

''Looking for you,'' he answered. ''You've been very elusive the last few days.''

''I've been here all the time,'' she pointed out. But she'd made sure he had no chance to catch her alone until now. She'd also renewed her vigilance over Carley, hovering not far away whenever they were together.

She sat on the high-backed leather chair behind the desk, opening the address book and trying to look busy as she compared it with the list of names she had laid on the pristine blotter. ''Excuse me,'' she said, ''I have something to do for your mother.''

She didn't hear him cross the Persian carpet, but a big hand suddenly slammed the book shut, making her jump.

He bent over with his hands flat on the desk, bringing his face close to hers. "Talk to me," he said.

Ghislaine sat stiffly, trying to still the hammering of her heart. "I'm busy."

"You're always busy! You're running yourself into the ground doing things for my mother. Don't *you* ever rest?"

"I'm young and fit. I don't need to rest."

"You're also rail-thin and getting hollow-eyed."

"That's not her fault. If I'm hollow-eyed it's because of you!"

The minute she closed her mouth again, she wished she hadn't said it.

He surveyed her with a rapier glance. "Losing sleep, Ghislaine?" He smiled. "So am I. There's a simple solution. Come share my bed, and we'll solve that problem together."

"You're disgusting!"

"What's disgusting about making love?"

"What you're suggesting isn't love. It's just sex—lust."

Silkily he said, "Was that a problem for you when you conceived Carley?"

She stared at him, chilled by his cynicism, frightened of his persistence. She knew he would never back down, never give up. Somehow she had to deflect him. With the quiet, implacable voice of truth she said, "I loved Carley's father."

She wasn't prepared for the sudden gaunt pain in his face. Her lips parted on an indrawn breath as he straightened, and before she could move he was round the desk and hauling her out of the chair.

He held her arms in a paralysing grip as he said between his teeth, "You loved *me!* Damn you," he said, *"you loved me!"*

"I wanted you."

His eyes narrowed to chips of green glass. "You still do. And I can make you admit *that* any time I like!"

"You arrogant bastard!"

"I'd be careful about throwing stones if I were you. Bastard isn't a term you ought to toss around indiscriminately."

He caught her wrist as she lashed out at him, and whipped it behind her into the small of her back, pressing her close to him. "You can't win, Ghislaine," he taunted. "Why don't you give up and tell the truth?"

"I have."

He looked down at her, his mouth going hard and cruel. "You're so thin," he said, "I could break every bone in your body."

Hypnotised, she stared back, her mouth dry. "Is that what you want to do?"

"Frequently." He released her suddenly, and she fumbled for the edge of the desk behind her to help her remain standing. "And that's only the half of it," he said.

Ghislaine moistened her lower lip with her tongue. "I wish..."

"What?" His gaze was alert, intent.

I wish I could tell you everything...

"...that you would stop molesting me," she said aloud. "It isn't going help you."

"Tell me what will, then," he invited her.

She looked away from him. "Be patient," she said. "Try to—to fit back into the family."

He laughed. "You think that will help?"

"It might. Your mother is prepared to meet you halfway. She's organising this party mostly for your benefit."

"Is that what she told you?" he asked disbelievingly. "Anyway, by her own admission, *you* are doing the organising."

Ghislaine dismissed that with an impatient gesture. "She wants to show people that you're—well, home again. She wants to introduce you to them."

"The prodigal forgiven?" he jeered. "I'm sure there's a price. What am I supposed to do? Resign myself to the role you've cast me in as Carley's father?"

"Can't you accept a generous, loving gesture for what it is? Is that what prison does to you?"

"Not prison," he said. "I learned when I was child that there is always a price to pay."

"For *love?*"

"Especially for love. I forgot that, for a while, with you. But debts are always recalled sooner or later."

"I don't understand you. I never tried to put you in my debt."

"Until now."

Ghislaine shook her head. "I haven't—"

"You love your daughter, don't you?"

"Of *course* I do! More than anything in the world!"

"Yes," Seth agreed. "So who's paying the price of that?"

Her lips parted and closed again. She flushed and then paled, speechless before the almost compassionate accusation in his eyes.

"Think about it," he said, and left the room.

The words echoed in her head for the rest of the day. Was she making Seth pay for her love of Carley? He thought so, and if so it was unfair. Unjust.

But Carley *wasn't* her only consideration. She wasn't fooling herself about that. Roald Keegan had made his wishes very clear, and he had a right to leave his estate as he wanted to. His reasoning had been spelt out in his will. Seth, he'd decided, had forfeited his rights to any share in the house, the business or the farm, not so much by what he had done, as by cutting himself off from his home and his family afterwards. He had shown no interest in any of it while his father lived, and his father saw no justice in leaving it to him when he died. Mr. Keegan might have been a hard and perhaps unforgiving man, but he had always done what he perceived of as right—right and just.

And that being so, it wouldn't be right for her to upset what he had decided. While Seth might feel that he'd been wronged, nothing she did could alter things in any constructive way.

Yet a small, nagging doubt remained.

Mrs. Keegan became absorbed in the preparations for the party, continually remembering some detail that Ghislaine

might have overlooked, and reminding her of everything
that had to be done.

She had always signed the invitations herself after Ghislaine had hand-printed them. Ghislaine had learned to do
copperplate at school, and Mrs. Keegan had been delighted
when she'd offered to help with the invitations the first time.
"It makes them so personal," she'd said. "Thank you, my
dear, they're beautiful."

There was a problem this year because usually Ghislaine
had used engraved letterhead paper, but since Roald Keegan's death Mrs. Keegan had none that did not include his
name.

It was too late to have new letterheads properly printed,
and Mrs. Keegan vetoed photocopies. Having rejected the
packets of cheap pre-printed all-purpose party invitations
that the shops in Tangihuna stocked, Mrs. Keegan decreed,
"We'll have to get some nice stationery from Auckland,
something tasteful."

"When would you like to go?" Ghislaine asked her.

But Mrs. Keegan looked doubtful. "It's getting so hot
now, and with Christmas coming up the city will be
crowded. Do you think you could choose something on your
own, dear?"

"Of course, if you'd prefer that."

"Mind if I cadge a lift?" Seth asked casually. "I've some
things to do in Auckland, myself."

Ghislaine could scarcely say no. She accepted the prospect of his company with as much grace as she could.

They had to pass through Tangihuna in a northward direction before they could reach the highway and turn south.
Part of the main route to Auckland ran parallel to the old
road where the Keegan house stood, but between the two
roads lay several large paddocks sheltered by belts of trees
that hid the house from the main highway.

Ghislaine always hated this early part of the journey, not
simply because of the hilly curves and steep fern-covered
banks falling away at the side of the road, but because she
could never drive along it without remembering the night
Seth's car had come out of River Road, narrowly missing a

truck travelling toward Auckland, and had been pursued by Traffic Officer Stanhope who had seen the near-miss.

The car had failed to stop, the officer had told the court, giving his evidence from a wheelchair. After pursuing the vehicle for some distance at speeds of up to a hundred and fifty kilometres per hour, the officer thought he'd lost it when the lights ahead abruptly disappeared. But then in the headlights of a vehicle travelling toward him he had seen his quarry again, taking a corner too wide, smashing into the oncoming car and sending it over the low roadside barrier to roll down the steep bank beyond.

"He must have turned off his lights," Mr. Stanhope said, "so that I couldn't see him. Probably hoped I'd think he'd gone down Kotokoto Road—that's a dead end."

The lawyer Seth's father had hired challenged that as speculation, but there wasn't much he could dispute in the evidence. Seth's car had been swung around by the impact, and although badly damaged on the passenger side had been sliding at speed toward the patrol car. "I had almost no chance to avoid it," the officer declared. "I took evasive action, and skidded into a tree."

Ghislaine glanced at Seth sitting beside her in the passenger seat. She'd felt the familiar clenching of her muscles as they passed the signpost saying River Road. And her palms on the steering wheel were damp as she followed the course that his car had taken that night, past Kotokoto Road, up a long rise and round a deceptive curve where the fatal impact had occurred.

Seth was staring straight ahead, his face impassive, but she noticed that his fist, resting on his knee, had clenched.

Officer Stanhope's injuries had been extensive. It was a good twenty to thirty minutes before a passing motorist travelling the uninhabited stretch of road in the early hours of New Year's Day had alerted emergency services, telephoning from the nearest farmhouse. There was no sign of the driver of the silver-grey car that had caused the accident, although a mortally injured woman passenger was trapped inside. But as the police and breakdown services cleared up after the accident Seth had pushed through the rescuers and onlookers, looking shaken and asking urgently about Crystal.

"He asked where she was and how badly she'd been injured," the witnesses said. "Yes, he asked after her by name." But by that time the girl was dead and on her way to the hospital mortuary. "There was blood on his shirt," they testified. And he'd smelled of whisky.

A breath-alcohol reading and later a blood test showed that more than an hour after the crash he was over the legal limit for driving. And afterwards forensic tests matched the blood type on his clothes with Crystal Summerfield's.

Ghislaine swallowed as she carefully drove along the straight after the curve. She had never been able to banish from her mind a picture evoked by one sentence in the forensic evidence, relating to the blood on Seth's shirt. "The material under the stain was creased." And when questioned the scientist had added unemotionally, "Consistent with someone holding—clutching the shirt in their hand? Yes, while it was being worn. Yes, it might have been the person whose blood was on the fabric we tested. Probably."

Everyone in the hushed courtroom must have pictured in their minds a dying girl reaching out for help. It was a picture she had never been able to banish, like a waking nightmare.

"Are you all right?" Seth's voice was harsh in the cocooned stillness of the car's interior.

"Yes." There was moisture along her hairline, and she felt a slight nausea, but that was usual when making this trip. She glanced at him again. Had he paled a little under his tan? But she didn't dare ask if he was all right. "I'll be okay now," she assured him, and slightly increased the pressure of her foot on the accelerator. She was always tempted to put it down hard, get away from the place as fast as possible, but had to hold herself back.

"You'll have made this trip often," he said, almost accusing.

"Yes."

"Does it always affect you like that?"

"It's getting better," she lied. And repeated, "I'll be all right."

The judge must have had the nightmare picture in his mind, too, when he summed up the case and told Seth, standing white and rigid in the dock, what he thought of a young man who drank and drove and ran away from the consequences of his actions, who made no attempt to get help for the victims of his criminal behaviour, and could walk away from a girl who was bleeding to death and pleading for his help. And who claimed, in the absence of any medical reason for a lapse of memory, that he could recall no single detail of the accident.

It had been obvious that not only the prosecutor but the judge and even his own counsel had become increasingly irritated with Seth's woodenly repeated answer. "I don't know. I don't remember."

"Damned lawyer shouldn't have put him in the witness box," his father had remarked much later. "But he said refusing to enter a plea was bad enough, he didn't think Seth could damage his case much further, and maybe the judge would believe he was suffering from shock."

That his father didn't believe it was obvious. Ghislaine was the only one who had. Who'd clung to her belief that only shock and a temporary loss of memory could have led Seth to behave the way he had. And perhaps, too, she'd felt in some way guilty herself.

Ten miles down the road she was able to relax a little, and take some mild pleasure in the feel of the car responding to the wheel in her hands. Hills covered with white and palest pink flowering manuka gave way to more hills cropped to a brilliant green carpet by flocks of sheep. The road ran down into a valley, and at the bottom they crossed a bridge spanning a broad, clear stream flanked by scarlet and green ferns trailing their ladderlike fronds in the water.

A patch of bush shaded them for a few minutes, tree ferns overhanging the road and creepers and wildflowers covering the banks where machines had sliced through the clay to form the road. And then sunlight hit them and Ghislaine slowed, dazzled, as they climbed again and looked down across a lush valley protected by distant, misty hills. Farther on as they crested a ridge the road allowed them a stunning view of blue sea glittering ahead, with a small dark island floating in sunlight.

"It's a beautiful country," Seth said. "I'd forgotten how beautiful."

Unexpectedly, Ghislaine felt an ache in her throat, a pang of sadness for all the time he'd spent away. "Isn't Australia as beautiful?" she enquired.

"In its way. Not like this. I suppose we all grow accustomed to our own landscape, the one we grew up in."

"Did you miss it?"

"I suppose I did. I've never thought of it until now. But some things you don't know you're missing until you see them again. Then it hits you like a punch between the eyes. And you wonder how you lived without it."

She turned her head briefly to look at him, finding his eyes on her face. Had he almost forgotten her until he'd arrived home and found her there? She tamped down a flash of anger. She'd never managed to eject him from her mind for a single day, but that didn't obligate him to feel the same.

She was tempted to ask him: If I hadn't been there when you came home, would you have come looking for me?

But the obvious answer was, No. He'd had the chance to come looking for her when he left prison.

"He asked after you," Roald Keegan had said. "I told him you were well. I expect he'll be here some day soon, and you can talk to him then."

But he hadn't. They'd waited and there was nothing. He had just dropped out of all their lives.

And now he was back.

"How did you find out," she asked him, "about your father?"

"Someone gave me a bundle of New Zealand newspapers," he said. "They thought, being a Kiwi, I'd be interested. There was a small item in the business pages about changes in the organisation of the Keegan group of companies since Roald Keegan's death. I almost missed it.''

"And you came straight over."

He seemed to hesitate. "I had to think about it for a bit."

"About whether it was worth your while?"

She hadn't meant to sound waspish, but perhaps she'd been more hurt than she liked to admit even to herself by the apparent ease with which he'd turned his back on her and all she'd thought she meant to him.

He turned a little in his seat, leaning back to look at her. She could feel his steady gaze even though hers didn't leave the road ahead.

"Yes," he said finally. "I guess you could say that."

"I'm sorry," she said, "that it didn't turn out as you expected."

"You can't be sorrier than I am," he assured her dryly. "I wonder what you'd be prepared to do about it?"

Ghislaine's hands tightened on the wheel. "There's nothing I can do."

"No? I could think of one or two things."

"I won't jeopardise Carley's future for you," she said brutally.

He laughed suddenly, a harsh, unfriendly sound. "I'm not asking you to do that."

"You don't know what you're asking," she muttered. "That's the trouble."

"What?" He frowned at her.

"Nothing. We'll be coming into the start of the city traffic soon. I'd like to concentrate on my driving, if you don't mind."

He looked fed up, but subsided obediently in his seat, folding his arms. He knew perfectly well it was an excuse, of course, but it was true that his presence was unsettling, and while he was probing and asking questions she found her concentration impaired. Having a passenger who made her nerves jump every time he turned his head toward her did nothing for her driving.

Chapter 9

After they had passed over the high smooth arch of the Harbour Bridge across the glittering blue of the Waitemata, with the tall buildings of Auckland's waterfront etched in misty pastels on the shore, Ghislaine asked, "Where do you want me to leave you?"

"Anywhere it suits you. There's no need to wait for me, by the way. I won't be coming back with you."

For an instant she felt an extraordinary mixture of shock and relief.

Then he said, "I'll find my own way home." And she realised that he wasn't planning a repeat of his disappearance four years ago. "How will you do that?" she asked. "Hitchhiking again?"

"I could." He looked slightly amused. "Do you disapprove?"

It wasn't for her to approve or disapprove of anything he did. "Your mother does." She glanced in the rear vision mirror, indicated and smoothly changed lanes.

"I'm rather past the age where my actions depend on my mother's approval."

"You might consider her feelings."

He said rather remotely, "If I did that every time I made
decision my life wouldn't be my own. Haven't you dis-
overed that?"

"I don't know what you mean."

He made a scornful sound. "You don't want to know.
Has she made life so comfortable for you that you can't even
ee what you've given up?"

"I haven't given up anything. I've had a lot given *to* me.
've been very lucky."

"Or very clever."

Ghislaine trod on the brake to stop at a red light. "I didn't
lan it, Seth!"

"It all just happened?" he asked sceptically. "With my
other playing fairy godmother?"

She shook her head despairingly. "You'll never under-
tand."

"Try me." His eyes were suddenly piercing as he leaned
oward her. "Trust me, Ghislaine."

She stared back at him, tempted, but terribly afraid.

The driver of the car behind tooted at them. The light had
hanged, and she wrenched her mind back to her driving.

Seth muttered a curse and looked back impatiently at the
ollowing car.

"It isn't his fault," Ghislaine said.

They didn't speak again until she had driven into a cen-
ral city carpark and pulled on the brake. "If you change
our mind," she said crisply, releasing her seat belt, "I'll be
eaving at about two o'clock." She reached back to pick up
er handbag from the floor and unlatched the door.

Seth got out and his eyes met hers across the roof of the
ar as she locked up. "I have a fair amount to do," he said.
Don't wait for me."

Dismissing from her mind a natural curiosity about what
was he had to do, Ghislaine headed for an exclusive card
nd stationery shop near the carpark, and took her time
hoosing some thick cream-coloured linen notepaper with
discreet gold design in one corner and matching enve-
opes.

Then she carried out a couple of other messages that Mrs. Keegan had given her, and spent the last hour before two browsing the clothing boutiques.

It wasn't until she saw the dress she wanted that the half-formed thought in her mind took definite shape.

For the past three years she'd worn the same dress to the annual pre-Christmas function. She had rarely needed a special dress and the slim-fitting beige sheath with the narrow gold belt was timeless and suitable. Mrs. Keegan had wanted to buy her something new last year, but she'd declined, as she had always declined the Keegans' offers to buy her clothes or jewellery or anything she considered personal, accepting them only as birthday or Christmas gifts.

She had counted herself terribly lucky that she had not needed to go on a benefit when Carley was born. The Keegans had been horrified at the idea, and she'd allowed them to pay for some of Carley's clothing as well as accepting their offer of living as members of the family. But mostly she made her own and Carley's clothes, having learned to sew from her mother, and learned also how to make a simple outfit take on a different and elegant look with the judicious use of inexpensive accessories or with a quick and easy alteration.

Her mother had been frugal and invested what little she could afford in interest-bearing accounts that still brought in small amounts of money each year. And until recently Ghislaine had her own secondhand car, successor to the one she had inherited from her mother, bought by trading that in as a deposit and paying off the rest in instalments. When Mr. Keegan died, his wife had urged Ghislaine to sell it. "You might as well use the Rover. It needs driving, and you can do all my messages in it." Mrs. Keegan had never learned to drive. "With my heart," she explained, "there's too much risk, not only to myself but to others."

Using the big car made sense, although Ghislaine had needed to push down a small, ridiculous panic that she was giving up the last remnant of her independence when a thrilled young couple expecting their first child drove her reliable old Mini down the drive.

With the money from the sale, though, she could afford to buy herself a new dress—this new dress, she decided recklessly, gazing at a window model wearing an oyster pink creation in heavy crushed silk. With clean, uncluttered lines that suited the lustrous fabric, it was strapless with a short skirt, and had a matching revered jacket in sheerest organdie, cut on severely classic lines, its unexpectedness both mocking and complementing the romanticism of the material. It was utterly perfect, utterly stunning and utterly expensive.

She had a few qualms after trying it on and saying firmly that she'd take it, almost changing her mind before the saleswoman wrapped it. Never in her life had she paid so much for a garment, and how often, her practical self demanded censoriously, was she likely to wear it?

Never mind, she might not wear it much but the style was a classic and she knew she'd still love it in ten years' time. It was, she told herself, a good buy. Besides, it had looked even better on her than on the lifeless plaster model.

Not once did she allow herself to speculate on whether Seth would like it. Or even notice it.

She'd been home for a couple of hours and she and Mrs. Keegan and Carley were sitting down to dinner when the sound of a car coming up the drive made them look questioningly at one another.

"I'm not expecting anyone," Mrs. Keegan said. "This is an awkward time to call."

Ghislaine said, "I'll find out who it is." But before she reached the door of the dining room, they heard the car drive around to the back of the house, and Ghislaine said with certainty, "It's Seth."

He came into the room a few minutes later, glanced at the table and said to Ghislaine, "Sorry I'm late." Then to his mother he said, "I've bought a car. May I park it in the garage? There seems to be plenty of room."

A quiver of surprise and perhaps displeasure crossed Mrs. Keegan's face, but she said in gracious if distant tones, "Yes, of course."

"What kind of car?" Carley asked.

He flashed her a smile, wickedly amused. "I'll show you later," he promised.

When he did, Ghislaine accompanied them. Expecting to see a rather shabby vehicle, she was brought up short, gaping in astonishment at the sleek dark blue Saab.

"You can't afford that!"

Carley danced into the garage ahead of them. "It's neat!" she pronounced. "Is it new?"

"A couple of years old," Seth told her.

So it wasn't brand new. But Ghislaine knew that even secondhand, this car wasn't a cheap buy.

"Can we go for a drive in it?" Carley asked.

"*No!*" Ghislaine said unthinkingly.

Carley looked round at her, astonished at the sharpness of her voice.

Seth said quietly, "I've had my licence back for a couple of years now, you know. And it's clean. No accidents. The rental car broke down, I didn't crash it."

Ghislaine looked at him blankly. "Rental car?"

"Oh." He looked at her rather strangely. "I never told you, did I? When I arrived in Auckland from Australia I hired a car. It broke down and I had to leave it at a garage about halfway here. Rather than wait for a replacement, I left the major part of my luggage with it and hitched the rest of the way. It was quicker."

"Rental cars don't break down."

He raised his brows. "This one did."

Carley said disappointedly, "Why can't we go for a ride, Mummy? Seth won't mind, will you, Seth?"

"Apparently your mother does," he told her. "Maybe another time."

Carley looked mutinous. "Why, Mummy?" she wailed. "I want to go now!"

Ghislaine gave her a stern look. "Don't whine, Carley."

"I am not!"

Carley rarely threw tantrums but it looked as though she was working up to one now. Ghislaine said, "Another time. Seth's had a long drive already from Auckland. He must be tired."

Seth cast her a sardonic look but said nothing.

"Can I sit in it, then?"

Seth said, "Sure," and opened the door for her.

"Where did you get the rucksack?" Ghislaine asked Seth.

He looked blank, and she said, "The rucksack you arrived with."

He shrugged. "I bought it somewhere in the years I was working around different parts of Australia. Guess I'm attached to it in a funny way. When I fly I use it for carrying a change of clothing and the bare essentials in case my luggage gets lost. Seemed logical to grab it when I had to leave the car behind. I didn't think to unpack some clothes that my mother would find respectable for dining at her table," he added ruefully.

Carley, bouncing on the leather seat, said, "It smells *lovely*. What are all these things for?"

Seth slid in beside her and introduced her to the intricacies of the dashboard, allowing her to switch on lights and windshield wipers and the radio. Ghislaine stood by remembering that in just the same clear, tolerant way he had once shown her how to read unknown words, how to operate a camera, how to understand a mathematical equation.

At last Carley grew bored and wriggled out of the car.

"Time to get ready for bed," Ghislaine reminded her.

"I want to say goodnight to Stardancer. I couldn't ride him today because you weren't here and Granna was too tired to watch me. Can I, please?"

"Five minutes," Ghislaine said. "But only to say goodnight," she called after her daughter's flying figure. "You're not to ride him without someone there."

Seth locked the Saab and slid the keys into his pocket. "You're very careful of her."

"Horses can be dangerous," she said defensively. "Even old plodding ponies like Stardancer can accidently kick a rider who falls."

"I wasn't criticising. Will you let me take her—and you—for a drive, perhaps at the weekend?"

Ghislaine shivered. It was silly to be frightened. Seth had always been a good driver. After the accident Darrell had been of the opinion that he'd been plain unlucky. "Could have happened to anyone," he'd said loyally. "Everyone makes mistakes, it was just bad luck there was someone coming round the corner at him."

Darrell had never expected his brother to go to prison, although the lawyer had warned them that with the recent public debate on a widely perceived judicial leniency over drinking offences, and the judge's obvious displeasure throughout the hearings, they might expect him to throw the book at Seth. Darrell had been totally, speechlessly shocked at the severity of the five-year sentence. That was what had broken Darrell, sent him into a tailspin of despair and desperation.

Seth's hands closed over her shoulders. "It's all right," he said roughly. "If the idea upsets you so much I'll tell Carley I can't take her for a drive."

She'd told Carley that other people ought to help ex-prisoners rehabilitate themselves. It struck her that so far she had done very little to help Seth. "No." She swallowed her irrational fear. "No, it—it will be nice for her. Thank you."

"Thank *you*." He was surprised, she could see. "Thank you very much, Ghislaine. You'll come, too, won't you?"

"Yes." She still didn't trust him alone with Carley.

He released her and stepped away, ready to close the garage doors. She waited for him, and as he turned toward her in the slowly falling dusk she said, "*Can* you afford it?"

"I can now."

"Your mother's given you some money? She must have been very generous."

He regarded her mockingly. "Why don't you ask her?"

She couldn't do that. She would never question Mrs. Keegan's use of her own money, and presumably she had more than enough for her needs, but it bothered Ghislaine that perhaps the older woman was being persuaded to part with funds that her husband had meant her to have for her own use.

On the other hand, if Seth's story of the rental car was true—and why should he have made that up?—her assumption that he'd arrived almost destitute had been wrong.

Although everything he'd said and done was consistent with that—wasn't it?

She couldn't remember all that he'd said or done. Only that he'd never denied that he was short of money. And if he wasn't, why had almost his first question to his mother been a query as to how much money his father had left? Why had he not told Mrs. Keegan he didn't need to take advantage of her offer to fund him through some arrangement with the lawyers? And he'd said, hadn't he, that he'd come to find out about his father's will? And been furious that everything had gone to his mother and Carley.

Seth quirked a mocking smile at her. "Worried about your investment?"

"Investment?"

"Of time and—deceit," he said quite conversationally. "Afraid I'll talk my mother into giving me the lot before you get your greedy little hands on it?"

He'd done it again. Changed from Dr. Jekyll to Mr. Hyde without warning. Ghislaine blinked, her heart sinking like a stone to lie in a cold hard lump in her chest. She closed her eyes. "It isn't greed."

As she turned away he said, "What, then? A need for security? Or some kind of status for your daughter that you never had yourself?"

Ghislaine kept walking steadily toward the house, but he strode beside her. "I can understand that," he said. "I just don't like your methods."

Ghislaine refused to answer him, ignoring his presence. When they reached the steps to the kitchen she turned away from him and called into the clear evening air, "Carley!"

Carley's distant voice answered, "Coming, Mummy!"

Seth said insistently, "Did you want to give her a head start in life, a better social position—?"

She turned on him. "Than whose? I'm as good as you, or anybody else, and I always will be. So was my mother. And so is Carley. I don't want any special position in society for her, I don't even want her to go to the supposedly best schools or be part of Auckland's pitiful social elite, although I know your mother pictures that in her future. I want her to be healthy and well cared for, and happy. And to have her rights. That's all.''

Seth drew in a harsh breath, but then Carley came scampering toward them, and Ghislaine went to meet her, scooping her into a hug. And when she turned around again, Seth had gone.

On Sunday after lunch Mrs. Keegan declined to join them for the promised drive, but Carley and Ghislaine accompanied Seth out to the garage.

He opened the back door and ushered Carley into the rear seat, leaning over to help her fasten the safety belt. But when Ghislaine would have joined her he caught at her arm and opened the front passenger door. ''I don't like playing chauffeur,'' he said.

He backed out and took the drive slowly, and once on the road never passed the speed limit. His driving was competent and relaxed, and even when he turned off the main road past Tangihuna and took a winding unsealed route toward the coast the ride was still remarkably smooth.

''You'll get your new car all dusty!'' Carley told him, transferring her attention from the scrubby bush at the roadside and a high granite rock face looming over paddocks speckled with white sheep.

''I'll clean it,'' Seth tossed over his shoulder. ''Want to help me?''

''Yes. Where are we going?''

''To a waterfall.''

Ghislaine asked, ''Do we have time? I need to be back to cook dinner.''

''We'll buy something,'' he promised.

''Mrs. Keegan doesn't like takeaways. Greasy food upsets her digestion and it's bad for her heart.''

''Don't worry about it,'' he advised with a touch of impatience.

''What kind of waterfall?'' Carley was asking.

''A big one. We have to tramp through some bush to get to it, though. Think you can do that?''

''Yeah, 'course,'' Carley answered. ''Is it miles and miles?''

"Maybe a couple, there and back. If you get too tired I'll carry you."

"You said a drive," Ghislaine reminded him.

He glanced at her. "It's an easy walk. You can stay in the car if you like."

She wouldn't, of course. She wasn't going to leave Carley alone with him for that long.

There were no other vehicles in the small carpark surrounded by tall native trees. Seth locked up and they passed through a gap in a post-and-rail fence and started up a well-maintained track through dense, humid bush. A heavy, white-breasted native wood-pigeon startled Carley, low-flying between the trees with a whoomph, whoomph of bishop's-purple wings, settling on a nearby branch to regard them fearlessly, its coppery green-feathered head cocked.

Carley said, "It's a kereru!"

"That's right." Seth put a hand on her shoulder. "Haven't you seen one before?"

"Not this close," Carley said. "He's not the least bit frightened, is he?"

"No need to be, he's a protected species."

"What's that?"

The pigeon flew away through the trees and they walked on while Seth explained. Ghislaine lagged slightly behind, using spindly, shaggy-barked kanuka for handholds as the path narrowed and became steeper. Bigger trees—miro and matai and rewarewa—soared not far away, some festooned with parasitical palm-like plants and trailing vines. Tiny mosses growing over the roots held beads of moisture on their miniature fronds, creeping teardrop-leaved ground plants covered the low banks on either side of the path cut through the forest, and a damp, rainwashed smell permeated the air.

After a while the path began a steep descent, and as they quickened their pace, Carley running on ahead, the sound of rushing water joined the rustling of the treetops and the penetrating chirps of flitting piwakawaka teetering on swaying twigs with their tails spread in tiny, perfect fans.

The dimness of the bush gave way to a burst of sunshine pouring into a clearing below the waterfall: Carley stood awed, holding Seth's hand, her head tipped back and her mouth slightly open as she squinted toward the top of the white, moving spill of water over the face of an invisible cliff. As Ghislaine joined them, she turned her head to her mother and said loudly, "It's big!"

Seth had turned, too, but Ghislaine avoided his eyes to smile down at her daughter. "Yes, it is," she agreed.

Seth asked, "You've never been here before, Carley?"

"No." Carley shook her head. "Can I sit over there and watch it?" She pointed to a large grey rock protruding from the bank into the deep, swirling pool below the fall.

"Okay." Ghislaine followed her as she ran along a narrow path worn in the soft grass and scrambled onto the rock.

Ghislaine stayed beside her, her eyes on the hypnotic movement of the waterfall, trying to ignore Seth as he sat down on the bank, his back against a tree and his knees hunched in front of him with one forearm casually resting on them.

A long time ago she and Seth had sat here on this rock, his arm about her shoulders, his mouth nuzzling that special, vulnerable spot just below her ear while she pretended to concentrate on the endless, driving fall of the water, the sparkle of the sunshine on its surface.

Until she could pretend no longer, and she'd turned her head to meet his mouth with hers, and they'd kissed until, as naturally as the water curving over the edge of the cliff, he'd borne her backwards to the sunwarmed rock and kept on kissing her with his hand covering her breast through the cotton of her thin shirt, making all her senses sing. When his hand left her she'd made a small sound of protest, but then she'd felt his fingers on the buttons of her shirt, and her mind had silently cried, *Yes*. Until his hand was on her skin, and his mouth relinquished hers and touched her throat, and then the warm curve that he'd bared.

It was the first time he'd touched her in that way, and the roaring of her blood drowned the sound of the waterfall as she gasped with the sweet sensation he created.

Seth had looked up, his eyes glazed, and said quietly, "You're beautiful, Ghislaine. You're so beautiful and so trusting."

"Trusting?"

He'd smiled then, ruefully. "You shouldn't let me do this."

"Why not? I like it," Ghislaine said, reckless with aroused passion.

"I know," he said, and his hand caressed her again briefly, regretfully. "I know. So do I. Too much."

He sat up and pulled her with him, and then he carefully, concentratedly buttoned her blouse again. Accustomed to following Seth's lead, she let him do it, swallowing disappointment but at some deep level relieved that he'd called a halt. She was seventeen and had been brought up to respect her body and insist on respect from others. She wasn't yet ready to explore the wilder shores of passion. Not even with Seth, whom she would have trusted with her life.

She helped Carley off the rock and Seth stood up, coming toward them.

"I want to paddle," Carley announced.

There was a small, shallow pool at the edge of the larger one, almost enclosed by rocks, and the two adults watched as she removed her sneakers and socks and splashed in, squealing at the cold.

She found a rock to sit on and sat kicking her legs, showering Seth and Ghislaine with droplets of water.

They stepped back, laughing, and Ghislaine stumbled over a large stone half buried in the ground.

Seth shot out his hand, his arm going around her, bringing her against his hard, warm body.

She saw the flare of awareness in his eyes, and knew that he'd seen the same in hers before she could hide it. Then he eased his hold, and she said, "Thank you," and tried to move away from him.

But he still kept his arm about her waist as she stood beside him. Carley was absorbed in staring into the water now, watching the current swirl about her ankles, and inspecting the coloured pebbles on the stream bed.

Ghislaine kept her eyes on the child, knowing that Seth was willing her to look at him again, her back rigid with the effort not to relax against him, to let her shoulder rest under his.

"You remember," he said softly. "Don't you?"

Ghislaine shook her head.

"Yes, you do." His breath warmed her temple. "You remember being here with me."

"I remember a lot of things," she said, finally meeting his eyes. "I remember," she said deliberately, "that you were down River Road with Crystal Summerfield."

Carley had hopped off the rock and was standing knee-deep in the water, plunging her arm in up to the elbow. "Look, Mummy! Look, Seth." She held up a fist-sized pink stone. "Can I take it home?"

Ghislaine walked away from Seth's slackened hold and went to the water's edge. "Yes," she said. "It's pretty. And it's time we were going."

She stuck close to Carley all the way back to the car park. And on the way home Seth seemed absorbed in his driving, his eyes on the road and a slight frown between his brows.

At the only takeaway bar in Tangihuna that was open on Sundays, he bought a rotisserie chicken, and at Carley's request a bag of French-fried potatoes and a hot dog.

"It won't hurt her," he said, catching Ghislaine's dubious look.

"You don't mind if she drips sauce on your upholstery?"

"It'll wash. Sure there's nothing else you'd like?"

Ghislaine had declined to state any preferences, leaving the purchase to him and Carley. "No, thanks." The chicken looked delicious, and it would be nice not to have to prepare a meal when they got home. But she wasn't sure how Mrs. Keegan would react.

In fact Mrs. Keegan seemed to enjoy the chicken, although she refused to touch the fries. Ghislaine had made up a quick salad with lettuce, tomato, cucumber and chives, and emptied a jar of preserved peaches into a glass dish, whipping up some cream to go with them.

Seth said, "I'll clear up, you take a break." And because she didn't want to share the kitchen with him, Ghislaine obeyed.

She took her time over Carley's bedtime ritual, and lingered in her own room until she went down to make Mrs. Keegan's night-time drink. The evening was warm and Seth seemed absorbed in a Sunday paper he'd bought at the takeaway. While Mrs. Keegan was having her hot milk, Ghislaine changed into her swimsuit and pulled her towelling wrap over it. When she'd collected the cup and saucer and washed them up, she unhooked the key and went out the back door, closing it quietly behind her and, crossing the patio in the cool dusk, unlocked the gate and slipped into the pool.

At first it seemed cold, but the sun had been on it all day and the water soon warmed. When she got out, though, the night air felt chilly and she was glad to pull on the wrap, belting it round her as she went silently barefoot back to the shadowed patio.

She'd almost reached the lounger before she saw Seth lying full length on the cushions, his shirt a pale blur, but his eyes showing twin gleams in the darkness.

She kept walking, making to pass him without a word, but he shot out a hand and captured her wrist, bringing her to a halt beside him.

And said, "Why didn't you ask me about Crystal Summerfield eight years ago, Ghislaine?"

Chapter 10

Ghislaine stood motionless, and Seth swung himself out of the lounger. "Why?" he asked her again.

"I didn't need to hear you say it," she said at last. "I might have been young and naive, but I wasn't so stupid I didn't know what you were doing down there with her!"

"And didn't want to know?" he asked her.

"If you want me to spell it out, I didn't want to hear you admit to it, and I didn't want to hear you lie about it. So there was no point in asking, was there?"

"But you thought you knew, and in spite of that you stuck by me, right up until I went to prison."

"It seemed the right thing to do."

"Duty?" he asked. "Was that all?"

"No," she admitted. "Of course it wasn't. I loved you. You know that."

"Past tense?"

"Definitely past tense." She pulled at her wrist and he released it. "And besides..."

"Besides?"

"I was young enough then to hold myself partly to blame."

"*You?*" Seth exclaimed. "How could you be to blame?"

''I figured it was my fault that you'd . . . needed a girl like Crystal. Because I was too innocent and too scared to give you what you wanted.''

''My God!'' Seth's voice shook. ''How long did you go on thinking like that?''

''Quite a while. Well, there was some truth in it, after all. You told me that Crystal knew how to—''

''I know what I told you!'' he interrupted harshly.

''Yes, well . . . it was a couple of years before I grew up enough to see that kind of reasoning for the masculine blackmail that it was.''

''I never tried to blackmail you! And I certainly never tried to blame you! Nothing that happened that night was your fault.''

''No, it wasn't,'' she agreed. ''But it took me a long time to accept that.''

And even longer to come to terms with the fact that she hadn't been responsible for the other events that were set on their inexorable course that night. ''We're all responsible for our own actions, in the end,'' she said. ''Including Darrell,'' she added, half to herself.

He said strangely, ''How did you know I was thinking of Darrell?''

She'd been following her own train of thought. But she knew instantly what brought the note of pain to his voice. ''You didn't cause his suicide,'' she said, ''any more than I caused your car to crash.''

''I don't think it was exactly unrelated.''

''Nothing's unrelated. Everything is woven together, and what we do reacts on other people who are close to us. But we all have the capacity to . . . to decide our own destiny. Darrell ended his life because he wanted to, it was his decision, and it can't be laid at anyone else's door.''

''I know that's true,'' Seth said slowly. ''But I can't help regretting—'' He gestured hopelessly with his hands. ''He was so *young!* It was such a bloody *waste,*'' he added.

''I know.''

''*Why* did he do it?'' Seth demanded almost with anger.

She couldn't tell him that, but she instinctively touched his arm in comfort, and he lifted his hands and drew her to him, holding her tightly, his face against her hair.

"I went through hell when they told me," he said. "I kept telling myself it wasn't true, it couldn't be true."

"So did I," she whispered.

"Darrell was always so alive, so... vital. I just couldn't imagine him being... not here any more."

"Yes." She closed her eyes. That whole year had been like some horrible continuing nightmare, and she'd kept hoping she'd wake up and it would all be over. But instead she'd had to live through it, and somehow retain her sanity for the sake of the baby she carried. "I know how you felt."

Seth drew slowly away from her. "You do, don't you? It must have been like losing a brother for you, too."

"I think it was. I kept remembering what he was like at four years old—giggly and still a bit pudgy with baby fat."

"He was a solid little crittur at four, wasn't he?" Seth remembered, his voice soft with affection. "And even at that age he had a primitive sense of humour. He was the only one of our family with that spontaneous ability to laugh."

"You had a sense of humour, too," she said. Seth had seldom laughed aloud, even as a child. Sometimes she'd been uncertain whether he'd made a joke or not. But she'd learned to recognise the slight crinkling at the corner of eyes and mouth, the lurking gleam that betrayed him when he sounded deadly serious but was in fact speaking tongue in cheek.

She'd noticed that Carley, young though she was, was learning to recognise it too. She'd seen her daughter look at him uncertainly and then break into giggles when she realised he was joking.

Those moments of humour were seldom directed at Ghislaine nowadays. She experienced a sudden piercing thrust of grief.

Seth said, "What?"

She was sure she'd made no sound. "Nothing," she said, and shivered. "I'm cold. I have to go inside."

"I could warm you," he offered.

Ghislaine took a step back on the cold tiles. She shook her head. "No."

Nothing he did could warm her, ever again.

Ghislaine went into Tangihuna to post the invitations when they were complete with Mrs. Keegan's flowing signature.

"Christmas cards, Ghislaine?" a voice enquired as she pushed the two bundles into a slot at the Post Office.

Ghislaine looked up, smiling. "Hello, Jinny. No, invitations to Mrs. Keegan's pre-Christmas gathering." On impulse she added, "Why don't you come? And Ralph, of course."

"Us, at a Keegan party?" Jinny grimaced, laughing.

"Why not? Mrs. Keegan's always told me I could invite whoever I liked." She'd never taken advantage of the offer, but somehow this year she felt she needed all the moral support she could get. "Please, do come. I'll send you an official invitation if you like, with her signature on it."

"Oh, I don't know. Though I've always wanted to see inside that place."

"I promise, you'll be very welcome. Where's Melinda today?"

"Playcentre. I'm off the leash for a few hours. Hey, how about we have that coffee? Are you free?'

"Yes," Ghislaine said almost instantly, mentally rearranging her morning.

"This is great," Jinny said, as they were settling into a corner booth with a plate of savouries and cakes and two cups of aromatic coffee. "We ought to do it more often. There's not many of our generation left in town, you know. The ones you and I were at school with."

"I know. And I seem to have lost touch with...everyone."

"It's living out of town, the way you do. Cuts you off. And you don't belong to any groups, do you? Heck, I have so many meetings and things to go to every week, I hardly know where I'm supposed to be from one minute to the next. So...what *have* you been doing lately?"

"Nothing much," Ghislaine admitted. "Looking after the house, helping Mrs. Keegan, being a mother, I guess."

"Mmm." Jinny picked up her coffee, then put it down and said, "Oh, what the heck! You know I'm dying to hear about Seth. Is he still there? How are you getting along together? S'pose you didn't take my advice, you didn't before. Is he going to make an honest woman of you at last?"

Ghislaine almost choked on her first sip of coffee. Then she burst into laughter. Jinny's frank curiosity was a welcome antidote to the sidelong glances, manufactured excuses and thinly disguised fishing expeditions that had come her and Mrs. Keegan's way lately.

"Tell me to shut up and mind my own business if you like," Jinny offered cheerfully, "but I figure if you don't ask you don't find out."

Ghislaine shook her head. "You haven't changed." They had talked only briefly and occasionally since they left high school and spent the summer celebrating their new adulthood, but Jinny had always had the knack of picking up their friendship where they had left off. She felt as entitled to ask personal questions and offer her trenchant opinions as if they were still children and "best friends."

"That's what Ralph says," Jinny grinned. "Well?"

"He's still here, it's difficult sometimes, and no, he isn't going to make an honest woman of me," Ghislaine told her.

"I'm glad, actually. There are worse things than being a solo mum."

"Like marry Seth? You never liked him, did you?"

"Nope. You said once I was jealous of him, and I probably was, too," Jinny admitted. "I think it was terrific of you to stick by him the way you did, right through the trial and everything."

"He needed me." The only time he'd ever shown that naked need was in the long weeks between the accident and the sentence. And she'd been there for him, supporting him, accepting that he didn't want to talk about what had happened, didn't want her to help him recall what he said he didn't remember. From her what he'd needed just then was purely physical comfort.

Ruthlessly suppressing her own hurt and anger, she'd accepted his kisses and caresses even while she wondered if he had kissed Crystal this way, touched her this way, minutes before she died beside him that night. Tried to respond when his passion became so intense it was almost violent, only to find herself shivering inside with revulsion and fright that she made a supreme effort to hide.

Until their last evening together, the night before he was to appear for sentencing, when she'd driven out to see him in her mother's car and they'd gone for a walk. Coming back, reluctant to go inside the house or to part, they'd ended up in the orchard where she'd first spoken to him. And there, lying in the shadow of an old plum tree, he'd kissed her very gently, and touched her as though he was almost afraid to, and she'd been able at last to kiss him back without reserve, and let him bury his face in the softness of her newly washed hair. And holding him in her arms, she'd found it quite easy to whisper, "Seth . . . if you want to, we could make love properly."

He'd lifted his head from its warm resting place on her breast, where he'd opened the buttons of her blouse, and looked at her. "Do you want to?"

Ghislaine swallowed and said steadily, "Yes."

"Ghislaine," he said, his voice deep and quiet. "Oh, my sweet, lovely Ghislaine!"

And she'd closed her eyes as he gathered her into his arms and muttered something that sounded like, "Forgive me!" before his mouth opened passionately over hers.

"If Ralph had done what Seth did, I think I'd have left him to stew," Jinny remarked.

"The crash was an accident," Ghislaine reminded her.

"I didn't mean that. Although that was awful, and he caused it, didn't he? I suppose he panicked, knowing he'd been drinking. No, I meant, going with another girl, and then leaving you with a baby."

"He didn't know about Carley."

Jinny gaped. "Didn't know?"

Ghislaine shook her head. "I wouldn't let them tell him. Jinny, does everyone—I suppose everyone thinks the same as you do."

"Pretty well everyone in town. Well, if he didn't know, I s'pose it makes some difference," Jinny mused. *"Why* didn't you tell him?"

"What does it matter? You advised me not to tie myself up with him."

"Yes, but he could pay maintenance. Not while he was in jail, I suppose, but now…"

"I'm not sure he's got anything to pay it with. And anyway, his father made sure Carley was taken care of."

"Well, that's something, I guess."

Ghislaine felt lighter as she completed her shopping and headed for the big house. It was a long time since she'd had a chat with a woman friend. In fact, she didn't have any real friends left, she realised. Like Seth's, the friends of her younger days had moved on, and the people she saw now were mostly of Mrs. Keegan's generation. Her life revolved around Carley and Mrs. Keegan, and apart from church, school meetings and shopping, she seldom went out.

Perhaps she ought to make more of an effort. She'd enjoyed seeing Jinny, and hoped that she and Ralph would attend the party.

"That's a new dress, isn't it, dear?" Mrs. Keegan, wearing black crepe with a draped neckline and pleated skirt, had come into the dining room while Ghislaine was putting the finishing touches to the buffet table. "I hadn't noticed you'd been sewing."

"I bought it," Ghislaine confessed, feeling stupidly guilty at the extravagance, "when I went to Auckland."

Seth was standing in the doorway behind his mother, urbane and darkly handsome in a white silk evening shirt and burgundy bow tie worn with a black dinner jacket and trousers. "Ghislaine's been too busy preparing for this party to have time for sewing, I should think," he said, coming into the room.

"I hope you haven't tired yourself out," Mrs. Keegan said anxiously.

"Of course not, I've enjoyed it," Ghislaine lied. "The caterers do most of the work," she added, looking at Seth.

"Oh, do make sure they use champagne flutes for the sparkling wines this time," Mrs. Keegan reminded her. Turning to Seth, she added, "Last year they served it in sauterne glasses."

"Shocking!" Seth murmured, catching Ghislaine's eye.

Mrs. Keegan asked, "What did you say?"

"I've told them," Ghislaine said hastily. "I think they'll remember."

"And tell them to count when they're washing up. I don't want to find a dirty glass hidden under the sofa again."

"Yes, I will," Ghislaine promised. "Why don't you sit down while we wait for people to arrive? You shouldn't be standing about." She noticed that Mrs. Keegan's colour was a little high.

"Yes, perhaps I will." Putting her hand to her throat, Mrs. Keegan made an exclamation of annoyance. "Oh, I meant to put on Roald's pearls!"

"I'll get them for you," Ghislaine offered.

Seth interjected, "No, I will."

"You wouldn't know where to find them," his mother told him. "In my bureau, dear," she said to Ghislaine. "You know the drawer."

"Yes, I won't be a minute."

When she came down with the double string of pearls in her hand, Seth was at the bottom of the stairs. "I've persuaded her to wait in the front room," he said. "Here, I'll give them to her." He held out his hand and she placed the pearls in it. "Is there anything else that needs doing?"

Ghislaine shook her head. "I'll just go and talk to the caterers again, make sure they have everything under control and get Carley out from under their feet." Her daughter had been enthusiastically helping in the kitchen, and when Ghislaine tried to remove her the caterers had said she was no trouble, leave her. A motherly woman in a smart black dress and frilled apron had volunteered to ensure Carley didn't stain the white broderie anglaise dress with the pink sash that Mrs. Keegan deemed suitable for the party. But Ghislaine didn't want to stretch their tolerance too far.

When she returned from the kitchen with Carley, the first guests were arriving. From the moment Seth stepped forward to shake their hands, the party acquired a vitality that the Keegan pre-Christmas gathering had never had. His presence was a catalyst that heightened the curiosity and the enjoyment of at least half the people there. The female half, Ghislaine thought cynically, watching him as he stood talking easily to a group of women who appeared to hang on his every word.

"I must admit I never realised how gorgeous your Seth would turn out to be," Jinny Price said in her ear, "when we were kids."

"Gorgeous?" Ghislaine turned. She'd been glad to see Jinny and Ralph arrive, Ralph looking slightly nervous and very scrubbed, and Jinny wearing a bright red sheath dress, sparkling pendant earrings, a lot of makeup, and a defiant air of being determined to have a good time. Mrs. Keegan had blinked in a rather taken-aback way before holding out her hand when Ghislaine said to her, "You remember Jinny? We were at school together. And her husband, Ralph Price."

"I wonder where he gets his expensive gear?" Jinny mused, still looking at Seth. "Probably made for him. Maybe Ralph... But no." She shook her head regretfully. "My Ralphie couldn't look like that no matter how much he spent on clothes."

"I thought you didn't like Seth," Ghislaine reminded her, feeling rather betrayed. She'd expected Jinny, at least, not to be dazzled by Seth, even in this fresh, bewildering incarnation of sophisticated, charming and even occasionally smiling host.

"I didn't say I like him," Jinny replied calmly. "Just that he looks like a million dollars."

He did, too, Ghislaine realised, now that she'd had it pointed out. His clothes looked expensive in spite of their discreet colouring and style. Where had he got them? Certainly not in Tangihuna. Auckland, perhaps, the day she had driven him there? Or had he brought them with him from Australia in that scuffed leather case? They were immaculate but without that indefinable air of never having been worn before that brand-new clothes had. Would a labourer, travelling about between—what had he said? mines and building sites—have a use for such clothes?

Don't be a snob, she chided herself. Labourers are just as entitled to have evening clothes and places to wear them as anyone. Seth had always liked music, and a couple of times he'd taken her to the theatre in Auckland. And to good restaurants, too. He needn't have stopped doing all that just because he was employed as a manual worker. He'd said, hadn't he, that the wages in the places where he'd worked were high? And given her the impression that he'd spent his money as soon as he made it. Maybe it had all gone on fast living.

Carley had approached the group where Seth was standing, slipping a hand into his.

He looked down at her, then bent and picked her up, introducing her to the women he was with. Carley's arm hooked trustingly about his neck, her face close to his.

"Cor!" Jinny said. "He can't blame that one on the milkman."

"What?" Ghislaine stared at her.

Jinny was abashed. "Sorry. Me and my big mouth."

Ghislaine looked again at her daughter, held in Seth's arms. "She looks like me! Everyone says Carley's like me."

Jinny said, "Yes, she's got your hair and eye colouring, but there's something about the eyebrows... it's more an expression, though. And the way she holds her head, just slightly at an angle, with the chin forward. They were both doing it just now. That's what made the resemblance so striking. Mrs. Keegan does it, too. It's a family trait. Like the way Melinda stands pigeon-toed with her head down when she's feeling shy. She's more like me in most things, but that's Ralph." She chuckled. "Look at him now!"

Following her gaze, Ghislaine saw Ralph standing with one of Roald Keegan's business partners and his wife, gazing into his wine glass with an unhappy air, his toes in their meticulously polished black shoes pointing inward.

"I'd better go and rescue him," Jinny said. "One thing I've never suffered from, thank heaven, is shyness!"

As she walked away, Ghislaine returned her gaze to Seth, but Carley had wriggled down and was walking away to where Mrs. Keegan held court from the sofa.

Seth, though, looked across at her and as he had once before, a long time ago, he excused himself briefly from the group and came across the room, holding her eyes with his. "Something wrong?" he asked when he reached her.

"No." Jinny was right. He was standing with his head slightly tilted, his strong chin appearing aggressive. In Mrs. Keegan the mannerism looked like brave determination, and Carley's pointed little chin gave her a look of sweet, childish stubbornness that sometimes made Ghislaine want to laugh when she needed to be firm. Of course, Carley had been around Mrs. Keegan all her life.

"No," she said. "Nothing's wrong. It's going very well, I think. Your mother will be pleased. Have you talked to your father's business colleagues?"

"Yes. Why, particularly?"

"She thought—" Suddenly sure that he didn't need it, she said, "She thought one of them might offer you a job."

"Did she tell you that?"

"More or less. She cares about you, Seth."

"About me, or the family reputation? She doesn't like the idea of having a layabout, unemployed son."

"I don't suppose she does. Would anyone?

He smiled wryly. "You're a very good advocate. You're probably right, and I'm a selfish, unfeeling swine."

"You said it."

He grinned suddenly. "Don't pull your punches, do you, Ghislaine?"

"I think you're unfair to her."

"Maybe." He shrugged. "Has it occurred to you that it's mutual?"

It had, but she had loyally tried to ignore the uneasy feeling that Mrs. Keegan was hypercritical of everything Seth did. "Perhaps if you made more of an effort—" she suggested.

"To please her? Do you think I haven't tried?" he asked bitterly. "Even as a teenager I was—" He stopped, watching the appalled compassion on her face. "It doesn't matter now. Water under the bridge."

"I'm sorry," Ghislaine said. She hadn't realised how deeply hurt he'd been. "But she's hurting, too. Surely you can—"

His face had closed. "Leave it, Ghislaine. It's too late to change anything. I want to congratulate you."

"Congratulate—?"

"You did a great job of organising this. But it's time you began to enjoy it, yourself."

"That's not what I'm—"

But he'd taken her arm and was leading her outside to the slightly less crowded patio under the patterned shadows of the vines, stopping here and there to talk to the guests, his hand still on her elbow, smiling down at her, drawing her into the conversation.

And in a strange way she did enjoy herself as she never had before since she'd been living at the house. She had moved among these people every year with a smile and a word for each of them, but always acutely conscious that she was an object of veiled curiosity, perhaps pity, perhaps even resentment, and that she was not really a part of their world.

Seth's presence at her side somehow made things different. There was still curiosity, even accentuated by the fact of them being together, and when Carley joined them, swinging on Seth's hand, or briefly winding her arms about her mother's waist while she asked if she was allowed another sausage roll or some more fruit punch, and wheedled to be allowed to stay up just a little longer, Ghislaine was acutely aware of several pairs of eyes covertly watching them. But with Seth there it didn't matter. She felt sizzlingly alive and almost happy for the first time in years, and although Seth made sure her glass of sparkling wine was refilled several times, she knew that wasn't the only reason.

After everyone had left she put a finally sleepy Carley to bed while Seth helped the caterers clean up. They were almost finished when she entered the kitchen to make Mrs.

Keegan's hot drink, and she took the opportunity to thank them. When she came down again they were packing the last crates into their van, and she and Seth were checking the front room as the vehicle receded down the drive.

"I didn't ask them to close the gates," Ghislaine said. "I'd better do it now." Usually she shut them in the late afternoon, sometimes as early as three-thirty when Carley came home from school, but lately Seth had been doing it more often than she.

"I'll take care of it," he said now. "You go up to bed. You must be tired."

It wasn't very late, although the party had continued longer than usual. Ghislaine retrieved a forgotten plate from behind a curtain, removed some crumbs off the carpet with a hand vacuum cleaner and got a bottle of polishing oil and a cloth to rub at a faint ring on the lid of the piano. When he came back she was plumping cushions on the sofa.

"Don't you ever stop?" he asked, pulling his tie undone so that the ends hung at the sides of his collar as he unbuttoned it and came into the room.

"I've finished now," she said. "Your mother doesn't like coming into a mess in the morning, and it's no trouble."

"Nothing's too much trouble for you to do for her, is it?" he asked her, coming to stand before her.

"No," Ghislaine answered simply.

"What has she done to deserve such devotion?"

"She's been kind."

Seth stood regarding her with enigmatic eyes. He said, "Is that why you didn't dump me immediately after the accident? Because I'd been kind to you?"

She swallowed. "Perhaps." It was his kindness that had made her love him in the first place, she supposed. But by then she had loved him for himself, for what he was. What she'd thought he was.

He said, "There's something I've been wanting to do all night."

"What?"

He raised his hands to the front of the sheer jacket she wore over the strapless oyster pink dress. "This," he said, and began slowly undoing the pearl buttons.

She ought to stop him, Ghislaine knew. She had to stop him, but he'd reached the third one now and she didn't move, didn't speak.

He glanced up at her, his fingers on the last button, and she told herself that she'd call a halt if he tried to go further, that the dress was perfectly decent, and he wasn't revealing anything he couldn't already see through the transparent material of the jacket. But there was something dangerously erotic in having him open those buttons, all the same. He parted the front of the jacket with both hands and touched the dress underneath, and said, "Silk?"

She had to draw in a quick breath before she could answer steadily, "Yes."

"It's beautiful," he said, pushing the jacket from her shoulders, down her arms and tossing it aside onto one of the armchairs.

Breathlessly she said, "I don't think—"

"Then don't," he advised, and his hands about her waist drew her to him, fitting her body against his as he bent to take her lips under his.

It just felt so perfect, she sighed into his mouth and her hands slid up his arms and about his shoulders without conscious thought. He stroked her waist, her hips, and his mouth left hers and touched her on her throat, her shoulder, and the slight curve that rose from the top of the dress. "Silk," he repeated, his mouth on her skin. And Ghislaine sighed again, her head thrown back, her eyes closed as she savoured the exquisite pleasure of his leisurely, almost lazy kisses.

"Beautiful," he whispered. He kissed her throat again, then the sensitive pulse below her ear, making her shiver with delicious sensation, and when he paused she turned her head seekingly, wanting his mouth on hers.

He gave it to her, passionately, giving, taking, increasingly aroused and arousing. His arms tightened on her body, and his hands moved down over the heavy silk fabric, lifting her closer so that she felt what the kiss was doing to him.

A primitive surge of triumph brought an answering heat, a warm, throbbing longing deep inside her.

He raised his head, staring at her and still holding her in that close embrace, his hands on the firm rounded curves of her behind that he could feel through the smooth silk. "Beautiful," he said, his eyes glazed with desire. "How can you be so beautiful and so deceitful?"

It was like having a door slammed in her face. He moved one hand up to cup it round her head, his mouth coming down again, but she pushed against him even as he captured her lips, holding her so that she couldn't escape.

But now he was getting no response, and he stopped kissing her and said, "What?"

"Let me go, Seth." She tried to draw her lower body away from his, but he jerked her against him, the lids falling over his eyes so that they were green, watchful, catlike slits.

"You want me to let you go?" He made a slow, suggestive movement, and watched her eyes dilate, the colour stain her cheeks before she turned her head aside.

"Please," she said. "No more, Seth."

"A minute ago you couldn't get enough of me."

Ghislaine closed her eyes against his taunting voice. He let her go, only to capture her head between his hands, his fingers raking into her hair as her eyes flew open and he stared down at her face.

She met his eyes and inwardly shrank from what she saw in them, the angry, contemptuous desire. He released her with a suddenness that was almost violent in itself, and said, "All right, you little hypocrite. Run away if you want to. But I warn you, one day there'll be nowhere to run."

Chapter 11

Two days later she went into the study to dust, and found Seth bending over the rolltop desk in the corner.

As she entered he flicked on the computer. She watched him bring up a list on the screen. None of it meant anything to her, but she said, "That may be private. You'd better ask your mother if it's okay to use the machine."

"I have," he told her absently, frowning at the list. "Check with her if you like."

Ghislaine shook her head. Of course she'd take his word for it. Anyway, neither she nor Mrs. Keegan could operate a computer.

"Do you know if it has a modem in it?" he asked.

"I've no idea. What's that?"

"It enables a computer to communicate with other computers off-site," Seth explained, still pressing keys. "There are various ways—ah!" He peered interestedly at the screen.

"Mr. Keegan used to communicate with his offices in other towns, I think," she told him. "After he got the computer he sometimes stayed home for several days a week, working in here."

"Mmm-hmm." Seth had something else on the screen now. He put a chair in front of the computer, sat down and pressed some more keys. "Come over here and I'll show you how it works."

When she didn't move, he glanced over at her standing with a cloth clenched in her hand.

"I was going to dust," she said.

He shrugged. "Feel free."

But she didn't feel free around Seth, even when he was pointedly ignoring her, keying something into the machine. She wondered if he was looking for documents or information that Mr. Keegan might have left, or was just bored and wanting something to do.

She dusted as quickly as she could and was about to walk out of the room when Seth turned in the chair and said abruptly, "I haven't heard you play since I've been here."

"Play?"

"The piano. It's still there in the front room."

Ghislaine shook her head. "I haven't played the piano for years."

"Why not?" He stood up and came toward her. "You were so talented. I thought it meant a lot to you."

Ghislaine shrugged. "I lost interest."

Seth was frowning. "Why?"

"I don't know why! I just did!" She jerked open the door and left him staring after her.

Her heart pounding and her eyes filled with tears, she hung the duster in the broom cupboard near the kitchen and then walked outside. Sunlight dazzled her, shining on the tears, and she dashed the back of one hand across her face and blindly walked into the garden.

Jerry Wallace looked up from staking some chrysanthemums and stared at her curiously. She veered away from him and walked toward the tennis court, meticulously maintained although no one ever used it now. She felt stifled.

There was a garden seat near the court and she sat down, taking deep breaths, trying to steady herself and be sensible.

Mrs. Keegan had encouraged her to play the piano after she came to live at the big house. When she was a child she'd sometimes been allowed as a great privilege to practise on the mellow old instrument, a dramatic change from the cheap secondhand upright that was all her mother had been able to afford. She was no child prodigy but she had, her teachers told her, an ear for music and with hard work might make a career teaching or more ambitiously, a modest name for herself as a performer.

She knew she probably didn't have a major talent, but she loved music and had looked forward to pursuing her musical studies at university, until her pregnancy and the drastic changes in her life had killed those hopes.

And more than her hopes. After moving in with the Keegans, the first time she had opened the piano, while Mrs. Keegan sat expectantly by with an encouraging smile, she had frozen. Totally. Looked at the keys, placed her hands on them and found herself unable to play. Unable to remember the notes, her mind absolutely a blank. "I can't!" she'd said, sitting there whitefaced and puzzled. "I...I just can't."

"Of course you can, dear," the older woman had said reprovingly. "You've always played so nicely."

Ghislaine had looked up at her, shaking, her eyes wide and panic-stricken. "I can't," she repeated, and got up, looking down at the keys with something like horror. "I'm sorry. I just—can't do it any more."

Later she'd tried again, on her own, with as little success. She didn't understand it, and Mrs. Keegan had continued to coax her, encourage her. Until her husband said loudly one night, "Leave the girl alone, Lucille. She's lost it."

Lost it. He'd put it into words for her, and for a moment she had a most extraordinary feeling, composed of both terrible grief and utter relief. She'd lost her music. Something she'd had all her life had gone from her. And she grieved for that, on top of all the other griefs that had gone before. But from that day she stopped trying to force herself to play, and accepted that her musical life was over.

Now Seth's casual query had brought the grief, the puzzlement, the frustration, flooding back. *Why* couldn't she play? In theory she knew how to do it, what notes to touch, how to work the pedals. It must be some kind of psychological block, and for a time she'd assured herself that if she just relaxed everything would come back one day. But it had been eight years now, and sometimes she looked back on her younger self, who had found such joy, passion and solace in music, with a piercing nostalgia.

Tears ran down her cheeks, blurring her view of the tennis court and the trees beyond it. She wiped them with her fingers, but it was a long time before they stopped falling, leaving her drained and sore-eyed. She sat there for some time afterwards before making her way back inside the house to go upstairs and rinse her face in cold water.

At lunch Seth looked at her sharply and said, "Are you okay?"

"Of course," she answered, casting him a fleeting glance.

Mrs. Keegan said, "What do you mean, Seth?" And, turning to Ghislaine, she asked, "Is something the matter, dear?"

"No, nothing," Ghislaine assured her with a smile. "I'm fine."

"Her name's Ghislaine," Seth said with sudden irritation.

His mother stared at him frostily. "I know her name, Seth." Transferring her gaze back to Ghislaine, she said, "You have looked a bit pale lately. Perhaps I should ask Dr. Turner to give you a check-up."

"Please don't," Ghislaine said, conscious of Seth's raised brows. "There's no need—"

"I upset her this morning," Seth told his mother.

Mrs. Keegan bridled protectively. "What have you been saying to her?"

"I asked about her music," he said deliberately. "She tells me she's lost interest in the piano."

"Oh, yes," Mrs. Keegan said. "Such a pity. I tried to encourage her to keep it up—"

"Did you?"

Ghislaine said, "Yes, she did. If you don't mind, I don't want to discuss it any more." She got up, taking her empty plate to the sink, and noisily clattered some cups from the cupboard for coffee.

* * *

In the following days Seth spent a lot of time in his father's study. Going in there to search for a pen, since all others in the house had simultaneously disappeared, Ghislaine pushed open the door to find him in his father's swivel chair, turned sideways, speaking into the telephone on the big desk. "...arrange the delivery," he was saying. "Thirty thousand? Yes, of course I can raise it, if you're sure...?"

As Ghislaine was about to withdraw he swung the chair around and saw her. He lifted a hand, gesturing her to wait while he listened intently to whoever was on the line. "Okay. Yeah. I don't know how much longer. I'll keep in touch." Then he laughed. "No, I don't think they'll track me down here. Merry Christmas to you, too."

He put down the receiver and stood up. "Did you want me?" he asked Ghislaine.

She shook her head. "I'm hunting for a pen."

He came round the desk and, as she rummaged in one of the drawers, stood watching her, his hands in his pockets.

Straightening with a ballpoint in her hand, she said, "Are you in some kind of trouble?"

He gave her an alert, wary look. "What makes you think that?"

"Nothing." She walked round the desk and made to pass him. It wasn't her business, and why should she care, anyway? "I just wondered...who it is you're afraid might track you here." Defensively, she added, "You did tell me to stay."

"The Mafia," he told her. "They're after me."

She looked at him witheringly, and he laughed.

"All right," she said, "don't tell me. But if you put your mother and Carley at risk—"

"If the hit man arrives," he promised, "I'll tell him we have to move away from the house for the shoot-out."

Ghislaine bit her lip. No doubt she was being melodramatic, but he had been in prison, and maybe he'd been doing more than bumming about as a casual labourer since. Supposing he'd disappeared like that because of something that had happened in the prison? And now that he was back, they were after him, wanting money, or even wanting to silence him?

"Thirty thousand," she said boldly, not letting up. "Dollars?"

"Mmm," he nodded, his eyes light and assessing. "Australian."

"Where are you planning to get that kind of money?"

"You don't think my mother will lend it to me?"

"What if she doesn't?"

The almost invisible lines at the corners of his eyes deepened just a little. "I told you I'd learned a lot in prison," he said. "Like how to make a great deal of money in a short time."

"Then why haven't you?" she shot at him.

He looked away from her for a second, as though framing an answer. "What makes you think I didn't?" he asked finally. "I don't need to borrow from my mother, Ghislaine."

"You have money?" She wasn't really surprised.

"Enough," he told her.

Enough to promise someone thirty thousand dollars without batting an eyelid apparently. "Then why," she challenged him, "are you so anxious to benefit from your father's estate? Why did you come running back here as soon as you discovered he was dead?"

He looked at her in silence, his eyes darkening as they held hers, with a kind of weary contempt. "Work it out for yourself," he advised her shortly, and turned on his heel to go to the computer table.

She said to his back, "Are you dealing in drugs or something? Is that why 'they' are after you?"

She thought at first he wasn't going to answer. Then he turned and said, "You have a charming idea of the sort of character I've become, don't you?"

"You just said that you learned how to make money in prison."

"Yes, I did. Come here."

Ghislaine didn't move, and he said again, impatiently, "Come *here!* I want to show you something."

Reluctantly she walked over to him, and he took her arm and placed her in the chair in front of the computer, bending over her to press some keys, his breath stirring her hair. She could feel the warmth of his body heat, although he wasn't touching her.

"Know what that is?" he asked her as a list of words and figures came up on the screen.

"No," she said. "Oh—sharemarket prices?"

"Right," he said. "I shared a cell for a while with a clever young man who'd been in the money business and got caught gambling with other people's funds. He had an amazing knowledge of stocks and shares and international trading. Taught me a lot. And before you ask, I use my own money, not other people's. And I've been lucky."

"Isn't it risky?"

"Financially, yes. I only risk what I can afford. When I first started, that meant whatever was left after I'd paid for my food and clothes and a roof over my head. Now I have a solid investment in a transport firm based in Perth, with a partner. If I lose on the markets, there's that to fall back on. And I never risk the business."

"Does your mother know this?" She must now, Ghislaine supposed, turning in the chair to look up at him. If she hadn't provided the money for Seth's car she'd be aware he must have been able to raise it somehow himself.

Seth shrugged. "She knows I've no need to borrow from her. She wasn't interested in the details."

"If you didn't need money," she asked, "why *did* you come back?"

He straightened away from her, and she stood up.

Seth folded his arms and leaned back against a bookcase. "Would you believe," he asked mockingly, "because I wanted to make sure that my dear old mother was all right?"

She might have believed it of the Seth she'd once known, she wasn't sure what to believe of this new, sarcastic stranger.

"And I found," he went on, "that dear old mother was being conned by a clever little fraud with a nice line in invention."

Ghislaine turned her head aside, her eyes shuttered by the lids. "Your mother isn't deprived of anything," she said. "She has the use of all the money, and the house, as long as she lives."

"Which, given the apparent state of her health, you didn't expect to be very long, I suppose."

Ghislaine gasped, her eyes returning to him. "I'm not *waiting* for your mother to *die!*"

He was looking at her with uncanny concentration. "I hope," he said in silky tones, "you don't mean that the way it sounds."

Ghislaine, at first bewildered, whitened. "Of course I didn't mean—how dare you suggest anything like that? I would *never* harm Mrs. Keegan in any way!"

"No," he said slowly. "I don't believe you'd go that far. But when someone is obviously not what you had always thought, it's difficult to know what they might or might not do."

That went double for him, Ghislaine thought. She had no idea what to expect from him next. "You don't really think I'm capable of murder!"

He shook his head, something that was almost a smile hovering on his hard mouth. "I don't know what you're capable of, Ghislaine. Obviously a lot more than I ever dreamed."

That was true, she thought bleakly. But not in the way he was suggesting. A bitterness that she hadn't been aware of welled inside her. "If I am," she said, "you can blame yourself."

He seemed to flinch slightly from the accusation in her eyes. But he said, "Didn't you tell me, we are all responsible for our own lives?"

"I also said, our actions affect those close to us," she reminded him. "What happened to me wouldn't have happened if you had been better at controlling your—your—"

"Animal lusts?" He grinned without humour. "Is that the term you're looking for?"

"It's as good as any," she told him. "And fairly accurate."

"Why do I get the feeling," he said, "that you haven't yet grown out of your adolescent fear of sex?"

"Fear?"

"I knew I'd scared you rigid, the night of the crash. Why do you think I'd been drinking so much later? You were too damned young, and I was going crazy, wanting you and trying to wait for you to grow up enough to want me as much—to even know what you wanted."

"I knew I wanted you," Ghislaine said starkly. "I wasn't frightened. Just a bit nervous, and inexperienced. And—I didn't want just sex."

"I wasn't offering 'just sex'," he claimed harshly. "Did you think I was trying to seduce you? And you only seventeen?"

"You wanted to make love to me!"

"Of course I did! But I was capable of some self-control!"

"How much?" she asked scornfully.

"A hell of a lot!" Seth answered loudly. "More than you'll ever know!"

"You don't even remember what happened that night!" she accused him. "You said so—you swore it on oath!"

His face was taut and angry. "I said I didn't remember the accident. I remember very clearly what happened earlier in the evening."

The door opened and Mrs. Keegan said, "I heard raised voices. Are you upsetting Ghislaine again, Seth?"

He looked across at his mother and then back at Ghislaine, his eyes very green. "Probably. It doesn't seem hard to do."

"Perhaps you might apologise," Mrs. Keegan suggested with dignity.

"Do you want an apology, Ghislaine?" His voice was laced with mockery.

"No." Turning to his mother, she said, "I've found a pen. We can get on with that list now."

Lately Ghislaine had allowed Carley sometimes to walk or to ride her pony across the paddocks to play with the farm manager's children, making the excuse that Carley was growing older and had enough sense now to be allowed to go on her own. But Seth was teaching her to use the computer and play games on it, and that was a powerful counter-attraction. It was no longer easy for Ghislaine to monitor so closely the time they spent together.

Then one night after her bedtime story, Carley confided, "Seth says he's had lots of injections."

Ghislaine felt a prickling apprehension between her shoulder blades. "Has he?"

"But he says he's not frightened of them any more."

As if he ever had been, Ghislaine thought grimly. "Is that right?"

"He said it helps if you hold someone's hand really tight."

"Mmm." Ghislaine thought of all the times she'd held Carley's hand while a doctor or nurse administered an injection or took a blood sample.

"And he says he bets me *six* computer games for my birthday that if he's there next time I have a needle, I won't cry and I won't feel sick."

"Did he indeed!" Ghislaine said between her teeth.

Carley looked startled. "What's the matter, Mummy?"

"Nothing." Ghislaine managed to smile at her. "Time to go to sleep, darling." She bent to kiss the soft, childish cheek.

Carley wriggled down in the bed. "So can he come with us next time?"

"You're not due for any needles for a while," Ghislaine assured her. "Don't worry about it."

"But that means I won't get my computer games," Carley said disappointedly.

"You don't *want* a shot, do you?"

"No...I don't think so," Carley admitted doubtfully. "But I'd like some more games. Seth showed me this catalogue that's got *hundreds* of them, and he said I can choose any six I like, if he wins the bet."

Ghislaine gave up on explaining the normal outcome of a bet, tucked the sheet firmly around her daughter, and went in search of Seth.

* * *

"He's in the pool," Mrs. Keegan told her, looking up from her library book. "At least, he said he was going to swim."

That was another resentment that Ghislaine had against him. She didn't swim much because Seth was often using the pool, or he'd come out to join her when she went in. And she didn't like sharing it with him. She was hot and sticky now, and she could have done with a cooling, calming dip. But more urgent was her desire to confront Seth, and she marched out to the poolside, fully dressed in a sleeveless top and flared skirt, and waited for him.

When he saw her he heaved himself out, picked up the towel he'd left on the tiles and gave his hair and face and chest a quick rub, then slung the towel about his neck and padded toward her. "Did you want me?"

"Yes." She was so angry she could scarcely bear to wait but, remembering Carley's open window, she added, "We'd better go inside." The second the back door closed behind them, she turned on him. "I might have guessed you weren't being nice to Carley out of the goodness of your heart. Where the *hell* do you think you get off, offering her bribes?"

"Bribes?"

"Yes, bribes! I told you, she's not having any tests. And don't you *dare* go behind my back, trying to talk her into it!"

"I see." He looked at her speculatively and said, "Why don't we go and sit down and discuss this—"

"There is nothing to discuss! Just leave her alone from now on. I'm warning you—"

Seth laughed harshly, making her itch to hit him. "Or what?" he asked.

Ghislaine glared at him, frustrated. "If I complain to your mother, ask her to tell you to leave—"

"On what grounds?" he asked, seemingly unbothered.

"On the grounds that I don't want you around my daughter!" Ghislaine said heatedly.

His breath hissed. *"You bitch!"* His hands shot out to grip her arms and jerk her forward, his eyes alight with an-

ger. "Even my mother wouldn't believe that I'd harm my
own child—"

"That wasn't what I meant, Seth!" Ghislaine was horrified that he thought it. "Anyway," she reminded him, "you
keep denying that she *is* your child."

He let her go, his chest heaving, his face taut. "You've
convinced my mother that she is," he said pointedly. "So—
hoist with your own petard, Ghislaine?"

"I want you to keep away from Carley in the future," she
said, trying to sound assertive.

"What, from my own little girl?" he jeered.

"Oh, shut up!"

He laughed. "You might as well give in," he told her.
"I'm going to get those tests, if I have to obtain a court order to do it."

"Court order?" Surely no court could force Carley to
have a test—could it?

"I've talked to Teddy Trounson," Seth told her. She recalled seeing him going into the solicitor's office, and went
cold. "We can do it that way and drag us both—and Carley—through the full legal process if you like. Or you can be
sensible and let me arrange it quietly and privately through
Mr. Trounson. It's up to you."

Ghislaine swallowed. She didn't think he was bluffing.
She tried to recall all she had read about blood tests and paternity. "A test won't necessarily prove anything," she said.

"Until quite recently," Seth agreed, "a blood test could
prove only that a man either couldn't be or could have been
the father of a child. DNA testing is much more reliable."

"I don't know anything about that." Her mind was trying to sort the implications of this new direction of attack.

"Briefly, it would mean a simple blood test for all three
of us. DNA characteristics in Carley's blood that match with
yours would be eliminated from the comparison, leaving
others that must have come from her father. It's almost
foolproof."

Almost. Supposing the tests were inconclusive? Would
that make things better—or worse? And supposing they
weren't inconclusive? What might Seth do then? She
scarcely dared think about it.

"There'd be very little doubt," Seth told her. "I've got some pamphlets you can read, if you like. After you've done that, you may decide to call a halt to this farce without going through the process at all."

"All right," she said tensely. "I'll read your pamphlets." She might as well know what it was all about. Forewarned was forearmed—maybe.

If he was surprised, he didn't show it. "Come on up to my room in five minutes," he offered, "and I'll give them to you."

She allowed ten minutes to make sure he'd have time to get fully dressed. He opened the door to her knock and said, "Come in."

He had combed his wet hair and pulled on jeans and a shirt. She stepped into the room and he crossed to the bank of drawers next to the wardrobe and pulled a sheaf of papers from one of them.

"Here," he said, putting them into her hands. "Read them carefully."

"I will." She turned to go, and he walked beside her to the door.

"Ghislaine," he said.

"Yes?" She swung round to face him.

"I don't want to see Carley hurt any more than you do."

"How can I believe that?" Ghislaine demanded. "You've been utterly unscrupulous. You accused me of worming my way into your mother's confidence. Well, what about you, manipulating a child with pseudo-friendship and promises of expensive presents?"

"I'm sorry if it looks that way to you. If you decide not to fight this thing, I'll see that Carley's protected from the major consequences."

"Oh, thanks," Ghislaine said bitterly. Hugging the papers he had given her, she made swiftly for her own room. She'd fight him to her last breath, she decided. There was no way she was going to give him the easy victory he wanted.

"Well?" he said when she returned the pamphlets the following morning after breakfast.

Armed with her determination, she looked him in the eye and said, "Well, what? It's a very expensive process."

"I'll pay for it," he said shortly. "If you're going to force us all to go through with it."

"You're the one who's doing that," she countered. "Unless you've changed your mind?"

His chin thrust forward. "No, I haven't. Do I have to get a court order, then?"

She thought about it, looking away from him, her lids lowered. "No," she finally conceded. He was right about one thing, she shrank from involving herself and Carley in court proceedings. It would be almost impossible to keep that secret, and probably exceedingly expensive. Seth might be prepared to pay for tests that she'd reluctantly agreed to, but there was no one who could help her pay lawyer's fees for a court hearing, which she had a hazy idea might turn out to be astronomical. She couldn't imagine asking Mrs. Keegan to provide her with funds for that. Besides, the whole process might put too much strain on the older woman. She took a deep breath. "Will you promise me one thing?"

"What?" He looked wary.

"If Carley panics, we call the whole thing off."

"Can I trust you not to engineer a panic?"

"What kind of question is that? I'm not likely to do anything that might make her even more scared than she is!"

"No," he conceded, "I don't suppose you would. Okay, if she's really frightened on the day, we needn't go ahead with it."

"What do you propose to tell Carley?" she asked him. "You don't want me to explain what the test is about?"

"Of course not," he said curtly. "I'm sure you'll think of something."

"I won't lie to her."

His brows rose. "You make an exception for her, do you?"

Ghislaine flinched. "You really hate me, don't you?"

He looked at her broodingly. "I haven't made up my mind about that."

"*You* think of something to tell Carley," she suggested. "I'm fresh out of invention, myself," she added with weary sarcasm.

"Okay," he said. "How about—it's to do with my father's will, and the lawyers have had to ask for tests. Would that satisfy her?"

"She'll want to know why."

"It's to find out whether her blood looks like yours, or like mine and my father's. If you have to tell her that they could only find characteristics like yours, it would hardly upset her, would it?"

"I suppose not." She was left with no more arguments.

Carley sat on Seth's knee while the technician took blood from him, and when it was her turn he passed her to Ghislaine, popped a sweet into her mouth and held her hand, telling her a story about a kangaroo joey he said he'd seen in Australia peeking from its mother's pocket. When the needle went in she made a face and gave a muffled "Ouch!" but Seth went on calmly talking and in moments it was all over.

"Mummy's next," he said cheerfully, swinging Carley off Ghislaine's knee. "And you were a very brave girl."

"I didn't cry, did I?" Carley said as the technician swabbed Ghislaine's arm.

"No, you didn't. Have you picked which games you want?"

Carley began a list, and Ghislaine bit her lip as the needle slid into her flesh.

Seth had told her he'd asked for the results to be sent to Mr. Trounson. "That way you'll be sure that it's all being done aboveboard, and we can go and get the news from him together," he'd said. "Sound fair to you?"

She'd agreed, unable to think of an alternative. At least they'd be on neutral ground. She could only pray that the result would not make things worse than they already were.

Carley's birthday had usually been a quiet affair. The approach of Christmas in the same month overshadowed it, and Mrs. Keegan's health wasn't up to having children's parties, but she had always presented the little girl with a new dress and several expensive presents. This year, Seth added his pack of computer games and a handsome red flannel cover for Stardancer, and Ghislaine had invested in a transistor tape player and earphones for which Carley had been heavily hinting.

Soon after her birthday Carley's school broke up for the long holidays at the end of the year. A few days later Seth came out of the study as Ghislaine was crossing the hall. "Mr. Trounson wants to see us tomorrow," he told her. "He's got a Christmas present for us both."

Sitting in the lawyer's office the following day, Ghislaine found her palms damp and her mouth dry. They'd had to wait fifteen minutes for Mr. Trounson's previous client to leave, and then listen to his apologies. He, too, seemed nervous as he found the long envelope and fumbled with opening it. "Do you want me to read all of it aloud?" he asked.

"Tell us what it says," Seth advised. "The conclusion that they came to."

"The conclusion," Mr. Trounson told him, looking down at the paper, and then up at Seth over the top of his glasses, "is that you are the father of this child."

Chapter 12

There was a thundering silence, and then Seth erupted from his chair and snatched the white paper from the lawyer's hand. He was saying something violent, but Ghislaine didn't hear the words; she was concentrating on staying upright while black spots danced before her eyes and the blood in her face drained away. She eased herself back in the chair that fortunately had a high back, while Seth scowled over the letter he held in his fist.

She took three deep, steadying breaths and gradually her vision cleared, although now she felt clammy all over.

She heard the lawyer say, "I've had two copies made, one each for you and Ghislaine. The odds against a random result of this nature are one in twenty-five thousand. The technicians are quite confident of their findings, although as you will see from their letter, if there was any question of a close relative—hypothetically speaking—the chance of a similar match would be in hundreds rather than thousands. The analysis is not able to exclude the possible involvement of an identical twin."

"I don't have a twin!"

"No, exactly." The lawyer sat back. "So in this case there's no argument. Well, I'm glad you took my advice. I hope it's—ah—clarified a few things for you."

"Not particularly." Seth turned to Ghislaine. "Can we go?" he said baldly. "You look as though you could do with some fresh air, too."

He drove home with ferocious concentration, never once looking at her. And Ghislaine sat perfectly still, her hands clasped tightly on the bag in her lap, not daring to look at him. She felt a bit light-headed, not quite real. She wondered what Seth would do now.

They had not mentioned the reason for their absence to his mother, just as they had not told her about the blood tests. Ghislaine had said she didn't want his mother worried, and he'd looked at her with glinting eyes and agreed not to mention it. Ghislaine had felt uncomfortable asking Carley not to tell, but so close to Christmas she was accustomed to keeping secrets, and it was less awkward than Ghislaine had feared.

Seth drew up at the front door. The day was cool for summer, but Mrs. Keegan had settled for her afternoon rest on the patio before they left, and Donna Hemi was looking after Carley. Ghislaine had said she had some things to do before Christmas and let the farm manager's wife draw her own, no doubt erroneous, conclusions.

"I don't know about you," Seth said roughly, as he pushed open the driver's door, "but I could use a drink."

He came round and opened her door. "Come on," he said, taking her arm.

In the drawing room he poured her a dry sherry and took a whisky for himself. Ghislaine stood uncertainly holding her glass, and he said, "Let's sit down, shall we?" and steered her to the sofa, seating himself at its other end while he narrowly surveyed her.

Ghislaine took a gulp of her sherry.

"You must be pleased with yourself," he said.

"Not specially." Her voice was husky.

She nervously sipped at her drink again. She could see that behind the concentrated stare he was directing at her, his mind was in overdrive.

Unable to sit still under that gimlet-eyed scrutiny, Ghislaine got up. "It was you who insisted on the test." She walked to a table, put her glass down and stared into it. "I wish . . . you could believe in me, Seth."

She heard the rustle of paper, and saw that he'd pulled out the copy of the report that Mr. Trounson had handed him. Nervously, she said, "Rereading it won't make it say anything different. You might as well do what you advised me to do, give in."

"Rereading it might help me to believe the unbelievable," he said.

He lifted his glass and downed the whisky in one gulp. "Because that's what this is, whichever way I look at it." He gave her a strange, baffled, considering look and came to join her by the table, putting his empty glass on it with a small thud. "I need to think this through."

After he'd gone, she sat on alone finishing her sherry. She heard him start the car and drive it around the back to the garage. She didn't feel triumph, or even relief. She felt numbed more than anything. Seth still wasn't accepting the situation. What would it take to make him back off?

She phoned Donna Hemi and asked her to send Carley home.

"Get your shopping done?" Donna asked cheerfully.

"Shopping? Oh—yes, thanks. I've finished now. Thank you for keeping Carley out of the way."

She put the phone down, staring unseeingly at the Christmas tree in the hall that Carley had helped decorate. This year instead of Matiu Hemi, Seth had gone to cut it, taking Carley with him. He'd subtly changed the routine of their lives in a few short weeks, and seemed intent on changing it still more.

On Christmas morning Seth accompanied them to church again. There was less overt curiosity about him now, and several people greeted him quite easily. They'd got used to seeing him around Tangihuna.

As Mrs. Keegan was talking to the minister, Ralph and Jinny Price stopped to chat with Seth and Ghislaine, while Melinda interestedly eyed Carley from behind her mother's skirts, a thumb in her mouth. Before they parted Ralph said casually, "We're having a New Year's Eve party next week. How about the two of you coming along?"

Ghislaine opened her mouth for a gracious refusal, but Seth was saying, "Thanks. We'd like that."

Ghislaine cast him an astonished glance, but he wasn't looking at her. Jinny gave her an apologetic look and then transferred her exasperated gaze to her husband, who appeared quite oblivious.

Carley was impatient to get home, because apart from the small trinkets and cheap toys her mother had crammed into a sock at the end of her bed last night, she'd not yet been allowed to open her presents. When Mrs. Keegan detached herself from the minister's side, Carley grabbed at her hand and begged, "Can we go home now, Granna?"

Opening the presents took some time. Carley inspected the names on the various boxes and packages and handed them to the recipients, saving her own for last. She had insisted on buying Seth a present, and Ghislaine had helped her choose a pictorial diary and matching address book, inscribing the card from both of them. She had also, following Mrs. Keegan's instructions, bought him a good quality tie and two pairs of socks on his mother's behalf. He thanked them all gravely and assured Carley that he would use the diary every day.

Mrs. Keegan held up the crystal vase she had unwrapped and said to Ghislaine, "It's beautiful, you have very good taste, dear." And waited expectantly as Ghislaine drew from its box a set of white satin underwear.

"They're lovely." Ghislaine kissed Mrs. Keegan's cheek.

"Very nice," Seth commented dryly, and his mother gave him a frosty look as Ghislaine hastily dropped the lace-trimmed panties and camisole back into the box.

"I'm afraid my present isn't nearly so exciting," he said as Carley pressed another parcel on her mother, commanding her to open it.

She thought at first that he'd given her a safe box of chocolates, relieved at the square chunky shape under the Christmas wrapping. But it was a book, *Christmas Carols and Traditional Songs*. She opened it, finding it charmingly illustrated with coloured plates of historical pictures, and on each facing page, the words and music of a song. The music danced before her eyes, and she blinked hard before looking up and saying in a cool voice, "Thank you, Seth. You didn't need to—"

"I thought you'd like it," he said.

"Let me see, Mummy?" Carley demanded. Thankfully, Ghislaine turned her attention to her daughter.

Carley admired the book briefly but she'd contained herself long enough, and was soon engaged in an orgy of unwrapping, scattering bright coloured paper and ribbons as she discovered the gaily striped overalls and matching peaked cap that Ghislaine had made for her, and the complete set of Tolkien.

"I'll read them to you," Ghislaine promised, "and when you're older you'll be able to read them again for yourself."

From Mrs. Keegan she received more books and clothes and a fluffy poodle pyjama-case to set on her bed. Then she tore open the wrapping on a large box marked, Carley from Seth. And sat back, her mouth open in an astonished *"Oh!"*

Ghislaine felt much the same. She watched, stunned, as Carley opened the box and carefully removed the plastic packaging.

"I'll help you set it up, later," Seth offered.

Ghislaine, at last finding her voice, said, "You *can't* give her a *computer!"*

"I did," Seth told her calmly, and got up to join Carley on the floor, helping her lift the screen, keyboard and disk drive out of the box.

Carley was flushed with excitement, her whole attention on her wonderful present. She flung her arms about Seth's neck and said, "Thank you! It's the nicest present I've ever had—except when Mummy and Granna gave me Stardancer."

Ghislaine stood up, looking at Seth as he gently freed himself from the embrace and got up to face her. His voice low, he said quickly, "Don't spoil it for her."

And of course she couldn't, but for the rest of the day, while she tidied up the mess with Carley's help, and got the midday Christmas dinner ready and cleared up afterward, fiercely rejecting Seth's offer to help, she seethed inwardly with tension and anger.

Carley and Seth disappeared to set up the computer in her bedroom, and Mrs. Keegan went off to rest in her room, because the afternoon had turned breezy and cool. Ghislaine was sitting at the kitchen table staring into space when Seth came in and said, "There you are. What's the matter, Ghislaine?"

"What do you think?" she asked him, pushing back her chair to face him standing. "How dare you buy Carley expensive presents without my knowledge?"

"It wasn't a particularly expensive one—"

"I know how much computers cost! It may not be expensive by your standards, but it's a hell of a lot of money by mine!"

"Are you jealous because *I* bought it for her, and not you?"

"That's not the point! You have no right to give my daughter—"

"She's supposed to be my daughter, too! That might give me some rights, don't you think?"

Ghislaine was brought up short with a sickening jolt.

"Hadn't you thought of that?" Seth asked her. "You've handed me a weapon, Ghislaine, and it's a two-edged sword."

She didn't like the way he was looking at her. Something was going on behind the green eyes that made her skin go suddenly cold. "You don't want her!"

Seth shrugged. "I've taken a fancy to the kid. Maybe I want a say in the future of *my daughter*. Suppose I decided to apply for custody? Did you ever think of that?"

"You wouldn't—" Her voice wavered. Could he? She had no idea, but surely no court would take Carley away from a perfectly good home.

He laughed. "You don't have any idea what I might do."

Empty threats, she told herself firmly. But he looked as though he meant it, and a shiver ran up her spine. "You promised you wouldn't hurt Carley," she reminded him.

"I haven't hurt her, and I've no intention of doing so," he said. "But I have a strong desire to strangle her mother!"

"Well, that's mutual!" Ghislaine snapped.

They stood glaring at each other, and then Seth said, "Hardly Christmas spirit, is it? Not like the old days."

That last Christmas before the accident, Seth had called for her after she'd shared a turkey and salad lunch with her mother, and taken her to the big house, asking Mrs. Keegan if she could stay for dinner.

Darrell had given her a meaningful smile, and Mrs. Keegan looked slightly taken aback but quickly recovered, saying graciously that of course it was all right, and perhaps after dinner Ghislaine might like to give them some music?

Ghislaine knew, as they did, that Seth was claiming her, telling them she was special. Even his father had bent a long, thoughtful glance in her direction and then levelled a frowning look of enquiry at his son, and abruptly asked her how old she was, now?

"Nearly eighteen," she'd answered.

Mr. Keegan had given Seth another measured look, which Seth returned steadily and in silence.

"Christmas past," she murmured involuntarily, recalling how nervous she'd been at that meal, though she'd known the Keegans almost her whole life. Remembering how Seth, sitting beside her, had smiled at her now and then, and once clasped her hand briefly under the tablecloth. Darrell had been inclined to tease, grinning at her cheekily from his place opposite, and throwing out veiled, suggestive hints to his brother until Seth said quietly, "Cut it out, Darrell. You're embarrassing Ghislaine."

And Darrell, blinking at Ghislaine's burning cheeks, had said contritely, "Sorry, Ghilly." And started to behave himself.

"What are you thinking of?" Seth asked. His voice was soft, as though he didn't want to break too rudely in on her reverie.

Ghislaine blinked a sudden stinging from her eyes
"Nothing." She shook her head.

"I think I can guess," he said. His gaze was on he
mouth, and as she felt heat in her cheeks, he raised his eye
and met hers.

They had volunteered to do the clean-up after dinner tha
long-ago evening. Darrell had made a half-hearted effort a
helping and then slyly suggested that, "you two lovebird
won't mind if I take off."

Seth mock-punched at him as he passed by, but didn't at
tempt to stop him. And when he and Ghislaine had fir
ished, he switched on the dishwasher, then turned to her.

"Do you mind?" he'd asked her.

"Mind what?" She was leaning against the table, wai
ing for him, enjoying watching every small movement tha
he made.

"That I've marked you out as mine."

She said, "I don't mind. If you don't mind me doing th
same for you."

He came toward her and drew her into his arms. "I'v
always been yours, from the moment you wandered into th
orchard and interrupted my solitude. You walked right int
my heart and I've never been able to chase you out."

"Do you want to?"

He shook his head. "Never. You're still too young, and
should let you try your wings and not be tying you to me s
soon, but I'm dead scared that someone else will snatch yo
away from me while I'm waiting for you."

"No chance." She linked her hands about his neck
"There'll never be anyone else for me, Seth."

She lifted her mouth to his, and the kiss was all she'd eve
dreamed a kiss might be. Tender, and passionate, and sat
isfyingly long. He hadn't really kissed her since the nigh
weeks ago, that he'd taken her and her mother home afte
the Keegan pre-Christmas gathering, and she'd been wai
ing for this ever since. When he finally eased her away fro
him, he looked down at her shining eyes, touched her lip
with a firm thumb and said, "The minute you turn eigh
teen, I have things to say to you."

"Say them now!"

Seth shook his head. "I feel like a cradle-snatcher as it is. I've known you since you were five years old!"

"What difference does a few months make?"

"I want to do this thing properly. I'm trying not to rush you into anything you might regret."

"Regrets, Ghislaine?" Seth asked now, uncannily echoing her thoughts. Or perhaps reading her face.

"Some," she acknowledged. "But there's no point in dredging up the past."

"Maybe you're right," he said. "So what about the future?"

"No one can look into the future."

"We can influence it. Or do you believe fate orders everything, and we poor mortals have no say in it? No," he answered himself. "That wouldn't accord with your philosophy that we're responsible for our own actions, would it? And you've certainly proved adept at making your own destiny."

"No!" Ghislaine cried suddenly, stung by the unfairness of that. "I haven't!"

His brows went up sceptically, and Ghislaine, angered all over again, said, "You don't know what you're talking about!"

"Don't I? Tell me, then. Tell me how Carley comes to be my daughter, Ghislaine." He shot out his hands and took hold of her, his eyes boring into hers, as though he wanted to get inside her skull. "Tell me that!"

She shook her head, her lips tightly closed, and he flung her away from him, so that she collided with the edge of the table and clutched at it to steady herself. "Does it make you feel good, being able to throw a woman around? You won't get anywhere by bullying me!" she told him.

He was suddenly pale under the Australian tan. "No," he said. "It doesn't make me feel good. It makes me feel sick. But one way or another, I find it difficult to keep my hands off you." And then he swung around and left the room. A few seconds later she heard the crash of the front door.

* * *

He came back in time for the cold dinner she had made up from the lunch leftovers. He said little except to answer Carley's chatter. Mrs. Keegan was quiet, too, seeming tired, and Ghislaine watched her anxiously, noting that she was picking in a desultory fashion at the food on her plate.

Later in the evening, when she came down after giving Mrs. Keegan her hot drink, Seth was in the hall, and he followed her to the kitchen. "Do you have bruises?" he asked her as she rinsed the cup.

"What?"

"From my—bullying, earlier," he said. "Did I hurt you?"

"I'll live." She snatched the tea-towel from the rack as he reached for it, and dried the cup with quick efficiency. "Were you hoping for bruises?"

His jaw clenched. "That's a hell of a question!"

Ghislaine hung up the tea-towel and turned to leave. "I'm going to bed."

"It's early."

"For you, maybe."

"Is it worth it?" he asked her. "Living this kind of life? They tell me you never go out, don't have any friends."

"I have friends."

"Name some."

She hesitated. "Jinny, Donna." She stopped there, trying to think of another name.

"The only time Donna comes here socially is before Christmas, because Matt gets an invitation from my mother. You only visit her when you take Carley to play with the Hemi kids. And you've never set foot inside Jinny Price's house. The first time she's been here was for the party. Do you call that friendship?"

"We don't have to be constantly in each other's pockets to be friends, and how dare you go round asking questions about me?"

"I have things to find out," he reminded her. "And if you won't tell me, I'll do it any way I can."

"You won't find out anything—"

"Odd," he said, "but you're just about right. No one knows much about you, although most seem to think that since you moved in here, you feel you're too good to associate with the people you used to know."

Ghislaine gasped. "That's not true! Jinny doesn't think that!"

"Ralph says she told him off for inviting us to their party, because she didn't think you'd want to come."

"I never go to parties," Ghislaine said. "It's nothing to do with thinking I'm better than anyone else! The opposite, if anything!"

"Meaning?"

Ghislaine looked away. "Meaning I'm an unmarried mother," she said finally, "and Tangihuna is still a very conservative community."

"That's why you have no social life?"

"Partly." The other part she found hard to pinpoint. Mrs. Keegan had never said she couldn't have friends to visit, but at first both she and the Keegans had been mourning. And then Carley was born, and she'd discovered how much work was involved in caring for a new baby. By the time she surfaced from grief and exhaustion, some of her friends had drifted out of her life, and anyway, as a young mother her interests were radically different from theirs. Nor did she feel she could ask Mrs. Keegan to babysit while she went out. And gradually her life had settled into a new routine bounded and ruled by the twin needs of her child and the woman to whom she owed so much.

"Anyway," she said finally, "it's years since anyone's invited me to a party."

And she'd had no intention of going to this one, but if Jinny would be hurt by her absence—

"We're going to this one together," he said. And then, with a smile that held no sort of genuine humour, he added, "Just like before."

She hadn't wanted to think about that. Involuntarily, she shuddered.

"Perhaps we'll lay some ghosts," Seth said. He looked grim, too, his eyes almost grey, and brooding as Ghislaine walked past him and went on up the stairs to her bedroom.

* * *

It was a New Year's Eve party at Jinny's place—her parents' house, in those days—that had set off the inexorable chain of events a malevolent fate had designed for them. Jinny had invited all the crowd, and told Ghislaine, "You'd better bring Seth. You two seem inseparable now."

They had spent almost every day since Christmas together. Ghislaine, starry-eyed with the knowledge that Seth loved her, would have been happy to spend every moment with him, but Seth the loner had suddenly developed a taste for company.

The day after Christmas he'd driven her to the waterfall for a picnic, and at first there'd been other people there—a family party, a group of teenagers skylarking in the deep pool below the falls, another young couple with their arms about each other, gazing into each other's eyes. But gradually they all left, and the sun's heat became gold and soft while Seth and Ghislaine sat on the rock and watched the hypnotic spilling of the water together. Until he'd taken her in his arms and kissed her and started to make love to her.

But he'd called a halt to that, and from then until New Year's Eve they'd seldom been alone. Certainly not for long, although she'd come to look forward to his nightly farewell on her doorstep, when he'd hold her with the length of her body pressed against his, and kiss her until she was aflame with desire. Sometimes he began almost tentatively, pressing his lips briefly against her temple, her closed eyes, the throbbing pulse beneath her ear that he soon discovered made her shiver with pleasure when he explored it with his tongue. And she found she could do the same for him. She learned to open her mouth for him, to curve her body into his and caress his nape with her fingers as her arms hooked about his neck. She found he liked her to touch her tongue to the little groove below the swell of his throat, and to stroke the warm skin of his cheek as he kissed her, and that when she ran her hands over his shirt she could feel the tiny male nipples harden under her fingers, and that it made him moan deeply with delight.

She still dreamed about those nights, especially in summer when the air was hot and still, the only sound the pirrup of the crickets outside her window, and she'd be restless. She'd wake bathed in heat, the heaviness of remembered desire weakening her limbs, the thudding of her heart loud in the darkness. Sometimes she could feel the imaginary imprint of his lips on hers, the firm, faintly rasping skin of his cheek against her palm. And she'd lie very still until the dream inevitably faded, leaving her cold and alone.

The dreams had become less frequent with the years, but since Seth's return they'd increased again in number. Often in the morning she was afraid he'd seen the aftermath in the lethargy of her movements, in the slumbrous look of her eyes that she caught in the mirror, in the lingering warmth she couldn't banish from her skin even after a cool morning shower.

Carley wanted to bring the Hemi children to see her computer.

"You'll have to ask Granna's permission," Ghislaine told her. "She may not want a lot of children in the house."

Mrs. Keegan, sitting in the small back sitting room, with a garden catalogue and a pencil in her hand, looked a little doubtful at the request. One or two children sometimes came to play or to ride Carley's horse, but usually they remained outside so as not to disturb Mrs. Keegan, who didn't tolerate noise well. When she was younger Carley had sometimes brought on one of Mrs. Keegan's headaches if she became boisterous or fretful. Ghislaine had always felt guilty despite the older woman's assurances that it didn't matter, that she would just lie down for awhile and the headache would pass off, but perhaps Ghislaine wouldn't mind bringing her an aspirin and a hot drink to wash it down with?

Of course Ghislaine didn't mind. It was the least she could do. And she'd try her best to quiet her daughter, explaining to Carley as soon as she was old enough, that Granna wasn't as well as most people and they must be careful not to disturb or worry her.

"We promise not to disturb you, Granna," Carley was assuring her anxiously. "And they won't stay long."

"I'll stay with them," Ghislaine promised.

Mrs. Keegan smiled graciously. "Bring them, then," she said.

"Oh, thank you!" Carley gave her a hug and kissed her carefully powdered cheek. "Can I tell them to come now?"

Mrs. Keegan said, "Yes, tell them if you like."

As she scampered off, Mrs. Keegan said, "She's a good child. Sometimes she reminds me of my own boy."

"Seth?" Ghislaine was startled.

"Oh, no, not Seth! He was a difficult child from the start. A cranky baby, very wearing on the nerves. Not an easy birth, I thought I'd die of the pain. I really didn't want to see him afterwards, not for days, but of course I was expected to feed him. He cried such a lot—probably hunger, a nurse told me later, I didn't have sufficient milk. Well, with my constitution I was never meant to have such a big baby." She paused.

"You meant Darrell," Ghislaine said. Mrs. Keegan almost never spoke of him.

"Yes, Darrell. Such a darling boy. I can't believe that—"

She stopped there, closing her eyes, her lips trembling.

Ghislaine slipped to her knees beside the chair, taking her hand. "I know," she said. "Try not to think about it."

Mrs. Keegan opened her eyes, and wiped at the corners with an embroidered handkerchief. "I know it's wicked of me," she said, "but sometimes I wish it had been Seth."

Ghislaine felt a shock run through her. "It isn't wicked," she said. "You're not a wicked person. But..." she added hesitantly, "perhaps you're not always quite fair to Seth."

Mrs. Keegan sighed. "I know. I did try but... he wasn't an easy child to love. Until Darrell came, I thought I was an unnatural mother."

Ghislaine's throat ached with hurt. For her, and for Seth.

"Perhaps it's God's punishment," Mrs. Keegan said, almost to herself. "Taking the beloved son, and leaving the other."

"No! You mustn't think like that! It wasn't your fault. Did you—do you blame Seth for Darrell's death?"

"I can't help it." She moved her hands fretfully, and Ghislaine released her grip. "The poor boy must have been brooding over Seth and what had happened—"

"But it was months afterwards," Ghislaine reminded her. "You don't know what triggered it, in the end. It may...may have been something else entirely."

Mrs. Keegan shook her head. "If Seth hadn't—" She took a shaking breath, her voice firming. "Darrell hero-worshipped his brother. And Seth wasn't worthy of it."

"Seth isn't the only young man to have an accident after drinking too much. It happens all the time. Darrell said he was unlucky, and in a way he was right."

"*You* can defend him?"

"I'm not condoning it," Ghislaine said. "But he didn't deliberately hurt anyone."

"It wasn't just that," Mrs. Keegan said. "It was leaving you, as well. And Carley."

"But he didn't know about Carley!"

The other woman opened her mouth, then closed it again, frowning down at Ghislaine, still kneeling by her. "He did," she said at last. "He did, because Roald told him."

Chapter 13

Ghislaine looked up in horror. "Mr. Keegan *told* Seth? *Seth knew about Carley?*"

"That's why Roald made sure that Carley would inherit."

Ghislaine put her hands to her face, then dropped them into her lap. "In his will he said it was because Seth had shown no interest in the business or the family."

"Carley is family. And Seth had repudiated her. Roald told the lawyer why he was doing it, because Teddy said a will like that might be contested. But he didn't want it put in writing."

"He didn't tell me!" Ghislaine cried. "Why didn't he tell me?"

"You'd put up with enough from our son. There was no need to hurt you any more. Seth told his father that he didn't intend to contact you or see you after he came out. So Roald—let him know about the child. Roald was disgusted—shamed—by Seth's reaction, his refusal to face up to responsibility."

Ghislaine closed her eyes, trying to rearrange the shards of knowledge in her brain. This changed everything—or did it?

"Perhaps I shouldn't have told you now," Mrs. Keegan said, "but Seth being home has altered things. I've thought once or twice that you still have a soft spot for him. You ought to be aware that he deliberately deserted you, knowing about Carley."

Ghislaine stood up. "Yes," she mumbled. "I needed to know. Thank you."

The children spent the early part of the afternoon in Carley's room playing with the computer. True to her promise, Ghislaine was with them. What she had not thought of was that Seth might be there, too. Carley demanded his help, and he seemed quite willing to give a couple of hours to teaching a bunch of lively children how to access the computer's functions and make the most of them. And also to arbitrating when it looked as though a riot could break out over whose turn it was.

Ghislaine stayed in the background, but at one stage Seth joined her where she was sitting on Carley's bed, while the children gathered round and gave gratuitous advice to Midge, who had the present use of the keyboard and mouse.

"Still angry with me for buying it?" he asked her quietly.

Ghislaine shook her head. How could she be angry over something that gave her daughter so much pleasure, not least in sharing it with her friends? But she was uncomfortable at the amount of money that it had cost.

"If it bothers you," he said, apparently reading her thoughts, "look on it as a means of keeping her out of the way when I'm using the computer downstairs."

"Has she been a nuisance?"

"I didn't say that. The kid's a natural. She'll learn a lot from it."

"You're very patient with her," she said. But then, he'd wanted Carley's agreement to the blood test.

"I'm a patient man. You ought to remember that."

Her gaze flew to his, uncertainly. Had she imagined the warning note in his voice? She wanted to ask him about Mrs. Keegan's revelation, but she couldn't now, while the children might overhear.

"What's the matter?" he asked, lounging back against the wall and folding his arms. "You didn't really think I'd give up, did you?" His eyes were watchful, his face carefully emotionless.

She glanced at the children, but they were absorbed in the coloured figures on the screen. Unable to contain the knowledge any longer, she said, almost under her breath, "Your mother told me you knew about Carley."

He looked at her alertly. "Yes. My father mentioned it."

"I'm sorry," she said, looking down at her loosely clasped hands. "I asked him not to, while you were in prison."

"He didn't. It was the day I came out."

"*Then?*" Her head jerked up, the sequence of events shattered yet again.

"Then. In the car when he came to collect me."

"Is that why you—"

"Why I didn't come back with him?" He shook his head. "I hadn't planned to, anyway. But it certainly helped to convince me I'd made the right decision."

"What . . . did he say to you?"

Seth was staring at the far wall. "I asked him if he'd seen you lately, and he gave me a funny sort of look and said yes. I asked him if you seemed happy, and he said he thought you were, now. He said, 'You've caused her a great deal of distress in the past, but I hope you have enough character not to do so again.' Well, I told him I had no such intention. I had, in fact, no intentions at all in your direction. And then he hit me with it. 'You should know that Ghislaine has a child.'"

Ghislaine sank her teeth into her lower lip. Her eyes blurred with tears. She turned her head, looking down so that he shouldn't see. "I wanted to tell you myself," she said.

"Well, that was . . . noble of you," he said. "But I bet you were relieved that you were saved the trouble."

Shamingly, in a way he was right. When he hadn't come home with Roald, her stunned disbelief had been mixed with a feeling of reprieve.

"Your ten minutes are up!" one of the younger Hemis was insisting, trying to shove his sister from the chair.

"No, it's not!" Midge, her dark eyes flashing with temper, clung stubbornly to the seat. Ghislaine got off the bed and hurried to make peace.

When she turned around, Seth had gone. His help was no longer needed, and the children didn't even notice his absence. When they had all taken their turn Carley wanted to go off to their place to play, and Ghislaine agreed, provided she was back for dinner. She had no doubt that Donna would dispatch her in time. She went to the kitchen to start preparing the meal.

"Seth tells me you're attending a party on New Year's Eve," Mrs. Keegan said the next day as she settled for her rest.

"Yes, I think I—we are." Feeling an obscure need to justify herself, Ghislaine said, "Will you mind very much? Jinny came to ours, so I don't feel I can turn her down."

"Seth says her husband asked both of you, together."

"Yes, he did, more or less. I think Ralph feels that Seth should be made to feel part of the community again." Changing the subject in the face of Mrs. Keegan's doubtful silence, she added, "I could ask Donna if she can have Carley for the night."

"There's no need for that, dear. She isn't likely to wake, and if she's ready for bed before you go, I can manage."

"Well, if you're sure. Thank you."

She didn't want to wear the silk dress and voile jacket again, remembering Seth's long, clever fingers undoing the pearl buttons. She knew that wearing it would remind him, too. Besides, Jinny and Ralph's party, she guessed, would be much less formal than Mrs. Keegan's "gathering." She surveyed her wardrobe without enthusiasm and eventually settled for an all-purpose shirtwaister in crisp blue, aqua and black stripes on a white background, a dress that had served her in good stead for three years.

Slipping her feet into white sandals on the evening of the party, she saw that she'd acquired a faint colour on her legs, just a hint of a tan. Her face too, had the slight golden glow of summer. And her hair, she decided as she carefully applied a dusting of eye shadow and a dash of pink lipstick, needed cutting again. She must make an appointment.

She'd anxiously impressed on Carley that she must be very, very good for Granna. As the car purred down the drive she looked back at the child and the woman standing at the top of the wide steps and assured herself aloud, "They'll be all right."

"Of course they will." Seth looked at her searchingly. "You're not really worried, are you?"

"No, of course not. Only I'm not in the habit of going out at night."

"I know. Everyone says you live a remarkably uneventful life."

She felt her skin prickle. "What did you expect?" she asked him. "Wild parties and a list of lovers as long as your arm?"

"They say you've only had one lover," he told her. "Me."

Ghislaine swallowed. "And what have you been saying to *them?*"

He laughed shortly. "Not a lot. What's the point of denying it? I'll tell you this much, they don't think much of me for leaving you with Carley."

Ghislaine winced. "I told Matiu Hemi," she said, "that I didn't want you to—to—"

"Marry you?" He flicked a glance at her. "Matt did the decent thing by Donna, didn't he? *Would* you, now?"

"Would I what?"

"Marry me," he said almost casually.

Ghislaine's head jerked up. Of course he didn't mean it, he was throwing out a hypothetical question. This sweet longing that suddenly stopped her breath and flowed warmly through her body was a reflex triggered by memory. The memory of when they were young and in love and no bitter burden of anger and suspicion had come between them.

Huskily she said, "This is a stupid conversation. Of course I wouldn't. Any more than you would seriously ask me."

He cast her an enigmatic sideways glance, and she turned her head to stare out the window, winding it down a little and making her eyes wide so that the passing breeze would dry the tears in them, and Seth wouldn't know she was crying.

When they entered the Prices' house, she had an unreal sensation of déjà vu. It was more modern than Jinny's parents' place, where she'd last attended a New Year's Eve party, but had a similar happy, lived-in atmosphere. Only a few of the same people were here, but there were enough familiar faces, grown older, to bring back to mind that other party and the carelessly exuberant young people who had populated it.

One man who had been in that summer's crowd, now married with three children, hailed both Ghislaine and Seth with a friendliness for which she could only be grateful, and insisted on getting a glass of white wine for Ghislaine and a whisky for Seth. He had already had enough beer to make him less discreetly tactful than he might have been. "Like old times, you two being together again," he beamed, and started looking around, listing the people he thought they'd remember. "There's old Jack, and Roseanne," he said. "She was with Tony then, of course—you remember Tony Wilkinson the footballer? He went off to Wellington and got married to an Italian girl. So Roseanne married Jack instead. They've got two kids."

Ghislaine smiled politely. Seth was looking distant but courteous. The man went on, "Who else do you know? Not many of the old crowd left now. Hey, remember that party we had at Jinny's place, just after we left school? Great night. Although—" Apparently recalling who he was talking to, he looked embarrassed suddenly. "Of course, that was the night—well, we didn't hear till next day, though. I mean—" he mumbled. "Spoiled it a bit, but it was a great party."

Taking pity on him, Seth said evenly, "Yes, it was. Unforgettable."

* * *

There'd been a lot of people at Jinny's New Year's Eve party that summer when she and Ghislaine were seventeen. Jinny was a popular girl, and she must have invited everyone she knew. Some of her parents' friends were there, too, and she had two brothers who'd also invited theirs. So it had been a mixed group, but the older people tended to stay in the big comfortable sitting room while the younger ones gathered about the barbecue in the roomy, tree-shaded backyard, where Ghislaine and Seth and Darrell found Jinny dispensing punch and beer and breezy hospitality.

Crystal Summerfield, wearing a black leather dress laced up the front across two inches of bare tanned skin from waist to low neckline, was sitting on Jinny's older brother's knee. Later in the evening Ghislaine saw them standing together at the makeshift bar on the back porch, but Crystal suddenly flounced away and stalked across the grass to sit by herself on a garden seat under a tree. After a few minutes of sulking, one foot swinging a high-heeled black sandal, she'd got up and rejoined the party, flirting with a bunch of boys, laughing a lot and tossing a mane of curly blond hair out of her eyes as she stood with a hand on one out-thrust hip, a row of gold bracelets glittering in the firelight from the barbecue. Darrell ambled over to join the group, and Ghislaine saw Crystal give him a mildly interested glance and exchange a series of bright-eyed, smiling remarks before she turned her sparkling attention to a young man who had casually edged out the others and was giving her a lingering appraisal. He wasn't as good looking as Darrell but he had the advantage of him by a few inches and a few years. Crystal preferred her men a little older.

"I don't know what they see in her," Jinny had muttered in Ghislaine's ear, offering her a plate of slightly charred sausages as the outmanoeuvred younger contingent drifted away to console themselves with a crate of beer. "I can remember when her hair was plain mouse, and so can half those boys. They used to call her Pieface when we were kids, and now they're like bees round a honeypot!"

Seth, standing with an arm hooked about Ghislaine's waist, gave Jinny a look of sardonic disbelief. "It's fairly obvious what they see, isn't it?" he enquired dryly. "She doesn't exactly try to hide it."

Jinny snorted, and Ghislaine said, "Pieface wasn't fair, anyway. She's very pretty."

"Makeup," Jinny said succinctly.

As she moved away Seth said, "Your friend doesn't like Crystal much more than she likes me."

"Who said she didn't like you?"

"It's obvious. She never speaks to me if she can help it. And I keep intercepting these threatening looks. I think she's afraid of what I might do to you. Actually, I don't blame her."

"And what might you do to me?" she dared him, her eyes flirting with him.

Seth leered down at her and growled, low in his throat. "I'll show you later, when we don't have an audience."

Ghislaine laughed up at him. She would never be afraid of anything Seth might do to her.

She'd been helping Jinny pick up empty glasses to take inside for washing, because they'd almost run out of clean ones, when she noticed Crystal talking to Seth, standing close to him in the shadow of a tree. Ghislaine paused with two stacks of glasses in her hands, vaguely disturbed by the sight. Crystal's face wore a look of alert, overtly sexual interest as she raised one hand and thrust back her hair, making her breasts jut pertly under the tight black leather. Seth's gaze involuntarily flicked downward, then up again, and Ghislaine's hands tightened damply on the glasses she held. She wanted to march over to them and shove Crystal aside, to publicly stake her own claim to Seth. Instead, she watched Seth's expression change from polite near-boredom to faintly amused sexual awareness.

Crystal had put out a hand then, and touched him. And Ghislaine had turned her back on them and hurried into the house, her jaw clenched, to dump the glasses in the sink so roughly that one of them chipped.

"Sorry," she said to Jinny who came in a few seconds later. "I've damaged a glass."

"They're only peanut-butter glasses," Jinny reassured her. "Nothing to worry about. Are you okay?"

"Of course!" Ghislaine persuaded bright surprise into her voice. "I'm having a great time. Good party, Jinny."

"Darrell's having a great time, too." Jinny laughed. "He's not driving, is he?"

"Heavens, no! Seth brought him. His father wouldn't have let him take the car to a party, anyway."

"Talking of Seth," Jinny said, nodding out of the window, "he might need rescuing. Crystal looks as though she's about to eat him up."

"Seth can look after himself," Ghislaine said, more calmly than she felt. But she couldn't help glancing out the window, and at that moment Seth looked up, over Crystal's blond curls, and then he put a hand on Crystal's arm, gently moving her aside, and left her.

When he entered the kitchen Ghislaine was bent over the sink, assiduously washing glasses while Jinny dried. He came over and dropped a kiss on Ghislaine's neck, saying, "I wondered where you'd got to. I'll finish that if you like, Jinny. Go and talk to your guests."

Jinny gave Ghislaine a raised-brows look and relinquished the tea-towel. And Ghislaine went on washing glasses, her happiness restored.

Seth had a hand under her arm. "Come on," he said. "We'd better circulate."

The talkative man with the long memory had melted into the crowd. Ghislaine thrust aside the memories of summers past, pasted a social smile on her face and said to a dark-haired woman in a slim-fitting black sheath, "Hello, I should know you, shouldn't I? I'm sure I've seen your face—"

The woman was more interested in Seth, and Ghislaine introduced him with an ironic sideways glance at him that he intercepted with a glinting one of his own. She made to retreat from his side, only to have her bid foiled by his hand clamping about her waist.

When the woman finally drifted off Ghislaine said, "I'm not your Siamese twin. It isn't essential that we stick to each other all night."

He loosened his hold. "Am I cramping your style? I was counting on you to be my protection."

"From what?" Surely he wasn't nervous of these people? She'd seen that a few had moved away, obviously unwilling to talk to Seth. The three people in the car his had crashed into had been part of a large Maori family, respected members of the tribe that had settled in the district centuries before the Europeans. Family members and their friends might still find it difficult to forgive and forget.

"From women like that, for instance," Seth said, cutting across her speculations.

"She seemed rather attractive, I thought," Ghislaine commented, ignoring the strong desire she'd had less than two minutes ago to tell the woman to take her fluttering eyelashes and her come-hither smile elsewhere. "And she was certainly taken with you."

"You're still an innocent in some ways, aren't you?" Seth looked down at her.

"What do you mean?" She didn't feel like an innocent, she felt jaded and embittered and older than her years.

"Some women," he spelled out for her, "like to come on to ex-prisoners. It isn't me she's attracted to—it's some kind of danger or excitement that she wants, that she thinks I can give her. Because of what I've done, where I've been."

Ghislaine felt a sudden shock of recognition. She had sensed that aura about him since he'd been home, of a hidden violence ready to explode. A violence she would have once thought him incapable of. "Are you dangerous?" The question was totally spontaneous, arising from her subconscious.

Seth's eyes glittered. "Only to you," he said.

It wasn't possible to leave the party before midnight. Ralph and Jinny didn't deserve such a snub. There were times when Ghislaine almost enjoyed herself, times when she was surprised that former friends not only recognised her but seemed genuinely pleased to talk to her. And to Seth, who was never far from her side, although once or twice he allowed her to elude him.

But somehow she felt there was an invisible thread between them. With her back to him, she knew where he was in the room. She knew when he came to stand nearby, and once, as she walked across the carpet behind him, she saw him turn his dark head and flick a glance in her direction, as though checking to see where she was.

When the chiming clock on the mantel began its midnight run-up and everyone was hilariously shushed by Ralph Price standing before it with upraised arms, Ghislaine felt Seth's presence at her back although he didn't touch her, and heard the soft sound of his breath. She gripped the glass of wine in her hand and stood straight and silent as the party-goers chanted along with the chimes, "One—two—three—" and on to "eleven—*twelve!*"

Amid the whooping and cheering and whistling, Seth turned her into his arms, and she felt a cold droplet of wine slide down her arm as she tried to steady the glass, holding it away from them. And then felt nothing but the warmth and firmness of his mouth, the hardness of his body, the strength of his arms moulding her to him. The sounds of revelry receded before the drumming of her blood as he parted her lips in a hot, passionate invasion.

Time interlocked in that instant, and she was back in another party, another year, being kissed by a younger Seth and feeling the same sweet burden of desire. And as she had then she wound her free arm about his neck and kissed him back, following his lead and giving herself to him as ardently as she had when she was seventeen.

And when they reluctantly parted, while the noise all about them gradually died down, he looked at her with the same blaze in the green depths of his eyes as he had then, and said again, "Let's get out of here."

And as before, she whispered, against the longing inside her that matched his, "We can't. Not yet."

"Not yet," she'd said. "We can't." And stood staring at him as he stared back at her, both of them oblivious to everything around them, although then too there'd been a lot of cheerful noise to welcome in that new year. A new year full of changes and bright promise.

They'd managed fifteen minutes of post-midnight party-ing, then Ghislaine had said, "What about Darrell?"

"Oh, hell!" Seth said, making her laugh. "Damn the kid." He'd looked around for his brother and found him at the centre of a hilarious group toasting the new year, the end of their schooling, the end of the old year, the hosts of the party, and anything else they could think of. "I'll take you home," he said, "and come back for him. He looks as though he's planning to go on for at least another hour—unless he passes out first. I'll have to smuggle him into his room at home. Dad would skin him."

"He's not that drunk, is he? Very happy, but—"

Seth cast him an assessing look. "Mmm. *Very*. Hang on here. I'll let him know I'll be back to drive him home."

When he returned to her side, Ghislaine said, "*You're* all right, aren't you? You've been drinking more than usual." He'd had several glasses of wine throughout the evening after the spirits he'd started with.

"Do I seem all right?" he asked her.

"Mmm." He'd been noticeably less quiet and more out-going than she'd ever seen him, occasionally bursting into the laughter that was rare for him, but he wasn't slurring his words or stumbling over his feet.

"We could walk," he said, "if you'd rather. Takes longer to get to your place that way."

She smiled back at the teasing light in his eyes and said demurely, "I think it would be safer."

Seth grinned lecherously. "What makes you think that?"

It was a slow walk home, because every now and then they stopped to kiss under a concealing tree overhanging the path, or in the doorway of a deserted shop. When they reached her house he pulled her to him on the darkened porch and she said, "Would you like to come in? I can make you some black coffee."

"Think I need it, do you?" he asked, grinning.

She didn't, really, but he had to drive home and he'd drunk more than was normal for him. Mostly, though, she didn't want him to leave her. It had been a good party and a lovely walk home, and she wanted to keep him by her as long as possible.

She made coffee and they took it into the small, shabby lounge and sat side by side on the sofa.

"Another?" she offered, putting out a hand for the cup when he'd drained it.

"Okay." He didn't want to end the night, either.

She smiled at him dreamily, and after bringing the second cup for him, she settled herself into the circle of his arm where it lay along the sofa back. When he finished that cup she took it and placed it on the floor beside them and turned to him, raising her lips to his.

The sofa was the wide, old-fashioned sort, and after a while he eased her down and they lay together on the velvet-covered softness, their kisses increasingly passionate.

And of course kissing wasn't enough, for either of them. When Ghislaine felt his hand slide inside her dress she was only mildly surprised that the fastening was undone, and as his palm found her breast, barely covered by the flimsy lace bra, she gasped with satisfaction and arched her body, the better to feel and enjoy his touch.

He was kissing her throat, and she wanted his lips *there*, where his hand was, but she was too shy to ask. Instead she put her shaking hands on his head, guiding it down. And gave a long, ragged sigh of pleasure as he found her, pushing the lace aside, giving her what she wanted.

It was what he wanted too, and that knowledge gave her even greater pleasure. When he lifted his head and returned his mouth to hers she opened it for him in wild, sweet invitation, opening her legs too when he jammed one of his between them.

There was thunder in her head and lightning running in her veins. Seth lifted his mouth and whispered hoarsely, "You're beautiful, so beautiful—more than I ever imagined." His hands were on her breasts, and she felt them swell and peak for him. "Perfectly formed. Exquisite."

She'd always thought herself too small, but Seth's admiration made her feel as lovely as he said she was.

"I want you so much," he murmured. And he moved away from her, tugging at his belt with one hand, the other sliding under her skirt.

Perhaps it was the physical coldness that came between them when he lifted his body away from hers. Or perhaps it was, as he said so long afterwards, the natural fear of an inexperienced girl. At the time she only knew that the reality of what was happening hit her like a cold shower. She was half-undressed in her mother's sitting room, with her mother sleeping next-door and trusting her to keep to the values she'd insisted on in her daughter, and Seth was obviously intending to consummate their relationship.

She drew the edges of her dress together in a convulsive movement and said, "No!"

"Darling—" Seth stopped what he was doing, but she was acutely aware of his hand on her bare hip.

"I can't," she whispered frantically, her eyes wide and scared and pleading. "I'm sorry, Seth."

She saw him fighting for control. His face contorted, brows drawn together, neck muscles corded in anguish, his eyes tightly closed as he lifted his head.

Then his hand left her, and he stumbled to his feet and took a deep, shuddering breath. With his back to her as she sat up, trying to adjust her clothes, he said in a muffled voice, "No, of course you can't. I wish you hadn't—"

"I'm sorry!" she said again, guilt washing over her. "It was my fault."

He turned then, carefully not touching her. "No," he said. "It was mine. I shouldn't have drunk so much. I'd have had more self-control. I'm sorry, Ghilly. I'm a brute, frightening you."

"You didn't," she said. She had been afraid, but not of Seth. Of an unknown physical experience, perhaps, one she was not quite ready for in spite of her feelings for him. Of the strength of his male passion and male demands, a little. And of betraying her mother's teaching, her own values. But never of Seth. Never.

Chapter 14

It was different now, Ghislaine realised as Seth swung the dark blue car onto the main road, leaving the thriving sounds of the party behind. Now Seth was a different man. A man to fear.

He drove just within the speed limit, and this time she knew he had drunk a single nip of whisky when they arrived, then made two glasses of wine last all night. And besides plentifully supplied nibbles, Jinny and Ralph had sensibly served a substantial supper just before midnight.

Tiny shivers chased each other over Ghislaine's skin, and she stared straight ahead at the headlights eating up the night. She half expected Seth to stop somewhere along the way, take a detour down a lonely side road, and she braced herself for that. But instead he drove all the way home and stopped the car in the garage before he turned to her and said, "I want to come to your room."

Ghislaine shook her head. "I'm sorry," she said, and opened the door.

He shot out a hand and pulled her back into the car, into his arms, and then he was kissing her, forcing her head against the upholstery, until she raised a fist and aimed it awkwardly at his cheek. He fought down her hands and held them in a hard grasp, looking at her face and breathing heavily. "You kissed me before," he said.

She knew she had, transported back to an earlier time, another place, when they'd been two other people. "I was carried away by the party," she said. "Everyone kisses at New Year."

He let her go and she climbed out and walked from the garage to the house, but by the time she was inside the back door, slipping off her sandals so as not to wake Carley and Mrs. Keegan, he was behind her, emanating a kind of dark threat that made her go up the stairs almost running. Silently he took them two at a time and stayed beside her as she walked down the hall to her room.

She paused at the door, her hand on the knob, and said quietly, "Thank you for taking me. Goodnight, Seth."

He was too quick. As she opened the door and made to slip through the gap he gave the door a shove, and came in after her, closing it as he leaned back against the panels, looming in the darkness.

Then he snapped on the light, and she blinked in the sudden glare, her eyes caught by the raw, flagrant desire she saw in his.

"You want it, too," he stated flatly, making her turn her head aside and lower her gaze to avoid the brazen sexuality in his steady stare.

He stepped away from the door and she retreated, flinching from him.

Seth stopped. "Do I frighten you?"

Ghislaine swallowed and briefly her eyes met his. "Yes," she said honestly.

"Why?"

She looked at him again. "You—you've tried to, lately," she accused him.

He nodded. "Yes. I have." His hand reached out to her hair, then her cheek, the fingers trailing to her jawline. "But I don't want to hurt you now, little cat," he said huskily. "Believe me."

The intensity of his gaze was hypnotic. The feather-light touch on her skin burned. Ghislaine closed her eyes against the bittersweet sensations he aroused. Her mouth framed the

word *Don't!* but no sound came, and a stinging tear formed
at the corner of her eye.

Seth had bent closer, she felt his breath on her cheek, then
his tongue stroked the tear away, and when she shivered he
gathered her—so gently—into his arms and kissed her
mouth again.

She didn't resist when he picked her up in his arms and
walked to the bed, or when she felt the softness of the mattress beneath her, and Seth's firm body above her, pulling
her against him.

His mouth was on her lips, then on her cheek, her throat.
He pulled open the buckle of her belt and undid the buttons at the front of her dress, and she heard the quick
soughing of his breath as his hand splayed on the warm skin
of her midriff.

"You're as beautiful as ever." Then he was kissing her
mouth again, and his hand roved over her, seeking, touching, stroking.

She lay like a doll, accepting his caresses without protest
until he stopped suddenly and said, "Open your eyes,
Ghislaine!"

She opened them, and saw him frowning down at her, the
hard glitter of desire in his eyes mingled with angry frustration. "What's the matter?"

"Nothing," she said tiredly. "Do what you want, Seth.
Take what you want. I just don't care any more." She felt
nothing but sadness and despair, and a deep, deep lethargy.
What did it matter? Seth was determined he was going to
have her, although he despised her and perhaps even hated
her. And maybe, after all, she owed him this.

He stared at her for long moments. "History repeats itself," he said, and rolled away from her and off the bed.
"You've certainly come up with a sure-fire passion-killer
this time, Ghislaine." He turned and ran his eyes over her,
giving a short, breathy, contemptuous laugh. "A woman
who's just uninterested is even less of a turn-on than one
who's fighting tooth and nail."

He walked to the door and with his hand on the knob
turned and looked at her again. "Goodnight. I hope you
sleep better than I will." Then he switched off the light and

went out, leaving her staring, dry-eyed now, into the darkness.

New Year's Day was always somewhat tension-filled in the big house, the adults unable to avoid remembering the early morning police call, the chaotic events of the night, the nightmarish aftermath.

Surprisingly, it was Roald Keegan who, when Carley was only two years old, had instituted the New Year's Day picnic. Each year thereafter he had driven them all north or east or west—never south past River Road—to some beach or remote spot in the country. Mrs. Keegan, if somewhat startled at the idea, had always concurred with what her husband decided, and Ghislaine, glad enough to be away from all reminders, had naturally fallen in with any plans the Keegans made in any case. Once they had eaten, Mr. Keegan would go for a walk and his wife would settle for a nap on the picnic rug, while Ghislaine played with Carley or took her exploring. After an hour or two Mr. Keegan's return signalled time to open the thermos for a last cup of tea before packing up to return home.

Having grown up with the tradition, Carley took it for granted that this year would be no different, and that morning made sure to apprise Seth of her expectations. She seemed to have totally accepted Seth in place of his father.

Seth, looking almost as heavy-eyed as Ghislaine felt, instantly agreed. "Where to?" he asked Carley. He hadn't looked at Ghislaine since coming down for breakfast, a fact for which she was grateful.

"The waterfall?" Carley suggested.

"No," Ghislaine vetoed, ignoring the glance that Seth cast at her now. "Granna couldn't walk that far, and it's too steep."

They settled for a small, secluded bay within an hour or so of Tangihuna, where there was safe swimming for Carley and plenty of trees so that Mrs. Keegan could sit in the shade on the canvas chair that Seth packed into the back of the car.

Ghislaine had made sandwiches and brought along a bag of fruit and drinks including a thermos flask of coffee for Mrs. Keegan.

When they'd finished the picnic Ghislaine helped Carley make a sandcastle. Carley rather wanted to enlist Seth as well, but Ghislaine said firmly that he might want to talk to his mother. From time to time she glanced at him lounging with his back to a tree near his mother's chair, but they didn't appear to be talking much.

Later she put on her swimsuit and supervised while Carley showed off her water skills. It wasn't until they came out that Seth pulled off the T-shirt and light trousers he wore over his swim briefs and plunged into the sea.

He stayed in for some time, and Carley, shading her eyes, commented admiringly, "Seth can swim a long way!"

Mrs. Keegan said unexpectedly, "Seth was a champion swimmer at school. He rescued his brother once when Darrell got into trouble in the water."

Ghislaine hadn't known about that. Of course, Seth wouldn't have mentioned it, and Darrell wouldn't want to admit that he'd needed rescuing.

Carley looked impressed. When Seth at last emerged and came to collect his towel, she said, "Granna says you saved your brother."

Seth gave his mother a startled look, and she said, "That time he nearly drowned himself when he was seven. You were fourteen."

Seth was slowly drying his face and arms. "What brought that up?"

"Carley was saying what a good swimmer you are."

"Was he very brave?" Carley asked solemnly.

Mrs. Keegan looked faintly surprised, then said slowly, "Yes, he was very brave."

Seth made a deprecating sound, and Mrs. Keegan looked up at him and said, "I don't know if anyone told you at the time, we were all so concerned about Darrell."

Seth looked down at her, pausing with the towel in his hands. A slow flush of colour came into his face, and he said, "It wasn't anything wonderful. He was okay, that was what mattered." Then he dropped the towel and turned to pick up his shirt, hauling it over his head. His back was still wet, making damp patches on the fabric.

When he drew up in the garage and opened the front passenger door for his mother while Ghislaine and Carley got out of the back, Mrs. Keegan said, "That was a most enjoyable day. Thank you for taking us, Seth."

"No problem," he answered, giving her a rather puzzled look. "Leave that stuff, Ghislaine," he advised as she made to retrieve the picnic things. "I'll bring it in."

Dinner was quiet but relaxed that evening. Carley yawned a couple of times, and Ghislaine sent her to bed early. When she came downstairs she heard a murmur of voices from the small sitting room, and after a slight hesitation at the foot of the stairs she went outside and wandered round the garden, pulling odd weeds here and there that Jerry Wallace had missed or that had sprung up since his last visit before the Christmas-New Year break.

She looked up when she heard the back door open, expecting Mrs. Keegan on her nightly garden inspection. But two figures appeared. The older woman was leaning lightly on Seth's arm, and as they neared Ghislaine Mrs. Keegan said gently, "There you are, dear! I'm feeling a little tired tonight. I wonder if you'd mind making my drink for me soon."

"Of course." Ghislaine hurried inside to get it, and when they came in she had it ready.

"I'll keep it warm while you have your bath," she offered.

Mrs. Keegan said, "I don't think I'll bother with a bath tonight. I really am very tired."

As Mrs. Keegan and Seth left the kitchen, Ghislaine tried to quell a tiny stirring of foreboding. She poured the hot drink and followed them into the hall. They had reached the stairs, and Mrs. Keegan let go of Seth's arm and turned to him. "You needn't come up with me."

"Perhaps I'd better."

His mother shook her head firmly. "No. I'm quite all right." She put a hand on his chest and reached up to brush a kiss against his cheek. "Goodnight, son."

He watched her slowly climb the stairs while Ghislaine stood unnoticed in the shadows. She had never seen that expression on his face before, surprised and vulnerable. It made her throat ache to look at him.

Then he lowered his head and turned and saw her, and she came forward saying unnecessarily, "I'm just taking up your mother's hot drink."

"Yes," he said absently. "Fine." He glanced again up the stairwell, but Mrs. Keegan had disappeared into her own bedroom.

In the morning when Ghislaine went in with Mrs. Keegan's breakfast, she came out again calling, "Seth! *Seth!*

"Get the doctor," she said when he appeared in the hallway below. "Your mother's ill."

"A massive cerebral stroke," Dr. Turner told them an hour later.

"Not her heart?" Ghislaine queried.

He shook his head. "There's years of life left in her heart."

Seth looked at him sharply, and Ghislaine said, "But you said it was weaker, gave her pills—"

"She had a bit of a wee problem," Dr. Turner said gruffly. "A slight murmur. And everyone's heart slows a bit as they get older. Her main trouble was an over-sensitive temperament. And lately her blood pressure's been a bit variable. The pills should have helped that. But this—this is unpredictable. She's unlikely to survive it. We could send her to hospital, but there's not much they can do."

"I want a second opinion," Seth said bluntly.

The old doctor looked at him from under shaggy grey brows. "You can get as many opinions as you like," he said. "They won't tell you anything different. Lucille wouldn't want to be kept breathing by a machine, if that's all they can do for her."

"I don't want that for her, either," Seth said quietly. "But I will get another opinion."

* * *

The other doctor was no more hopeful. "She's dying," he told them bluntly. "It's a question of how long, and where. Can you care for her here? We could get her into hospital."

"She'd want to be at home," Ghislaine said.

"Do you need a nurse to help?"

"I'll do it," she told him firmly.

And Seth said, "*We'll* do it."

There wasn't, in the end, a great deal to do. Mrs. Keegan was unable to take food except in liquid form, spooned into her mouth, and her needs were the most basic, reduced to a regular change of position and clean linen.

Ghislaine took Carley in to see her, and when the little girl held her lifeless hand and kissed her cheek a flicker of awareness showed in the blank blue eyes.

"She will get better, won't she, Mummy?" Carley asked when Ghislaine ushered her out.

Ghislaine took her hand and led her to the pretty pink-and-white bedroom along the passageway, closing the door. "Granna's very ill," she said.

Carley's eyes went huge. "Is she going to die?"

Ghislaine went on her knees and put her arms about the child. "You've seen how sick she is," she said gently. "When people are not ever going to get well again, sometimes it's better for them to die. It's hard for us, because we'll miss her a lot, but we wouldn't want Granna to stay this way, and not be able to walk around or talk to us, or read, or do anything nice."

Carley sniffed, a sob shaking her small body. "Will she be with Grandad?"

"With Grandad, and with Darrell—her son. She loved him very much."

"I want her to stay with us!" Carley cried rebelliously.

"Yes, darling, I know." Holding her daughter while Carley expressed her pain and rage, Ghislaine, too, wanted to howl at the unfairness and cruelty of death. But she knew it would make no difference.

Carley spent most of the day at the Hemis', and when Donna phoned and offered to keep her overnight, Ghislaine accepted gratefully. Mrs. Keegan's condition hadn't changed, and Ghislaine and Seth took turns at sitting with her.

At midnight Ghislaine was nearly dozing in the armchair Seth had set by the bed when he came into the room and motioned her to go and rest. She bent and kissed Mrs. Keegan's cool, lined cheek, pausing as the closed eyelids flickered and the parched lips parted.

"Mrs. Keegan," she said softly. "It's Ghislaine. Can you hear me?"

A small sound came from Mrs. Keegan's throat. Her eyes briefly opened, with the awareness of recognition, then closed again.

Ghislaine turned to Seth, now standing beside her. "She knew me," she whispered.

Seth nodded. "I believe you're right."

Ghislaine went to lie on top of her bed without undressing, her heart full of hope. Perhaps the doctors were wrong, after all. Many people recovered from strokes, didn't they?

She woke to the burbling of magpies in the orchard, and a pale sun struggling through the clouds outside the window. If Mrs. Keegan had survived the night...

She was optimistic as she hastily dashed water on her face and thrust a comb through her hair before hurrying along the passageway and pushing open the door.

Seth's hand lay in his mother's on top of the sheet, and he was leaning forward with his dark head on the pillow beside hers, apparently asleep.

He stirred as she walked in, and sat up, looking round at Ghislaine. His eyes were bloodshot, and his cheeks were hollowed and held a shadow of beard.

"How is—" Ghislaine began, murmuring.

And Seth said quietly, "She's gone." He stood up and very carefully replaced his mother's hand on the sheet, then bent and kissed her forehead. "Some time ago," he said, answering Ghislaine's unspoken question. "There wasn't any point in waking you."

He walked over to the window, looking out at the grey-pink morning, and Ghislaine crossed to the bed and touched Mrs. Keegan's face, finding it chilled.

"There'll be things to do," Seth said remotely. "We should telephone old Turner, I suppose. It'll break his heart."

"Yes," Ghislaine said. She wanted to go to him, hold him close, but he was shutting her out, deliberately, with his back still turned to her. "Did she—wake?"

"Sort of. For a few seconds. And tried to talk."

"What did she say?"

He shrugged. "I thought she was trying to say my name. Or perhaps it was 'sorry.'" He turned, his eyes catching hers and then flickering away. "More than likely she thought I was someone else."

"No," Ghislaine said gently. "She knew Carley. And me. She didn't think you were anyone but you."

Ghislaine was mildly surprised at the number of people who turned up for the funeral. Mr. Keegan's had brought a large crowd, but he was well known in business and had a much wider circle of acquaintance than his wife. Perhaps many of them had come out of respect for his memory.

At the house later, Ghislaine tried to remember some of their names as she handed around trays of sherry and plates of sandwiches. There were a number of tall men with the Keegan family characteristics clearly stamped on their faces, and she was surprised when, thinking she recognised one of a group, she fairly confidently greeted him as "Mr. Keegan", and was corrected.

"I'm Phil Jones," he said. "My mother was a Keegan, though, and my father's mother was a Delbridge."

One of his companions, an older man sporting a dashing peppery moustache, laughed. "It's the nose," he said. "There's no getting away from it. Been turning up in both the Keegans and the Delbridges from when old Foster Keegan married Delbridge's daughter back in nineteen hundred or so. In those days," he explained to Ghislaine, "they were partners, Keegan and Delbridge, in the Auckland business."

"Keegan's son bought out Delbridge later on," Phil Jones told her, "but the families remained close."

"Phil here is doing a family history," the Keegan man explained. "Finding a few skeletons in the cupboards, eh, Phil?" He exchanged a covertly amused glance with the other man. "Well, poor Lucille isn't around to mind. Bit of a dust-up when she married Roald."

Startled, Ghislaine asked, "Why?"

The men looked at each other again. Then Phil Jones said, "Storm in a teacup. Family didn't take to the idea. Roald was a late starter in business. Dark horse, too. Handsome devil, but didn't have much to offer a girl except his name. Not a lot of money in that branch of the family."

"Still, Lucille wanted him, and in the end her parents were left with not much choice but to accept it," said the Keegan man. "Banished the pair of them to the country—I believe Lucille's father helped to buy this house and set Roald up in business—and let the poor girl rot here."

Ghislaine had sometimes wondered why Mrs. Keegan seldom saw members of her family, but assumed that the social life of Auckland didn't interest her. The house and her garden and the surprising number of charities and women's groups she supported in Tangihuna seemed to have consumed all her limited energy.

Catching her expression, Phil Jones said sympathetically, "Mediaeval, isn't it? The Delbridges were like that. Really behind the times."

The older man said, "Lucille was quite a beauty, you know, when she was young." He sighed. "Well, we all have to go in the end. At least it was quick."

The next few days were something of a hiatus. Carley was a little weepy, but Ghislaine encouraged her to ride Stardancer and play with the Hemi children, and all the signs were that her normal happy personality would soon reassert itself. Seth spent much of his time shut away in his father's study, presumably keeping in touch with his business partner via the computer. Ghislaine sorted through Mrs. Keegan's clothing and packed several boxes for the Salvation Army to collect.

"There's some jewellery of your mother's," she said hesitantly to Seth, catching him on his way to the study when she came down after reading Carley's bedtime story. "Perhaps it should go into a safe deposit or something."

"It's Carley's now, isn't it?" he said. "Do what you want with it. Wear it, if you like."

"I couldn't wear it!"

"Why? Wouldn't it suit you?"

"It's not mine! It wouldn't be right."

He looked at her. "Your ideas of right and wrong constantly amaze me," he said, and continued on his way to the study.

She gave Carley the ornate silver dressing table set that she had always admired. Mrs. Keegan would have wanted the little girl to have some personal keepsake. And she arranged with the bank to have the jewellery properly stored. But when she came upon a leather box full of obviously personal papers, the first one she lifted out and looked at being Darrell's birth certificate, she took it downstairs and knocked on the door of the study.

"Yes?" As she walked in Seth looked up from the big old desk in front of the windows.

"These are some of your mother's papers. I think you should have them."

She put the box on the desk and made to leave, but he said, "Sit down."

"I have things to—"

"Sit down," he said harshly. "You've scarcely sat down except for meals since my mother died."

How would he know? she thought. He'd spent most of that time in this room. She looked at the desk and realised that there were no papers in front of him, but on the leather blotter holder that Mr. Keegan had used stood a squat bottle and an empty shot glass.

"You haven't asked me to leave," Seth said.

"Leave?" A sudden hollow opened in her chest, as though someone had just reached in and removed a vital organ.

"The house is virtually yours now. Do you want me to leave?"

"Would you?"

"I may not have much choice if you choose to enforce your legal rights," he said. "Or rather, Carley's. Although perhaps you wouldn't. She likes me, and seeing me forcibly marched off the premises might be upsetting for her."

He didn't really think she'd do that, did he? She looked at his face, the dark mockery of it. "I—it's your home," she said. "I wouldn't do that." Legal rights or not, she wasn't at all sure she had any moral right to throw Seth out.

He watched her a moment longer and inclined his head. "Thank you."

"If that's all—" she said, and rose from the chair.

Seth got up, too, facing her across the wide, polished desk. "No, it's not all," he said. "Will you marry me, Ghislaine?"

Chapter 15

"Marry you?" Ghislaine repeated, stunned. *"Marry you?"*

"That's right," Seth said calmly. "Well?"

"I—" She glanced at the glass on the desk. "You're drunk," she said, as the obvious explanation presented itself.

"I'm not drunk," he informed her. "Crazy, quite possibly," he added thoughtfully. "But not drunk. I'm very careful these days about drinking."

"I can't marry you," Ghislaine said. "You can't marry *me!* Not while you—you despise me!"

"I want you," he pointed out.

"It's no basis for marriage."

"It's the only basis a lot of people have. But there are others in our case. Carley, for instance."

"Carley?" Ghislaine's head came up, scenting danger.

"If she's mine, as you keep saying she is, what could be more appropriate? A wedding seven—eight years late is surely better than no wedding at all. My mother would certainly have thought so."

"This is a sick joke," Ghislaine said.

"It's no joke," he said grimly. "Marry me and I'll accept Carley as my daughter. I swear I'll never deny my paternity again, to anyone. Think about it, Ghislaine."

She thought about it, trying to put aside her feelings, which were so complicated they made thought almost impossible. A rush of longing, of excitement that she'd deliberately fought down. Shock that he'd suggested it, and fear of what had prompted him to do so. Hope that, along with the physical want he had never denied, the aching desire that she shared, there was still, buried beneath the bitterness, a remnant of the love they had once had. A love that might yet be brought back into full bloom.

Putting aside all that, she tried to examine the cold, hard facts. Sort out the best, the wisest thing to do. And the fairest.

And she came to the conclusion that it was the only thing to do. As Seth pointed out, the simple yet tremendous step of marrying him would solve everything. Except the rift of distrust between them.

They were married very quietly on a hot summer afternoon three weeks later, the harsh rasping purr of the cicadas outside almost drowning Ghislaine's huskily spoken vows. Surprisingly, it was Seth who insisted on a church wedding. Ghislaine wore the oyster pink dress and jacket, and Carley, taking the idea of her mother marrying Seth as perfectly natural and much to be desired, was of course not to be deprived of a star part as her mother's only bridal attendant.

Ghislaine had made it a condition that Carley didn't object to the marriage, but there was no obstacle—or reprieve—there. Carley was ecstatic at the thought of Seth being her stepfather. It seemed to restore to her the sense of security that his parents' deaths had rocked.

Jinny, hiding disquiet under smiles and congratulations, kissed Ghislaine and wished her well while Ralph wrung Seth's hand. The Hemi family were all there, and after the guests had been given a few drinks and a meal at the big house, Donna and Matiu gathered up the children, including Carley, and left Seth and Ghislaine alone for the night.

Ghislaine had refused to consider a honeymoon on the grounds that it was too soon after Mrs. Keegan's death for her to leave Carley. Expecting opposition from Seth, she'd been ready to argue, but he only said, "Fair enough. I need to spend some time in Perth soon, though. I've been away too long as it is, and it's unfair to my partner. We could fly over there after the wedding, take Carley along, too."

"She has to go back to school, soon."

"A week or so missed won't hurt her. She's a bright kid and she'll soon catch up."

Ghislaine had killed an irrational spurt of irritation at his tone of calm authority. The weeks before the wedding had been a time of strangeness, like an armed truce, when she and Seth treated each other with marked politeness and never touched. Having Carley in the house had helped to maintain a spurious normality, but now it was their wedding night. As she stood beside Seth at the top of the steps and watched the Hemi station wagon retreat down the drive into the dusk, Ghislaine was conscious of a rising sense of panic.

Seth took her arm and led her into the house. The sound of the heavy wooden door closing behind them made her flinch. The hallway was very dim.

Seth said, "Another drink before bed?" Neither of them had drunk very much of the wine they'd served for the guests.

"Yes." Anything to fill in the time, make it longer. And anyway, it was surely too early yet to think of retiring for the night.

"On the patio?" he suggested.

It was hot and stuffy inside, and the night air wasn't yet too cool. "Yes," she said again. "That would be nice."

She thought he cast her a sardonic glance but it was too dark to see properly.

He fetched a bottle and two glasses, and they walked outside. Cicadas were still singing in a desultory fashion nearby, and the pool looked like black satin in the rapidly fading light. The passion flowers had fallen but there was a

faint sweet scent on the evening air of roses from the gar
den and frangipani from a tub in a corner of the patio.

Mrs. Keegan's lounger had gone, because Ghislaine
hadn't been able to bear looking at it. The small wrought
iron table was still there, and they sat on the chairs flanking
it while Seth poured the wine. He had discarded his jacke
and tie and was dressed in dark formal trousers and a white
shirt with two buttons undone at the throat and the sleeve:
rolled to the elbow.

Ghislaine half turned in her chair so that she could pre
tend to be admiring the slow creep of nightfall over the hill:
and across the paddocks, and watching a huge pumpkin
coloured moon climb into the velvet sky. Hoping it would
help her relax, she drank the first glass quite quickly. Seth
refilled it without comment.

The wine warmed her, and absently she started to unde
the buttons on her jacket, finding it constricting as well a:
hot.

"I was looking forward to doing that," Seth said, break
ing the silence.

His gaze had followed her hands, and she took a quick
choking breath, her head turned to him, her hands stilled.

"Don't stop," he said softly. "I enjoy watching, almos
as much."

She took her hands away and clenched them on the ta
ble.

After a heartbeat's silence, Seth said quite casually, "Hov
about a swim?"

"Yes," she said. The water would be soothing to he
jumping nerves. "I'll get changed." She stood up and made
to hurry past him, but he caught her wrist, swinging him
self out of his chair, and said with laughter in his voice, "N(
need. There's only the two of us here, and we're married."

"I don't swim nude!" she said sharply.

"Don't be a prude, Ghislaine. It's dark, anyway."

"The key—"

"I'll get it." He released her and strode to the house
leaving her standing uncertainly by the table.

When he returned he was swinging the key in one hand
and had two towels in the other. He put his hand on he

waist and guided her to the pool, leaving the gate swinging and dropping the towels onto the tiles.

He unbuttoned his shirt rapidly, pulled it from his pants and dropped it, then began to open the buckle on his belt.

Ghislaine said, "I don't think this is a good idea."

"We can go straight up to bed if you like," Seth offered. He slid down the zip and his trousers joined the shirt.

Standing in a pair of brief underpants that hugged his lean hips, he said, "Are you waiting for me to undress you?"

As he stepped toward her she put a hand to the front of her jacket and moved back. "No! Certainly not!"

Seth laughed. "I could almost believe your story of never having had a lover," he said. "I'm your husband, Ghislaine," he added grimly, "and I intend to spend the rest of my life with you naked in my bed every night. There's no point in being coy with me."

"I'm not being coy!" Ghislaine flashed.

"All right," he taunted. "Prove it."

Trapped, she stood looking at him, unable to discern his expression now for the shadows that the night cast over his face, making it look all angles and jutting curves.

Her face was flushed, and her pulses hammered. Lifting her chin, she began undoing the jacket and slipped it off, but hesitated about letting it lie on the ground, and Seth took it from her and draped it over the gate.

Ghislaine stepped out of her shoes, kicking them aside.

"Now the dress," Seth said.

She swallowed, and pulled down the zip at the back, letting the soft fabric slide over her hips, stooping to retrieve it. She'd hurriedly removed her sheer stockings when they returned to the house, too hot to keep them on, and now she wore only satin briefs and a skimpy strapless bra.

Seth took the dress from her and hung it with the jacket. Then he looked at her and said, "Turn around."

She did so, staring at the dark, lapping water of the pool. She felt his fingers part the fastening at her back, and the cool night air on her breasts as he took her bra away. Then his hands skimmed the satin panties down her thighs and she was naked. And Seth said quietly, "All right. Get in."

She dived blindly, welcoming the cold shock of the water. She was breaststroking to the other end when she heard the splash of his entry, felt it in the sudden wave lifting her body.

She waited for him to come near, to touch her. But he didn't. He swam parallel with her, apparently ignoring her, his arms moving in a strong, leisurely crawl.

When she was tired she climbed out by the ladder and wrapped a towel about her, sarong-wise, tucking in the corner and then bending to wring water from her hair. With her back to him she heard Seth padding across the tiles, and when she looked at him he was securing the other towel at his waist.

In silence she picked up her clothes and he gathered his, then locked the gate behind them.

The house was in darkness but Ghislaine knew the way, and she didn't falter until she reached the door of her room and Seth said as she paused there, "No. My room."

"I need to dry my hair."

"There are more towels in my bathroom. And a hair dryer. I'll do it for you."

He turned on the bedside light, stripped the cover off the bed and sat her down on it and fetched another towel, sitting beside her to rub her hair. He'd already rough-dried his.

He had brought a comb, too, and he drew it carefully through the tangles until her hair lay smooth on her head, quickly drying at the ends where they lay on her shoulders.

"I like it damp." He put the comb down and touched the darkened strands, his fingers lightly grazing her skin.

Ghislaine shivered, and he said, "Are you afraid of me?"

She forced herself to look into his eyes, unable to read what she saw there. "Should I be?"

"Not tonight," he said. His fingers stroked her shoulders, along the curve of flesh over bone, and up again, his hands holding her head. "Tonight I want you to love me."

Then his lips came down on hers, and he bore her backwards to the pillows.

In the humid, quiet night, with the moon carving a path through the sky and silvering the window, laying a soft light over the wide white bed, he made love to her with a tenderness she had known only in dreams, and a passion that she met with a wild, abandoned eroticism that fed on his and fuelled it, a deliberate blotting out of everything except this long-awaited culmination. She gloried in the warm, slick tautness of his skin under her palms, in the intimacy of his hard, firm hands discovering her nakedness as he threw aside the crumpled dampness of the towel and touched her thighs, her breasts, held her hands in his and kissed her mouth, and then urged her to turn so that he could admire her back, sweeping his hands slowly down the long line of her spine and over the gentle curve below, dropping a kiss on her hip and then several more along the firm flesh of her thigh until he reached her knee, before she turned on her back, wanting to touch him, too, sitting up to bring him back into her arms as he lifted his head enquiringly, twisting so that she huddled against him with limbs twined, while they tasted each other's skin, mouths, hands—her lips against his salty palm, her finger drawn into his mouth, teased by the hot, wet roughness of his tongue—and in the end every part of their bodies.

She opened her mouth against his shoulder and her teeth made a row of tiny, teasing bites, until he gave a muffled groan and tugged at her hair, drawing her head back and doing the same to her along the taut curve of her throat, eliciting a laughing gasp of protest.

"You started it," he muttered, and threw her on her back again beneath him, lowering his head to plunge his tongue into her open, laughing mouth, his muscular thighs holding hers snugly between them, the swelling evidence of his need for her lying trapped against the tender concavity of her belly.

"I want you..." he gasped, raising his head at last. "I've wanted you for so long, Ghislaine, my love. Tell me it's the same for you. Say you want me."

"Yes," she whispered. "Yes, I want you. I've always wanted you."

He moved, his legs shifting, nudging hers to part for him, and she raised her knees and cradled him between her thighs. His body lifted slightly, and he gazed down at her face, and she knew it wore the same tight, waiting look of passion that was on his. "Tell me you love me," he said.

And she said, "I love you, Seth." And felt him plunge into her inner softness—the warm moist flesh, unused to such invasion, at first reluctant so that she drew in her breath and stiffened momentarily until the slight discomfort eased and her body closed about him, accepting, welcoming, loving.

He gave a long, guttural sigh. "You've never loved another man. Have you?"

"No. Never." She felt his chest rise and fall against her breasts, and inside her his body moved, seeking the core of her, sending small shockwaves of darting pleasure all over her.

"I'm the first," he said. "The only one."

"Yes, yes. The only one I'll ever love, Seth. You—only you."

"Yes," he said. "Yes." And then he found what he'd been seeking, and gave a wordless, wrenching cry and her mouth opened too as all the breath seemed to leave her body on a swiftly rushing, uncontrollable tide that flung her into a void where nothing existed but the waves and waves of extraordinary, unbelievable pleasure that Seth was giving to her, that she was giving to him, until the heavy, beating, overwhelming surges of excitement washing over her quieted to tiny, tingling ripples, and Seth lay unmoving in her binding arms, breathing unevenly with his mouth against her temple.

After a long time he moved aside, and she murmured a faint protest when his body left hers, but he gathered her into his arms and kissed her softly on the lips, his hands stroking her back, and she shifted her legs, settling into the hard curves of his body, and he started making love to her all over again. She felt sleepy, but her senses were suddenly alert again to his every exquisite touch, and when she touched him in return she felt him stir against her and heard the quickening of his breath. With the tip of her tongue she investigated the sensitive spot she knew of at the base of his throat, and smiled when he made a small, pleased sound and pulled her closer to him. And this lovemaking was even better in its way than their first coming together, quiet and unhurried until Ghislaine, her slight body lying prone along the length of his muscular one, sat up, holding his hands, and eased herself onto him, her head thrown back in ecstasy as he dropped her hands and caressed her thighs and then took her breasts into his palms.

Watching her closed eyes, her parted lips as he fondled her, he said, "Do you like that?"

"I love it." Her voice was low, hardly audible.

"You love *me*," Seth insisted.

"Yes." She was very still, afraid to shatter the delicious feelings coursing through her. She bent her head slowly, until she could meet his glittering eyes, looking at him with her hair shadowing her face. "Yes. I love you."

He slid his hands up to her shoulders and said, "You're too far away. I want you close to me. Do you mind?"

She leaned down to him. "No. I want to be close, too." As their lips met, her feet slid under his thighs, and he gave a grunt of pleasure and turned over with her so that she lay under him again, and as he plunged into her over and over she cried out again and again until finally he caught up with her on the edge of that heaven where only they could take each other, and they spiralled into it together.

Ghislaine woke very late, the sun already streaming into the room as she opened heavy eyes and realised where she was. Only a sheet covered her, the rest of the bedclothes strewn on the floor beside the bed. Her body ached pleasurably, and her lips felt full, swollen. A shadow at the window resolved itself into Seth, dressed in casual slacks and a pale grey shirt.

She hadn't moved, but as if he felt her gaze he turned and looked at her. With his back to the light, she couldn't see his face when he said, "Good morning."

"What's the time?"

"Nine-thirty."

Ghislaine sat up, instinctively clutching the sheet over her nakedness. "You should have woken me."

"I was tempted, believe me. But I figured you needed the sleep." He came toward her, and she still couldn't read his face. "You're awake now." He sat on the bed and reached out a hand, his eyes on the slipping sheet.

The sunlight was very bright and, suddenly shy of him, the more so for remembering how uninhibited she'd been last night, she hoisted the sheet closer. "I need a shower. And we have to fetch Carley."

"There's no hurry," he said.

"But—" she remembered "—we're flying to Perth today. There are things to do—"

She thought his eyes cooled. "All right," he said, getting off the bed. "Do you want breakfast? I can make it while you shower."

"Just coffee," she said, "and a piece of toast."

He went toward the door, then hesitated before opening it. He turned and his eyes slid over her, glittery and cold. "By the way," he said, "I want to thank you for last night. You lie beautifully. But then, we already know how good you are at that, don't we?"

He hauled open the door without looking at her again and snapped it shut behind him. Ghislaine stumbled into the shower and turned it on hard, the cascading water mingling with the tears that ran down her face.

When she came down he had the coffee and toast on the kitchen table. "We could take it outside," he said. "It's warm enough."

"No, here's fine." The only way to survive this debacle, she decided, was to be as civilised as possible. She remembered last night on the patio, and realised the wine bottle and two glasses were still outside.

He poured himself a cup of coffee and sat opposite her.

"Have you eaten?" she asked him.

"Hours ago."

Her coffee was too hot to drink. She nibbled at the toast but wasn't really hungry. She felt nervous, ill at ease. Images of last night kept floating into her mind. She was glad when Seth began to talk. He said quite casually, "I didn't tell you, did I? In that box you gave me after my mother died, I found some very intriguing documents.''

She looked up, trying for an air of polite interest.

"My birth certificate," he said. "And my parents' marriage certificate." He paused, and she felt he was watching for her reaction. "They were actually married a year later than I'd always thought."

"Oh?"

"I told you once that people in glass houses etcetera. It's advice I could well have taken myself. I'd been under the impression that I was born eighteen months after their marriage."

A piece of toast fell from Ghislaine's hand to the plate. "Oh."

"Yes," he said. "It was six months, in fact. No wonder my mother resented me so much. It must have been a very inconvenient pregnancy. The permissiveness of the sixties hadn't hit New Zealand then, and her family were a fairly Victorian lot..."

Ghislaine recalled the covertly amused look between Phil Jones and the elderly Keegan at Mrs. Keegan's funeral. "She was so kind to me."

"But for the grace of God..." Seth suggested.

"It did surprise me," Ghislaine admitted.

"Perhaps I might surprise you, too, if you trusted me."

She glanced up and saw him scrutinising her with an air of taut expectancy.

She stared back at him, then looked down and said, "It's not a question of trust."

"Oh, I think it is," he said softly, still watching her.

Ghislaine pushed away her plate. "You don't understand," she said in a brittle voice. "I'll go and fetch Carley."

Seth shoved back his chair, standing up and coming after her to swing her round with his hands on her shoulders. "Make me understand!" he said. "I want to, Ghislaine!"

"I can't, Seth! Don't push it, please!"

"Hasn't Carley ever asked about her father?"

Ghislaine bit her lip hard. "Yes."

"So—what did you tell her?"

She said in a low voice, "I told her he was dead."

She almost thought he'd flinched, his eyes darkening. "How very convenient. So now she has a resurrected father."

"Stepfather."

"Make up your mind, Ghislaine! You're beginning to get your stories muddled."

"I've never told her you're her father," Ghislaine said. "All she needs to know is that you're her father *now*. The only one she's ever had. What difference does it make?"

"It makes some difference to me!" Anger glinted in his eyes. "Surely you can understand that?"

"I'm sorry," Ghislaine whispered.

His eyes narrowed. "You're not going to tell me, are you?"

"I can't. *Please*, Seth, I *can't!*"

"You will," he said. "Some day you damned well will!"

She was glad that getting ready for the flight to Perth and journeying to Auckland to board the plane meant there was scant time in the rest of the day for any private talk. Carley was excited by the trip, and she made an adequate buffer. It was her first flight, and Ghislaine's. Seth seemed to be a seasoned traveller. "Wear something comfortable and loose," he'd advised Ghislaine. "And soft shoes, not new. Your feet may swell with the pressurisation in the cabin. You don't want to arrive barefoot because your shoes won't fit back on."

They were met by Seth's partner, a big bluff man called Morton Hall who said happily, "Everyone calls me Mort—unless I owe them money." He ruffled Carley's hair with a huge, blonde-furred paw and wrung Ghislaine's hand while he studied her face with undisguised curiosity, eventually pronouncing to Seth, "She's a beauty, mate. Dark horse, aren't ya? See why you weren't too keen about the Aussie birds followin' you over the Tassie and trackin' you down. Had this one tucked away all the time, did ya? No wonder you didn't want to come back to work!"

He winked at Ghislaine. "Only teasing. Bit of a surprise ole Seth getting himself hitched in such a hurry. There'll be a few broken hearts around Perth, I can tell ya! But I can see he's done all right for himself.''

Seth said, ''You talk too much, Mort. Carley's getting tired, it's past her bedtime back home.''

Taking the hint, Mort picked up a suitcase as though it were filled with feathers, and led them out to his car. ''Hafta come an' meet the missus tomorrer,'' he invited them. ''But Seth reckoned you'd be going straight to his flat tonight, so you can bed down the little one.''

The flat, overlooking the river, had two bedrooms, each with a double bed. Carley fell asleep almost instantly in one of them, and when Ghislaine rejoined Seth in the lounge he said, ''I've unpacked my stuff, but I guess you want to deal with yours.''

She was glad of the excuse, and made the task last as long as possible, then had a shower and got ready for bed. When Seth came in she was about to slip under the sheet.

''Are you tired?'' he asked her.

''Yes,'' she said instantly. ''Yes, I am, rather.''

He stood surveying her with a twist at the corner of his mouth. ''I see,'' he said at last. ''Well, you'd better go to sleep, then.''

She still wasn't asleep later when he switched off the light and she felt the mattress depress under his weight beside her, but she pretended to be.

Mort picked them up the next day and Ghislaine and Carley went sightseeing with his wife, a small, dark woman with a wide, welcoming smile, while the men spent the day at their office near Government House. Afterwards the adults had dinner together at a restaurant, followed by a show, leaving Carley with the Halls' children and a babysitter that Mort's wife assured Ghislaine was utterly trustworthy and, ''terrific with children. I promise Carley will love her.''

Carley certainly seemed quite happy with the arrangement, and Ghislaine was only too glad to give the impression that she was having a great time and wanted to prolong the evening. She could legitimately plead tiredness again when Seth joined her in their bedroom at the flat.

But on the third evening as she made to leave him in the lounge, muttering something about an early night, he said, "You're going to run out of excuses eventually, Ghislaine. And in my book one night of bliss doesn't constitute a marriage. I'll be with you shortly."

Resentful of his forcing the issue, she tried to remain cool and uninterested when he joined her in the bed, but he was both patient and persistent, and also somewhat skilled, she realised with a flaring of jealous anger. This time he didn't ask for, and failed to elicit, any declarations of love. But he could have been in no doubt when she grappled her arms about his neck and cried out against his searching mouth, her body erupting into spasms of pleasure, meeting and matching his, that she was as lost in him as he was in her.

By the time they returned to the big house in New Zealand, that had become the pattern of their lovemaking—her initial reluctance overcome by her own sensuality under his expert ministrations. More and more Ghislaine was angered by that expertise. And aware that under a surface blend of mockery and an irritating confidence in her eventual capitulation, Seth was increasingly chagrined by her unwillingness to respond.

Another source of frustration was her instant veto on any suggestion of selling the house and moving to Perth. "I don't want to uproot Carley," she'd told him when he first broached the idea. "And I don't feel we have the right to sell the house, even if Mr. Trounson agreed as her trustee. It's part of her heritage. Your father wanted her to have it."

He looked savagely amused at that, but evidently decided not to attack her argument head-on. "We could rent it out if you're reluctant to sell," he said.

"I don't want to live in Perth," Ghislaine insisted stubbornly. "And I don't want to bring up my daughter there. This is a good place to grow up. It's what we planned for her—your parents and I."

"You're married to me," Seth reminded her grimly.

"So?" Her head lifted. "The days are gone when the little woman followed her man all over the world at his whim—"

"It's not a whim! My business is in Australia, and it isn't fair to leave Mort to carry it all on his own."

"You should have thought of that before you blackmailed me into marrying you!"

"Blackmail?"

"Whatever it's called when you marry someone under duress. I could probably get an annulment."

"Try it." His eyes looked very green, and dangerous. "I'll drag you—and Carley—through every court in the land, and every muckraking newspaper. Keegan is still a name that attracts publicity."

She looked at him helplessly, filled with rage and despair. "Why don't you call it quits and go back to Australia, yourself?" she asked, dreading the prospect but at the same time yearning for a peace and tranquillity that was no longer possible.

And Seth said, "You know why."

Chapter 16

Carley was back at school, and Ghislaine found it difficult to fill her days with housework, shopping and the little gardening that was left for her after Jerry Wallace's regular visits.

She attended one school Parent-Teacher Association evening with Seth and a public meeting called to discuss the setting up of an art and craft gallery in Tangihuna, but at both she was acutely aware that interest in her and Seth's marriage so soon after Mrs. Keegan's death, and speculation as to who had inherited the estate, had not yet died, and she shied from the covert glances and obliquely curious questions. She began to wonder if it might be better for Carley to move away, after all. Children adapted easily, and a new life might not be such a bad idea for all of them. Seth had never been truly happy in this house, and it held too many mixed memories for her, too.

The summer seemed relentless, the sun burning from an achingly blue sky every day, turning the green paddocks dry and brown, and the cicadas' insistent song seemed to echo the pulsating heat that sometimes rose in visible waves from the ground. The cattle gathered under the trees, their tails flicking incessantly at the flies that bothered them, and

Stardancer stood droopily in his paddock with his head and tail down. White cabbage butterflies haunted the garden, occasionally joined by their glorious cousins, the black-veined orange monarchs, and at night whirring flying huhu bugs and big green puriri moths batted against the window screens.

Even Carley was often cross as well as tired on her return from school in the stuffy, crowded school bus. Ghislaine blessed the swimming pool that cooled them both off in the afternoons and allowed them to be reasonably comfortable by dinnertime. Now she could let Carley bring home schoolmates or invite the Hemi children to come and enjoy the pool too, under Ghislaine's supervision.

"Midge is learning to play the piano," Carley told her mother one day as they dried themselves after a swim. "Can I show her the one in the front room? She's never seen a grand piano."

"When you're dressed," Ghislaine promised after the barest hesitation. There was no need to warn Carley to be careful, she had been trained from babyhood to treat everything in the drawing room with respect. And Midge was a polite and considerate child. All the same, she followed them into the room.

When she lifted the lid, Midge said in excited awe, "Oh, please, am I allowed to play it?"

Ghislaine looked at her eager face and beseeching brown eyes and said, "Yes, of course." The piano had been meticulously maintained and regularly tuned even though rarely used. Mrs. Keegan had occasionally played a small repertoire of pieces she'd learned as a girl, but confessed she had no great musical talent, and preferred listening to those more accomplished than herself.

Midge sat on the piano stool and played three simple tunes she had learned by heart, her feet barely reaching the pedals. Carley watched, entranced, and said, "Play another one."

"I don't know any more, not without music."

"Well, play that last one again."

Midge obliged, but soon wriggled off the stool, thanking Ghislaine politely before she went to fetch her wet towel and swimsuit and walk home.

At dinner that evening Carley announced, "I want to learn to play the piano."

Ghislaine felt an extraordinary sensation of pride, resignation and fear. "We'll see," she temporised.

"Oh, please, Mummy!"

"I'll think about it."

"Why do you have to think about it?" Carley demanded.

"Because, for one thing we'd have to find a teacher, and it costs money."

Seth looked up from his salad. "That's hardly a problem."

She would have liked to tell him to stay out of it, but that wasn't possible in front of Carley. Whatever their private differences, these were never allowed to impinge on her security.

Carley asked, "What about Midge's teacher?"

Remembering a recent conversation with Midge's mother, Ghislaine saw a reprieve in view. "She has too many pupils already," she told Carley. "There's a waiting list."

Seth said, "Why not teach her yourself?"

"Mummy can't play!" Carley said.

"Yes, she can," Seth told her.

Ghislaine gave him a murderous look.

Carley was gaping. "Can you, Mummy?"

"No," Ghislaine said. "Not any more. I've forgotten."

"Forgotten?" Seth looked sceptical.

Between her teeth, Ghislaine said, "I can't play any more. I haven't in years."

Slowly he said, "But you know how to play. It's not a thing you *forget*." He paused. "Even if you don't play yourself, it shouldn't stop you teaching Carley."

"*Leave me alone!*" Ghislaine said, and pushed back her chair, leaving them both staring after her as she fled the room.

Later she tried to explain to a subdued and puzzled Carley that she was tired and hot and hadn't meant to be so silly.

With the one-track tenacity of childhood Carley accepted the explanation and simply said, "Will you teach me, then?"

Ghislaine smiled wryly. "Maybe. Just leave it for a week or two and if you still want to, I'll try."

"Why can't you try now?"

"Carley, I—"

"Please, Mummy, please! Just for a little while, before I go to bed?"

Obviously, Ghislaine thought wearily, she would get no peace until Carley had tried it. Maybe if she found out it wasn't so easy she'd forget the idea. "All right," she said. "Fifteen minutes."

In the end it was considerably more, because Carley turned out to be a natural, easily learning the notes. She played "Mary Had a Little Lamb" several times with one hand and said, "Show me how to do it with two hands, like Midge."

"It's a little too soon for that," Ghislaine said.

But she was inveigled into teaching her "Chopsticks," and soon they were side by side on the piano stool, Carley managing the simple two-finger bass while Ghislaine played the tune, pausing to move her daughter's hands to the correct keys when necessary.

By the fourth time, Carley was almost able to manage the notes herself, although still with uneven pauses while she placed her hands for each shift.

"Okay," Ghislaine said at last. "Time you got ready for bed."

Carley bargained hard for the promise of another lesson tomorrow before going off, satisfied. And Ghislaine sat on, looking at her hands on the keys and, slightly stunned, realising that she had actually played something—a simple little tune that every beginner knew, but a tune all the same.

She felt a stirring of excitement, a tingling in her fingers, and tentatively she ran them up and down the keyboard, softly, almost afraid. And tried a chord, then another, then flexed her fingers and began the haunting air of "Greensleeves'' which she had learned long ago, followed by what she used to call her ''party piece'' that had been popular with the older residents of Tangihuna when she was a teenager performing at school concerts and fundraising functions, ''The Rustle of Spring.''

She finished and sat with her back very straight and her hands in her lap, offering a silent prayer of gratitude. And Seth's voice said, ''Why did you stop?''

Ghislaine swung around. He was lounging in the doorway, his arms folded as if he'd been there for some time. ''How long have you been listening?'' she demanded.

''A while.'' He straightened and came toward her. ''Why did you say you couldn't play?''

But her rediscovered gift was too new and too fragile for discussion. ''I'm very rusty,'' she said, getting up from the stool. ''I have to go and see Carley into bed,'' she added, making to walk past him.

''But you can play,'' Seth said, stopping her momentarily with a hand on her arm.

She looked back at the piano, then at him, and knew that he was right. What she had lost had mysteriously returned to her, unlocked at last from its long imprisonment. ''Yes,'' she said confidently. ''Yes, I can.''

Before she went to bed Ghislaine had a last swim, stroking lazily up and down the pool while the stars teased out of the darkening sky, weaving fantasies about completing her music degree after all, perhaps having the chance to do a few concerts, maybe teaching. Back in the bathroom she had now become accustomed to sharing with Seth, she had a brief lukewarm shower and towelled her hair dry, then ran the dryer for a few minutes and returned to the bedroom wearing her mother's blue robe, to sit at the dressing table. She was combing her hair when Seth walked in.

She looked up, briefly meeting his eyes in the mirror, and went on combing, wincing as a stubborn knot refused to yield. She felt Seth's presence behind her as she raked the hair with her fingers, trying to coax the tangled strands apart.

''Your hair is lovely like that,'' he said.

"I'm going to get it cut!" Ghislaine snapped, as she struggled with the knot, hurting her scalp. She was hot again already in spite of her swim, and the tingling awareness of Seth's nearness upset the precarious equilibrium she had found.

"Just because I happen to like it?"

Ghislaine bridled at the exasperation in his voice. "Don't be silly. I had it short before, I just haven't had time to get it done lately. Anyway, it's too hot in summer to have it long."

"You could put it up," he suggested.

The comb at last ran through the skein of hair, freeing it. "It would never stay. It won't hold pins." She put down the comb and stood up, walking past him. She wished she'd put on her nightgown before he came in. She was very conscious of having nothing on under the thin silk wrap, and from the way he was looking at her he'd noticed.

She said, "I'm going to check Carley." With any luck he'd be in the bathroom when she got back.

"I just did. She's fast asleep," Seth told her.

Ghislaine stopped on her way to the door. "Have you locked up?"

"I do every night," Seth pointed out. "What's the matter, Ghislaine?"

"Nothing," she muttered. "I just want to put on my nightgown."

Seth's cheek creased. He looked her over with deliberation. "Why bother?" he asked softly.

Ghislaine felt herself flush all over. She said, "Can't you think about anything else?"

But her voice sounded uncertain and husky rather than scornful, and Seth, coming over to draw her into his arms, said simply, "No. Not when you're looking the way you do now." And tipped her head back with his hand under her chin to lower his mouth onto hers.

It was a thorough, leisurely kiss, and Ghislaine stood quite still in his arms while he completed his gentle devastation of her mouth. When he lifted his head at last, he eased her away from him, his glance dropping briefly to the front of the thin gown where the faded blue material was taut over her breasts, a gleam of satisfaction in his eyes at what he saw. "Get into bed and wait for me," he said. "*Without* a nightgown. I won't be long."

Given little choice, she switched off the light and climbed under the single sheet, still wearing the wrap. She shivered in anticipation, resentful of her vulnerability to him. When he came out of the bathroom he slipped in beside her and reached for her. "Take this off," he ordered, plucking at the gown, "if you don't want it torn again."

He watched as she slipped it off, and then took it from her to toss it to the floor.

She tried to remain cold and unresponsive, and perhaps succeeded for longer than usual. And Seth became less patient. For the first time he took his pleasure without bringing her with him, and afterwards when he tried to make up for it she pushed his hand away and said sharply, "No— don't!"

"It's not the same, but I can make it good for you," he said.

"I'm sure you can," she said bitterly. "You know all about making it good for a woman, don't you? How many have you practised your undoubted skills on?"

Lying beside her rigid body, he said, "I don't think you really want to know that. Not that many, actually."

"Well, I suppose being locked away for several years must have cramped your style for the duration, but you seem to have made up for it afterwards."

"Mort," Seth said, sighing, "ought to keep his big mouth shut. I'm not the stud he likes to suggest I am. Last year there was a woman I saw a couple of times who for some reason was much keener than I was. I think she was slightly unbalanced. She started ringing me at the office and actually called round once or twice demanding to see me. It was difficult to shake her off. Mort took it into his head that I was some sort of Great Lover. At least, he likes to pretend that he thinks so. You know him. He'll milk a joke to the last ounce. As a matter of fact I had never been, as they say, intimate with a woman until after I came out of prison. Believe it or not," he said with savage cynicism, "I was waiting for you."

Ghislaine lay very still, listening to the suddenly loud beat of her heart. She felt as if she'd just been hit with a very blunt instrument. "But—all those girlfriends," she accused him. "You had girls all the time you were at university!"

"Lots," he agreed. "A man doesn't necessarily sleep with every girl he takes out. I was careful not to get too involved. That's why there were so many of them. Because if you see one girl for a time—the relationship has to either progress or end."

Ghislaine was still trying to take that in when a glaring, salient fact burst like an exploding rocket in her brain, and she sat up, trying to see his face in the shadowy dark. "Crystal Summerfield," she said. "You're not telling me you took Crystal down to River Road and *didn't make love to her?*"

Seth was silent for so long that she believed he'd realised that was a lie he couldn't make tenable.

"I see," she said, and lay back on the pillows. "Had you forgotten about her?"

"No!" Seth said violently. He reached over and switched on the bedside lamp beside her. "I had not forgotten. There's something you need to know," he said. "No one can be hurt by it now, and—it's time one of us, at least, was honest about what really happened eight years back."

Ghislaine blinked up at him, the light harsh on his face, the brown skin of his chest gleaming. "What are you talking about?"

Seth took a deep breath, and said, "It wasn't me in the car with Crystal. It was Darrell."

Chapter 17

Ghislaine's eyes were wide and disbelieving. *"Darrell?"* She sat up facing him. "But you—it was you who was there, asking for Crystal. It was your car! Darrell was at home, in bed!"

"Afterwards, he was. When the police came to the house."

Ghislaine shook her head, trying to take in what he was saying. "You never denied you were responsible!"

"I never admitted it," he reminded her. "All I said was I didn't remember anything about the accident. I couldn't remember anything, because I wasn't there."

"And Darrell was?"

"Yes. You remember, I'd left the car at the party while I took you home that night. When I went back to Jinny's parents' place, the car was gone. Darrell had decided not to wait for me, and taken it."

"Didn't you lock it?"

"I don't remember. I certainly had the keys, but Darrell and his friends knew how to hot-wire a car. One of the accomplishments that teenage males delight in, even those who'd never think of stealing a vehicle. It was smart to know how. They could probably open a locked one quite easily, too. And of course he wouldn't have thought borrowing his brother's car was stealing. It was just a bit of a lark. He even left a cheeky note under a stone where I'd had it parked, promising to deliver it safely home.''

"He'd drunk a lot that night."

"I know. So I was fairly worried. But there wasn't much I could do except walk home and wait for him, intending to give him a large piece of my mind."

"And meantime, he'd gone down River Road with Crystal?"

"Apparently. It took me some time to get home on foot, in the dark. Only one car passed me after I left the main road, but the driver was understandably not keen to pick up a lone hitchhiker in the early hours of New Year's Day. There was no sign of Darrell when I got back here, and I was thoroughly fed up by then. I was already disgusted with myself for what had happened at your place after I took you home.''

Ghislaine made a small sound. "Disgusted?"

"I had meant to be very careful, very circumspect with you, until you were old enough."

"Old enough—?"

"To marry me. To love me as a woman, not a girl. To know what you were doing when you said yes. I knew you weren't ready for real lovemaking, anyway. And I wanted everything to be perfect for us when it happened. I had so nearly spoiled it all, that night. With Darrell's prank coming on top of that, I was in a fairly foul mood. While I waited for him, I made some hefty inroads on my father's whisky, sitting in the dark in the front room and planning several interesting ways to kill my little brother.''

Ghislaine shivered.

Seth winced, too. "Bad joke, in the circumstances. Of all the people who died that night, Darrell probably most deserved to, objectively. But he walked away from the crash, and came home. I'm not sure exactly when. He'd trekked across the farmland from the highway, and because I was listening for a car I hadn't heard him come in. Well, he didn't want to wake our parents. He'd got quite good at arriving home at all hours without their knowing when.''

"He was totally unscathed?" Ghislaine said sceptically.

"Bruised, but mostly under his clothes. No one noticed how stiff and sore he was over the next few days, because for once everyone's attention was concentrated on me. Anyway, he managed to creep upstairs unheard, and when I finally gave up and decided to go to bed, he was in my room, waiting for me." Seth leaned back on the pillows, staring at the wall opposite, his eyes bleak. "He was in a terrible state. When I walked in he hurled himself at me like a kid, crying and shaking. At first I couldn't get any sense out of him. Then he managed to tell me that he'd crashed the car, and he thought Crystal was dead. There was blood on his hands, and his clothes."

"That's how Crystal's blood got on your shirt."

"He was clutching at me, begging me to help him. I had my arms round him." Seth put a hand to his eyes, closing them. "I hoped that he was panicking more than he needed to, that maybe Crystal wasn't so badly hurt, after all. He was pretty incoherent, he just kept saying, 'She's dead, she must be dead.' But I couldn't persuade him to come with me back to the scene of the accident. Someone had to go. In the end I told him to phone the ambulance and clean himself up, and I ran over the paddocks to where he said it had happened. Cut myself on some barbed wire and ricked an ankle on the way. By the time I got near I could see the lights of the emergency vehicles, and a lot of people. I had to try to find out about Crystal. I didn't realise then that others were involved as well."

"And it didn't occur to you that they'd think you were the driver?"

"Not then, no—stupidly. And when they arrested me, how could I tell them it was Darrell they wanted? My little brother, that I'd just left, terrified out of his mind and crying like a child with remorse and fear of what he'd done?"

"But afterwards!" Ghislaine said. "Surely when he realised—"

"Darrell wasn't a strong character," Seth admitted. "We all loved him for his other qualities, the qualities the rest of the family didn't have. I knew, and he knew, too, that he'd never stand up to being in prison, or even reform school, if that was what it came to. It would have destroyed him. I was the strong one, we both knew I'd survive it.''

''But the court might have been more lenient with him. He was so much younger!''

''Maybe. Neither of us had any idea what the penalty might be until the lawyers spelled it out, and I think then he just panicked all over again. A couple of times he said he was going to own up, and I wouldn't have argued. I didn't *want* to go to court, end up in jail. But he never did. He couldn't quite screw up the courage to do it.''

''So you let everyone think you'd done it.''

He shrugged. ''At the time, everything seemed inevitable. From the moment the police arrested me, events took their course and there was no stopping them. The more time went by, the more impossible it was to tell the truth. And even if I'd tried, would anyone have believed me?''

Ghislaine swallowed. ''Do you think Darrell would have denied it?''

''I don't know. I like to think not. But—maybe. And I'd have destroyed whatever was left between us—and the rest of our family, as well. I don't think my mother would ever have forgiven me if I'd pointed the finger at Darrell, whether he denied it or not.''

And all his life, Seth had tried to win his mother's approval and to protect his brother.

''They were very important to you, weren't they?'' Ghislaine, suddenly unable to remain in the bed, snatched up the silk robe he had taken from her and pulled it on, throwing back the covers and walking over to the window. The stars were hanging silent in the sky, brilliant and cold. The window was open but there was no breeze.

''What are you doing?'' Seth asked.

''Thinking. When Darrell died you must have thought of telling the truth.''

''Of course I did. And again, who would have believed me? Even my parents would have thought I was seizing a chance to get out of what I'd done, smirching Darrell in the process when he was dead and unable to defend himself. I'd been proven guilty in court. They had so much circumstantial evidence. It was my car. No one saw Darrell and Crystal in the car together—''

"She talked to Darrell earlier, at the party."

"She talked to every man present earlier," Seth pointed out, and Ghislaine remembered with piercing clarity that she'd been jealous, watching him and Crystal together. "Yes," she said.

"She'd had a flaming row with Jinny's brother and walked out sometime after midnight. Darrell picked her up along the street."

"I see." Seth standing in the shadows with Crystal Summerfield, watching the tilt of her breasts as she raised her arms and looked at him the way she'd looked at every presentable male. "None of you could resist her."

"I did." As if he read her thoughts he said, "She produced a superficial reaction, Ghislaine. It meant nothing but a simple male reflex. Darrell should have known better— would have, if he'd been sober."

She knew deep inside her that everything he'd told her was true. That he'd spent years paying for something he had never done. And that she'd paid for it, too. This made sense of everything that had seemed so senseless at the time, impossible and yet irrefutable. Her thoughts were chaotic, jumbled by a complicated mix of emotions, the chief of which seemed to be fury, and she wasn't sure why.

From her subconscious the reason came with blinding clarity. "I loved you," she said, her voice blurred with the angry tears that clogged her throat. "Unconditionally, from the first moment I saw you. I was ready to marry you the minute you asked me, to spend the rest of my life loving you, loving your children. None of your family loved you as I did. Your father ignored you for most of your life; and your mother—she tried, but she never appreciated you, never saw how much you needed her approval, her love. And Darrell only loved you as the big brother who would always get him out of trouble, not for yourself but for what you could do for him, because Darrell never grew up, emotionally he was still a child."

Seth got up and came over to her, standing facing her in the dim light of the stars. "I never realised you understood us all so well."

"I didn't, until now." Now she could see it all so clearly. And see the thing that was making her shake with rage. "How *could* you, Seth?" she cried. The angry tears welled up and spilled. Unable to contain the rage any longer, she raised her fists and thumped them at his bare chest. "How could you throw away what we had, turn your back on my love, on our future, our *lives*—for *them?* It wasn't just that no one would believe you, was it? You *wanted* to make some sort of heroic sacrifice of yourself, for Darrell. Because you loved him more than you did me. And for your mother— because if she'd known you were saving her baby boy, she'd have loved you, too."

He grabbed at her flailing hands, holding her wrists, staring into her face. "Is that what you think?" he said at last.

"*Yes!*" It had all come pouring out with no thought behind it, but she knew in her heart that it was true. "You never really wanted me so much," she added tiredly. "You told me so when I visited you, told me I was too young, that I bored you, but I didn't want to believe it."

"I did want you!" he argued. "I loved you and wanted you. Maybe there's something in what you just said. Maybe I was thinking of my mother, ultimately. I don't know. At the time I just knew I couldn't do that to Darrell."

"But you did it to me! Didn't you know what you were doing to *me?*"

"I was on the bloody rack about you!" he said, with remembered anguish in his voice. "About us. I thought some day I'd be able to tell you, that you'd understand. I was going to ask you to wait for me. Only no one had thought I'd get five years! Even the lawyer, although he warned us of the possible penalty, wasn't expecting it to be so severe, when I hadn't even had a speeding ticket in years. And how could I ask you to wait that long when you were so young? So I let you go. *I had to.* That was worse than all the rest."

"But—" she remembered "—when you came out you told your father you wanted nothing more to do with me! Even before he told you about Carley!"

Seth shifted his hands to her shoulders. "I didn't intend to contact you. Yes, I told him that. He'd said you were happy. And—I'd been in prison for almost five years, Ghislaine. The things I saw there—experienced—changed me. I wasn't the man you had known. I was someone much harder, rougher, capable of things that I'd never have dreamed of before. In that place I turned into someone you'd never known, someone I was afraid to let loose near you. In my mind you'd stayed the same as when I'd last seen you—innocent, vulnerable, pure in every sense. Do you see what I'm saying?"

Dimly she could understand that he'd idealised her memory, preserved it through the long years in prison as though she were a kind of Snow White in a glass coffin, an unreal fantasy figure.

He said, "I felt I had no right to inflict this new self on you. I could've hurt you. Then my father told me you'd had a child. And that made it even more imperative not to disrupt the new life I thought you'd made. I assumed you were married. Married, and happy and with a baby. So I—ran away. And forced myself to stay away. I could never come home, never risk myself near you, because my instinct would be to smash your marriage and make you come back to me. And maybe now I was ruthless enough to go with my instincts." He paused there, and then said roughly, "It never occurred to me that the child was already five years old!"

"He didn't say?"

"You knew my father. Not one to waste words. Those prison visits he made were agony for him, and for me in a way. But I was grateful that he made them. I suppose he figured that telling me you had a child was all the information I needed. It might have been, if his assumptions had been correct. I was too thunderstruck to ask any questions."

"I thought you didn't know about Carley until you came back. I'd asked your father to let me tell you myself. But I never got the chance."

His hands tightened on her arms. "You have to tell me now, Ghislaine!" He paused, looking into her wide, doubtful eyes. "I have to know how it happened, how you came to do what you must have done, before I told you those lies about not wanting you. Before I set you free."

She closed her eyes momentarily. "You hadn't asked me for any promises."

"You know we were promised to each other," he said.

"We were! That night in the orchard, before I was sentenced, you offered everything to me."

"I loved you. I wanted us both to have something to hold on to, to remember, to strengthen our love if you didn't come back the next day!"

He said, "And it was all I could do not to take you."

"Why didn't you?" She'd been ready for it, thought he was going to when he gathered her into his arms and asked her to forgive him. She'd wound her arms about him, and given him her mouth without reserve as his body pressed hers into the soft grass and the fresh summery scent of it rose around them.

And then he'd rolled away from her and sat up, pushing a hand through his hair, his elbow resting on an upraised knee. And said thickly, "Ghislaine, if you never do anything else for me, do one thing now."

And she'd sat up, too, putting a hand on his shoulder. "What?"

He shuddered away from her touch, leaving her bewildered. "Go home," he said. "Please, just walk away now and go home, will you?"

"But—"

"Don't argue," he said with clenched teeth. "After tomorrow I may be in jail. I'm sorry but I can't—do anything tonight."

"You don't have to—"

"I *need to be alone!*" he burst out savagely, as though she'd angered him. "You can understand *that*, can't you?"

She stood up. "Of course." She felt rebuffed. And stupid. She'd got it all wrong. He didn't need her tonight, he was still a loner who preferred to wrestle his own problems in his own way, without help. "I'm sorry," she said blankly.

"I'll be there tomorrow." She'd not been working long and she knew that her boss wasn't pleased about her having time off for the court case, but she'd insisted.

"I was afraid," Seth said.

"Of what?"

"Of hurting you—physically, emotionally. I knew that I'd scared you several times, wanting you as I did, needing you. And your first time might have been painful, even if I'd had the experience and the self-control to make it as easy as possible, which I knew I didn't. I dreaded leaving you with a memory of something that had been awful for you. And— this'll give you a laugh—you might have become pregnant, and what if I was in prison and unable to be with you? I couldn't do that to you, but it wasn't easy, refusing an of- fer made so generously, so sweetly." He took a deep breath. "You accuse me of failing my love for you, but what about you?"

Ghislaine was silent. After what he'd just confessed, did she dare to tell him the truth? Or even a part of it? She tried to frame the words, words that would assuage his pain without adding to it.

He said, "After I came home I had to wonder if I was mistaken that night. If I'd been wrong about you all along. Maybe you weren't the innocent virgin I took you for—"

"I was! You know I was!"

As if he hadn't heard, he went on, "And yet who else was there?"

Ghislaine said, "No one. You know there was no one for me. I've never loved another man."

"Except Darrell." He dropped his hands, and Ghislaine, her heart pounding, stepped back. "It had to be Darrell," Seth said.

He stared at her, his eyes tortured, and Ghislaine mutely shook her head, unable to voice a denial.

He said, "I've known, really, ever since we got the test results. Only I couldn't—wouldn't let myself—believe it. It seemed bizarre. Worse than some stranger, some secret lover that I'd never have guessed at. People would have noticed if you were seeing someone else. But Darrell and you—

you'd always been close, and during those holidays you were practically inseparable except when I was around. Were you sleeping with him all that summer?''

"No!" she cried. "Oh, Seth, no! We were never lovers!"

Almost wearily he said, "It's no use lying any more, Ghislaine. I've been round and round the facts, everything I could think of. Though I kept trying to deny it, to think of some other rationalisation, some fluke random test result, perhaps. But there's no other explanation. *Why,* Ghislaine?'' The pain in his voice was so raw that she felt tears burning in her eyes. "Why did you betray me—and with my own brother?''

And she cried, "I *didn't,* Seth! I would have waited forever for you!''

"*No!*" he shouted at her, coming after her as she instinctively retreated. "No more lies, Ghislaine!" He gripped her shoulders, shaking her. "Carley's not my child!" He held her, staring into her tear-filled eyes, and finally he threw her down on the bed. "*Is she?*''

Ghislaine sobbed, crying now in earnest. "You know she isn't.''

He knelt beside her, pulling her up to face him. "Then she's Darrell's. *You have to tell me!*" he said again. "We can make something of this marriage, Ghislaine, if we don't have secrets from each other. Can't you see what this is doing to me? It's made me cruel to you, it's eating at my soul. I want to understand!''

Ghislaine swallowed. "Seth—I love you. I'm afraid of making you hate me again.''

"I never have," he said bleakly. "I never will. You're part of me." He took her into his arms, rocking her like a child. "But I need to know, Ghislaine.''

"Yes," she sighed at last. "I'm sorry, Seth. You loved Darrell so much. I sometimes thought he was the only consistently good thing in your life.''

"And you," he said, kissing her hair. "You, Ghislaine." He lay with her head against his shoulder and said quietly, "Tell me.''

He was right. There could be no more lies between them, or even half truths. No evasions, no deceits. Even if the truth brought renewed pain, total honesty was the only thing that could heal their love.

After Seth was sentenced and taken to prison, she'd spent that day and the next in a kind of fog, stunned and disbelieving. Then there was a knock on the door about ten o'clock in the evening, and her mother came in with Jinny Price.

"Jinny's here to see you," she'd told Ghislaine. "She saw the sitting room light and knew we'd not gone to bed. I'll leave you two girls to talk." She was trying to sound casual, but Ghislaine was vaguely aware of the anxiety in her eyes that had been there since the trial.

For her mother's sake, and because she'd had good manners instilled into her all her life, she tried to rally herself, and mustered a smile. "Hello, Jinny. It's nice of you to call in. Sit down."

Jinny sat but, glancing after her mother, seemed edgy. "How are you, Ghislaine?"

"I'm all right." Ghislaine swallowed. "Well—" she tried another weak smile "—I will be. It's been horrible," she confessed frankly. "For all of us."

"Yes, I know. Ghislaine—I didn't come just to talk. I've got—well, we've—the boys and I, have a problem."

"Your brothers?" Jinny always talked of them as "the boys."

"I could kill them, but you know we always stick up for each other, help out when one of us is in a hole. So I said I'd ask you."

Ghislaine was bewildered. "How could I possibly help?"

"It's Darrell. He's at our place."

"What's he doing there?"

"Getting blotto!" Jinny said viciously. "Courtesy of my stupid big brother, who bought the drink for them. He's the one who looks old enough to go into the pub and buy a crate of beer. He was *sorry* for Darrell, he said. With Seth going to jail and all. Thought he should drown his sorrows. Honestly, boys are the limit! And of course it's not the first time that bunch has got drunk, even though they're all under-age. You know that. Generally they go down River Road with the grog.''

Ghislaine did know. She'd once remonstrated with Darrell but he'd laughed at her. Drinking parties on River Road were among the puberty rituals of Tangihuna's male youth that everyone knew about although many parents preferred to pretend that their sons were not involved.

"Darrell," Jinny said, "didn't want to go there tonight, and my parents are out so they came to our place instead. But Darrell is *rotten* with it, and the parents'll be coming home about ten-thirty, eleven o'clock. They'll be furious. We can't persuade Darrell to go home. He's been crying off and on, and not making any sense, but now he wants to go on partying all night, and when the boys called a taxi to take him home and tried to get him into it he got quite aggressive—''

"Aggressive?" *Darrell?*

"—and the driver said he wouldn't take him. I thought maybe you could talk him into leaving?" Jinny finished pleadingly.

Ghislaine's first thought was to refuse, but she knew why Darrell had drunk too much tonight, and the habit of looking after him was ingrained over many years. "How did you get here?" she asked.

"Walked. Ran, mostly."

"I'll borrow Mum's car and come and get him."

"Don't tell her why!" Jinny begged. "She might feel she ought to tell my parents about it."

Her mother looked askance at the request for the car, but when Ghislaine said, "Jinny wants me to come over to her place for a while. Some of the old crowd are there tonight, and maybe I should think about something else—'' she ca-pitulated. There wasn't much crime in Tangihuna but she preferred Ghislaine to have transport home if she was out at night.

"Why didn't you phone me?" Ghislaine asked Jinny as she backed the car out.

"Didn't want Darrell to hear. Honestly, Ghislaine, I've never seen him like this. I wouldn't have put it past him to rip the phone out if he saw me calling you."

"*Darrell?*" Ghislaine could scarcely credit it.

When she got there the boys had him in the bathroom and were running cold water on his head. He looked glassy-eyed but was no longer fighting, and Ghislaine declined Jinny's older brother's offer to accompany them. Darrell was still inclined to scowl at him for some imaginary remembered grievance, whereas he'd smiled sunnily if drunkenly at Ghislaine and allowed her to coax him into the back seat of the car.

She thought he'd gone to sleep as they left the outskirts of the town, and wondered if she'd be able to wake him. She debated taking him to her house instead of home, but they'd have to phone his parents and explain, so that Mrs. Keegan wouldn't worry. She might as well take him to the big house. At best she might be able to help him sneak in unnoticed and sleep it off before morning. And at worst, if she couldn't manage him alone, she'd just have to enlist his father's help. And hope that Darrell would eventually forgive her.

Halfway there he had to climb out to be sick. When he came back he seemed better and more lucid, and got into the front beside her.

"Sorry 'bout this, Ghilly," he muttered. "Thanks."

"You're a fool," she told him crossly. "Getting drunk isn't going to help Seth."

"I know," he said, and started quietly sobbing. "Oh, God, Ghilly. I want to help him, I do! Jus' a few drinks, Dutch courage."

Ghislaine's lips had tightened at that. He was talking drunken rubbish. She didn't ask why he needed courage, unless because he was due to start his first university term in two days' time. Perhaps he was, after all, nervous about leaving home. More likely he'd been trying to forget about Seth being in prison.

He lapsed into silence, his head bowed, until they were approaching a patch of trees edging the paddocks, casting a dark shadow on the road, when he said abruptly, "Let me out!"

She slammed on the brakes, thinking he needed to be sick again. Instead he stood swaying beside the car, then set off walking along the verge.

She expected him to disappear into the trees for a minute and then come back. But he walked for a few more yards, then veered into the long grass growing beside the road and seemed to collapse into it.

Ghislaine left the car and called, getting no answer. When she reached him he was lying on his back in the grass, staring at the sky.

"Darrell!" she said, exasperated. "What are you doing?"

"Walk 'rest of 'way," he said. "Sober up. Ol' man'll kill me, coming home like this. 'Sides, they'll hear the car."

He had a point. But, "You can't walk," she said. "You just tried."

He found that funny for a while. When he stopped giggling and lapsed into morose silence, she said, "Try to sit up. I'll walk you up and down."

He managed about ten yards leaning on her before he said, "Got to sit down." And collapsed again, his arm still about her shoulder, dragging her down with him so that they were both sitting in the grass, in the deep black shadow of a macrocarpa.

"Love Seth," he said after a while, sadly. "You do, too."

"Yes." Ghislaine felt tears on her cheeks.

He put his head against hers and they cried together, their arms about each other, cheeks pressed close. After they had stopped, Darrell was holding her tightly, clinging, and when he lay back with her still in his arms she let him, her arms about him in mutual comfort.

Even when he kissed her cheek and then her lips she didn't realise what was happening. He was her playmate, her younger friend, Seth's brother. His lips were soft and warm, and mingled with the bitter aftertaste of beer and a lingering sourness she could taste the salt of tears on them. He was Darrell and he needed her compassion, her gentleness.

When his breathing changed and he kissed her differently, turned so that his body was heavily on top of hers, she tried to repulse him, knowing he wasn't fully aware of what he was doing. She pushed against him, turning her face aside. "No, Darrell. You don't mean this. Come on, you have to go home."

"Not yet," he slurred. "Please, Ghislaine. I need this."

Weakly, she let him kiss her again, thinking that was all he wanted, the comfort of kisses. And what harm was there? She still thought of him as something of a child, a surrogate younger brother. And for a few minutes she tried to pretend that he was Seth, because she needed comfort, too.

But he wasn't Seth, and when he touched her breasts and burrowed a hand between her legs, through her dress, she said sharply, "No, Darrell! That's enough!"

"You can't stop me now, Ghilly! Ghilly, please. Be nice to me. I need this. I need it."

"No!" She tried to use her knee but she was lying on the skirt of her dress and it hampered her. She slapped him and he didn't seem to feel it. She realised then how strong he was, much stronger than her and a great deal heavier. Although he wasn't a particularly big young man, he was fit and muscular, and he was holding her down without much effort at all while he muttered coaxingly in her ear.

That was when she began to panic. And even then, in spite of her fright and anger, she kept thinking, This is *Darrell*. Darrell wouldn't hurt me, he doesn't mean it. He'll stop when he realises what he's doing.

Right up to the last, surreal moment, when she felt the sudden tearing pain and cried out her denial and her grief to the unheeding trees above and the cold night sky beyond, she didn't believe that Darrell—*Darrell*—would really rape her.

Chapter 18

"Darrell raped you?"

"Yes." Ghislaine eased herself from Seth's suddenly slack hold, and lay on her back against the pillows.

Seth shook his head, then passed a hand over his eyes. "I knew the man had to have been my brother, I just couldn't understand how either of you—"

Turning to look at him, she said, "Perhaps it was my fault. I wanted his arms around me, I let him kiss me. And I think that's all he wanted, too, at first. Maybe I let him think that I was willing."

Seth turned to her swiftly and gathered her back into his arms. "It was not your fault! You can't be blamed for being compassionate and for accepting comfort." He drew a shuddering breath. "He must have been crazy."

"He was very drunk. And very—guilt-stricken, I realise now."

"That's hardly an excuse!" Seth said harshly. "You didn't tell the police?"

Ghislaine shook her head. "I didn't even tell my mother until I realised I was pregnant. Until I was sure. We'd all been through enough as it was. And Darrell didn't remember what had happened."

"He didn't?"

"Not me talking him home, not anything."

"After *that,* you took him home?"

"I scarcely knew what I was doing. He'd gone off to sleep for a little while, but when I finally managed to push him off me he woke and he—he was just Darrell again. Still drunk, but sweet and happy. It was all unreal. I dropped him off— shoved him out of the car, by that time I was beyond caring if he got in without your parents knowing, but I guess he must have—and I drove home. My mother was in bed. I called goodnight through the door and had a shower and went to bed."

"And he never mentioned what had happened?"

"No. He left for Auckland the next day without talking to me again. And I tried to forget it. When I found out I was pregnant, my mother insisted that he had a right to know. So I saw him, and—he said he'd some vague memory of someone trying to get him into a taxi, and assumed that was how he'd got home. The rest of the night was a blank."

Ghislaine paused. And Seth asked the question she had dreaded. "When did you tell him?"

She closed her eyes. "When he was home for the May holidays. He hadn't been here at Easter, and anyway, then I was still trying to deny it had happened, even to myself. Pretending I couldn't really be pregnant. When I did tell him, first of all he said I must be joking, and when I pointed out I was hardly likely to joke about it—he was stunned. I think he didn't know what to say, what to do. He said he needed to think, that he'd see me before he went back to university, and we'd work something out. On the last day of the holidays, he shot himself."

He'd borrowed a gun from Matiu Hemi, saying he was going rabbit shooting. The coroner found that Darrell's death was clearly suicide. He had expressed sympathy with the family and made some general remarks about the tragedy of young people imagining their problems were insoluble. Darrell's university grades in the first term had been unsatisfactory. That, combined with his parents' presumed expectations and his brother's imprisonment had seemed

sufficient to explain his action to most people in Tangihuna.

Ghislaine had not gone to Auckland to see him buried in
the family plot. No one had mentioned a suicide note, but
if Darrell's parents had any idea what had happened, she
didn't think they would want the reminder of her presence.
And she'd heard that Seth was to be given leave to attend.
She couldn't have faced Seth.

She felt Seth's chest rise and fall, and waited for him to
push her away, to accuse her of the guilt she'd never quite
shaken off.

Instead, he held her tighter and said, his voice muffled, "I
suppose on top of the accident, and me taking the blame,
that was the last straw that tipped him over the edge. Finding out that he had done that to you."

"I should never have told him, Seth. I blamed myself for
ages."

"No, you weren't to know about the rest." He was silent, then gave a long, heavy sigh. "I'm sorry, Ghislaine.
Sorry for all the hell my family's caused you. No wonder
you felt we owed you, owed Carley something in compen-
sation."

"It wasn't that! When your father came and asked me if
I was carrying his son's child, I should have realised he
meant you."

She could feel his sudden intake of breath. "You thought
he meant Darrell?"

"Yes. It was only weeks later. I'd thought about almost
nothing else in that time, until my mother died. I hadn't
slept with you, or any other man. I knew it could only be
Darrell's baby. It sounds stupid, now, but it didn't cross my
mind that of course most people would have jumped to the
wrong conclusion. I thought that Darrell had told them
what he'd done, left a note or something."

"And when you discovered that it was supposed to be my
child?"

"I didn't discover it, exactly. It just gradually dawned on
me. I suppose I didn't want to face that I was here under
false pretences. I promised myself I'd tell your parents the
truth when the child was born, but then—tell them Darrell

had raped me? And if I just said we'd had sex together—
they must have known I'd never willingly make love with
any man but you. And they might have thought less of
Darrell for it. It didn't seem fair to do that when they'd so
recently lost him. So I let things drift. Waiting until you got
out of prison. I decided I'd talk to you first."

"But I didn't come home."

"No, and I was reprieved. When your father changed his
will, I almost told him, but the way he explained it, telling
would have made no difference. I didn't know then that he
believed you'd deliberately abandoned your daughter. He
kept that out in the will."

"He was protecting you, of course, but he told the lawyer the full story as he knew it, in case I contested. Mr.
Trounson passed that on to me. He had permission to use it
in court if necessary."

"No wonder you were angry. By the time you arrived
here, it was too late, too complicated, too fraught with the
possibility of hurt for everyone—your mother, you, Carley. And she was their only grandchild. If they'd known she
was Darrell's baby they'd have done the same. Because
Darrell did owe her something, Seth. And they'd have
wanted to make it right."

"Possibly more willingly," Seth agreed, "rather than out
of duty. Once I started looking, I thought I could see Darrell sometimes in Carley's features. Perhaps my mother did,
too."

"Jinny thinks she's like you."

"Me?"

"Yes. She has my colouring, but she's a Keegan too. You
all have family traits."

"And genes. That really rocked me, when they said I was
the father."

"I'm sorry I couldn't tell you. I was trying to protect your
mother, and Carley—and you. You and Mrs. Keegan both
adored Darrell. How could I shatter your picture of him,
spoil his memory for you both, when it was all you had
left?"

"That's why you wouldn't admit even to me that Carley
wasn't mine?"

"You knew it, anyway. But you were so different from what I remembered . . . so hard and bitter. I was sure that if I told you whose child she really was you'd have thought it was a lie, and hated me for it. Even if you believed me, I was worried about what it might do to your mother if you confronted her with the truth. She'd grown fond of Carley, and she was so highly strung. You were quite caustic about her sometimes."

He was tracing the line of her throat, her shoulder, and he didn't lift his eyes. "I resented the fact that she'd never been able to love me, even though that was hardly her fault. And I could see she was manipulating you."

"Wasn't it me you thought was doing the manipulating?"

"Mutually. It looked like a thoroughly unhealthy relationship from where I stood. Having been away so long I had a more detached view of her, perhaps, and I'd learned something about psychosomatic conditions—the prison library was limited and I had time to read all kinds of things. Apparently old Turner understood her better than I thought, but I'm not sure his treatment was the best thing. And also—" he added, giving her an oddly shamefaced glance "—maybe I was even, in a twisted way, jealous of her affection for you. And of yours for her. I'd come back home, and although everything had changed, nothing had. All through my childhood I'd felt shut out."

He stopped abruptly there, and Ghislaine touched his cheek. "I know." He'd come home and found a usurper—two—in his place.

He gave her a wry smile. "I'm a grown man. This is ridiculous."

"No." But he didn't need to explain any more. "Your mother did love you at the end, Seth."

"Perhaps. Or at least she tried to. It's your love I need now."

"You have it," she said simply. "When I told you I loved Darrell, it was true, but not in the same way."

"I think I *would* have killed him myself, if I'd known what he did to you."

"He didn't know what he was doing that night. Darrell was still a boy, just not mature enough to handle everything that happened."

Seth sighed. "If you can forgive him, I guess I can."

"As we have to forgive each other. We've both been guilty of lies by omission."

"Yes. Maybe if I'd come on less aggressively you could have told me sooner."

"You seemed bent on some kind of revenge."

"I thought I was. When I realised you weren't married, and that you had grown into a woman—that you weren't the vulnerable child I was still seeing in my head, my heart—at first I was astounded and excited by the thought that there might be a chance for me, that everything needn't be over between us."

"And then you met Carley."

"Yes. Seven years old, going on eight. Everything turned on its head for me. All I could think was that the prison gates must have barely shut behind me before you gave yourself to another man. The will was another shock—and your refusal to admit that there was no way Carley could be mine. I told myself I was staying here to expose you as a liar and a cheat. The truth is," he hunched himself up on his elbow, regarding her sombrely, "I couldn't bear us to be apart again. And that's why I asked you to marry me, to bind you to me somehow even though my head kept telling me I was mad, that you weren't the girl I'd been in love with all those years ago."

"I think I said yes for the same reason. I told myself it was because I owed it to you. You might not have needed the money, the estate, but I had decided that if you ever had children, I'd have to speak up. Because then what I had done would be taking their rightful inheritance. Only," she added, recalling the piercing, hot pain the decision had cost her, "I didn't want you to have children that weren't mine. I didn't marry you because you forced me into it. Or because I felt I ought to somehow make it up to you for being cut out of your father's will. I pretended that I was agreeing for all sorts of pragmatic reasons to do with fairness and justice and doing the right thing. But really I said yes because I wanted to spend my life with you. I hoped that your asking me meant you still loved me in some way, and that even if I could never tell you about Darrell, you would accept there was a good reason for what I'd done, and you'd learn to trust me again.''

He smiled at her. ''My heart has never believed that you were the mercenary, grasping opportunist I accused you of being. I've been brutal to you, haven't I?''

''Sometimes,'' she agreed. ''It's true, you've changed. I'd never have been afraid of you in the old days. But I've never stopped loving you. That hasn't changed.

''And I you. Some things are eternal.''

''Like this,'' she said, drawing him to her. ''I wanted you, too, Seth. Wanted so much to love you. But all the barriers between us seemed impassable. And even if you didn't love me, even if you went on hurting me, I couldn't live without you again. When you're not with me, I'm only half alive.''

''So am I,'' he said. ''I've had eight years of half-life. I can scarcely believe it's over at last. Hold me, Ghislaine, and make me believe.''

''I will,'' she whispered, touching his hair, his face, sliding her arms about him as he lowered his head and found her mouth, her throat, parted the fabric covering her breasts and touched his lips to the warm skin over her heart. ''Believe.''

The following day Ghislaine put Carley on the school bus and after tidying up inside took a red plastic bowl out to the orchard to pick the last of the peaches. The climbing plants over the patio had lost their blazing blooms. The clematis was covered in star-shaped fluffy seed-heads, its leaves going coppery. The days were still warm, but there'd been showers lately and the grass needed cutting.

When Seth walked out of the house and came looking for her, he found her seated on the ground, the bowl of furred golden peaches at her side, her head resting against the rough grey trunk of an apple tree laden with blood red fruit, while she watched a fat green beetle teeter through the grass from one blade to another.

She looked up at Seth's approach, and he said, "Are you all right?"

"Just lazy." The morning sun had warmed her skin, and a faint breeze moved through the orchard, stippling shadows over her blouse and skirt, tugging a few faded, curling leaves from the peach tree nearby. "A bit tired," she said.

His eyes glinted down at her. "After last night, I'm not surprised."

Her eyelids went down, and she turned her head slightly, a hint of a flush colouring her cheek.

Seth laughed softly, and took a step closer. "Still shy?" His dark hair brushed a low-hanging branch. An apple thudded to the ground.

"I was thinking." She shooed away a striped yellow wasp that was showing interest in the peaches.

He scooped up the apple and bit into it as he hunched down beside her, then offered it to her. Ghislaine shook her head, and he put his arm about her and fitted her into the curve of his shoulder.

"What were you thinking about?" he asked.

Her eyes were on the house, the tall stern chimneys and darkly glistening windows. This side didn't catch the morning sun.

"That you've never been really happy here," she said.

"Until now." He kissed her, his lips tasting of apple juice, and she returned the kiss gently, yearningly.

When their mouths reluctantly parted from each other, she said, "Carley liked it in Australia. I think...I could learn to like it, too. As you said, we could rent this place out. Carley can decide what to do with it when she's older."

"I could be happy anywhere, with you," he said. "And I promise, if you don't like it we'll come back to New Zealand. I've been talking to Mort about opening a branch here. But we're not ready for that kind of expansion yet."

"We need a new start," she said. Somewhere everyone didn't know them, wouldn't be eyeing them with curiosity and knowing looks.

The breeze freshened and a flurry of leaves swirled about them, one of them drifting into Ghislaine's lap.

Yellow in the centre, darkening to a line of red, but brown and brittle at the edges, it disintegrated in her fingers. She said, "Summer's almost gone. It's nearly autumn."

"It will always be summer for us."

"Oh, no," she said. "We need the other seasons, too. The peaches are nearly finished, but yesterday I picked the first bunch of grapes. The apples are just ripening, and the figs will be ready soon."

He looked at the fig tree with its gnarled, spreading branches, its huddles of small, bulbous fruit hard and ungiving. Within weeks they'd be swelled and soft and flushed with stripes of rich burgundy. Birds would punctuate the branches, squabbling over the musky succulence, digging recklessly into the ripened flesh. Yet there would still be an abundance of fruit for the house.

Later, too, the smooth green globes of the passion vine would turn purple and be milked of their deliciously sweettart, juicy insides before they could wrinkle and die on the vine.

"Autumn is a fruitful time," he agreed.

Ghislaine smiled dreamily. "Oh, yes. It is."

It was too soon yet to be certain. She didn't want Seth to be disappointed if she was wrong. But she'd noticed small signs that she'd experienced only once before, when she'd been too naive to guess what they might mean.

This new secret was no dark, destructive burden, like those she had kept so long and so desperately from Seth. It was a quietly shining, warming thing, a thing of light and life instead of death and shame and sorrow.

He looked contented and at peace with himself, with the world, and she knew that it was because of her. Her lips curved with a contentment of her own. It was tempting to share with him her barely formed suspicion. But for just a little while she would keep her lovely, tentative womansecret to herself. She pictured how he would look, what he would say, when she told him.

He said, "That's a cream-fed smile, my lovely cat. What are you thinking now?"

Ghislaine shook her head, still smiling. "I'm thinking of you," she said truthfully. "I love you."

She took Seth's strong wrist in her hand and bit a piece from the apple he still held, and stayed snuggled in his arms while they finished it between them.

Then he kissed her again and said, "If that offer you made me here a long time ago is still open, I'd like to take you up on it."

She opened her arms to him, and her mouth, and then later, her body. The laden branches of the apple tree sheltered them, the bees hummed through the air, while they lay together and loved each other in the sweet autumn grass.

*   *   *   *   *

For all those readers who've been looking for something a little bit different, a little bit spooky, let Silhouette Books take you on a journey to the dark side of love with

SILHOUETTE
Shadows™

If you like your romance mixed with a hint of danger, a taste of something eerie and wild, you'll love Shadows. This new line will send a shiver down your spine and make your heart beat faster. It's full of romance and more—and some of your favorite authors will be featured right from the start. Look for our four launch titles wherever books are sold, because you won't want to miss a single one.

THE LAST CAVALIER—Heather Graham Pozzessere
WHO IS DEBORAH?—Elise Title
STRANGER IN THE MIST—Lee Karr
SWAMP SECRETS—Carla Cassidy

After that, look for two books every month, and prepare to tremble with fear—and passion.

SILHOUETTE SHADOWS, coming your way in March.

Silhouette®

SHAD1

AMERICAN HERO

It seems readers can't get enough of these men—and we don't blame them! When Silhouette Intimate Moments' best authors go all-out to create irresistible men, it's no wonder women everywhere are falling in love. And look what—and who!—we have in store for you early in 1993.

January brings NO RETREAT (IM #469), by Marilyn Pappano. Here's a military man who brings a whole new meaning to macho!

In February, look for IN A STRANGER'S EYES (IM #475), by Doreen Roberts. Who is he—and why does she feel she knows him?

In March, it's FIREBRAND (IM #481), by Paula Detmer Riggs. The flames of passion have never burned this hot before!

And in April, look for COLD, COLD HEART (IM #487), by Ann Williams. It takes a mother in distress and a missing child to thaw this guy, but once he melts...!

AMERICAN HEROES. YOU WON'T WANT TO MISS A SINGLE ONE—ONLY FROM

IMHERO3R

Take 4 bestselling love stories FREE
Plus get a FREE surprise gift!

**Silhouette Intimate Moments
is proud to present
Mary Anne Wilson's
SISTER, SISTER duet—
Two halves of a whole,
two parts of a soul**

In the mirror, Alicia and Alison Sullivan both had brilliant red hair and green eyes—but in personality and life-style, these identical twins were as different as night and day. Alison needed control, order and stability. Alicia, on the other hand, hated constraints, and the idea of settling down bored her.

Despite their differences, they had one thing in common—a need to be loved and cherished by a special man. And to fulfill their goals, these two sisters would do anything for each other— including switching places in a life-threatening situation.

Look for Alison and Jack's adventure in TWO FOR THE ROAD (IM #472, January 1993), and Alicia and Steven's story in TWO AGAINST THE WORLD (IM #489, April 1993)—and *enjoy!*

SISTERR

INTIMATE MOMENTS®
Silhouette®